A DEATH ON BEAR CREEK

A SEQUEL TO COAST GUARD BLUES

A MARTY GALLOWAY MYSTERY

KENNETH ARBOGAST

Published in the United States by Vigilant Newf Books.

Cover art by Mariah Mason.

ISBN: (978-1-7348721-9-4) (eBook)

ISBN: (979-8-9873890-0-3) (Paperback)

Library of Congress Cataloging-in-Publication Data has been applied for.

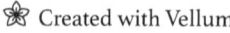 Created with Vellum

PRAISE FOR COAST GUARD BLUES

This compelling thriller centers on the vanishing of the crew of a U.S. Coast Guard vessel on the waters of Lake Superior. Arbogast shows a keen knowledge of security, waterways, and Coast Guard Special Investigations, while the novel is finely paced and action-filled.

— BOOK LIFE

I was spellbound from the very first page to the end and hardly could stop reading. One of the best crime stories I ever read.

— AMAZON REVIEWER

This novel is one of the best suspense ones I have ever read. The author has presented a realist view of the Coast Guard including how their operations work.

— GOODREADS

To my friend Pete
and all who befriended me in
the U.S. Coast Guard
and the U.S. Forest Service.

In memory of
LCDR Ray Massey, U.S. Coast Guard

April 1998

1

A dense snowfall reflected the yellow flash of a sedan's high beams as it came up the driveway. The lights cut through the late season snowfall and illuminated the big front window of the cottage where I planned to hibernate for six days. There was no worse time for visitors. Moments earlier, I had fixed a tumbler of Irish whiskey neat and settled into a comfortable armchair with the thick novel. George Richter urged the London Symphony Orchestra in a rousing version of the *Ride of the Valkyries*. On the weathered page, the novel described Benedict Arnold marshaling the cowering American forces in an assault on British and Hessian regiments at Bemis Heights. There are times, I said aloud to the whistling wood stove, when shooting trespassers is justifiable.

The small cabin on Lake Michigan's East coast was neither my home nor castle. Arriving early in the year, I managed to reserve the Coast Guard's recreational cottage behind the small lighthouse on Betsie Point for a week. On the drive up from Cleveland, the old Grand Wagoneer carried 100 compact discs, 20 books, five cases of beer, five bottles of liquor, a cooler of frozen dinners, and other sundry minimal preparation foods. For the first time since enlisting, I was on leave without either a fishing rod or a scuba tank.

The first of the late Winter storm began at mid-afternoon, not long after I returned from a long hike over the Sleeping Bear Dunes National Seashore. Going early on a winter weekday, I enjoyed the solitary run of the breezy dune peaks. At about noon, the wind blew up, coming first out of the West and raising white-capped breakers that rumbled onto the gravel shoreline down over the hill from the cabin. While I carried in extra firewood for the night, the wind coming off Lake Michigan brought a few lake-effect flurries. The storm strengthened across the afternoon and then began to dump a driving, wet hail and snow that cut visibility so that for a few hours, I couldn't see even the small lighthouse, which was less than a quarter-mile away.

The intruder came to a stop on the far side of the driveway, by the starboard side of my Jeep. The car's headlights blinked off. I placed a bookmark in the thick Kenneth Roberts novel, paused the CD player, and laid my reading glasses on the coffee table. Rising in a casual manner to avoid alerting anyone outside, I walked into the kitchen and then strode toward the dark bedrooms down the hallway.

Not expecting visitors in a snowstorm on Michigan's remote coast, my adrenaline red-lined. In the corner of the master bedroom, I located the leather valise that carried the various tools of my trade. I shoved a full magazine into the butt of a Colt .45 and tucked an airman's survival knife into my belt. I didn't pause to dress for the weather, not wanting to give anyone sufficient time to surround the cabin and block my exits. Holding a mini-flashlight in my teeth, I went through the smaller bedroom in silence, lifted the open window higher and slipped over the sill into a deep snowbank.

Stooped low to minimize my profile, I crept straight aft of the cabin about 15 yards into the white-covered sand dunes. Without boots, my socks froze, so they offered no traction. I peeled them off and walked barefoot into the snowdrifts, making a wide sweeping arc uphill away from the lake and the glare of the lighthouse. I moved slowly, partly to avoid hostile attention, but to a large degree because of cold, stiff muscles. I wished I had also grabbed the bulky leather jacket hanging from the back of a chair in the dining room. My feet began to feel leaden, and my sweater soon became saturated with cold, wet snow.

With an unknown presence in the driveway, I climbed the steep hillside on bare hands and feet in the night, through six inches of powder that would make a nice base at the ski resort northeast of Manistee, but would do nothing to satisfy the local snowmobilers. Most people might assume an unknown vehicle to be a lost motorist. I lost that luxury a few years earlier on a desolate, sandy location named Crisp Point. Despite the blowing snow, I held a good vantage point overlooking the cabin, driveway, and surrounding dunes from the embankment. A street light mounted behind the lighthouse illuminated the cottage's yard and driveway. Though it sat in the shadow of the larger Grand Wagoneer, I could see into the intruding vehicle, a mid-size four-door indistinguishable from any other sedan that rolled out of Detroit in the past decade. Years ago, I could distinguish a Ford from a Chevy at night by seeing the arrangement of their headlights and parking lights at a distance. Now it's easier to sex a condor than guess simple make and model of a product out of Motor City.

The sedan appeared empty. One man stood alone on the cement porch, rapping on the front door of the cottage. He appeared to be about six feet tall, wearing a dark trench coat. I waited on the bluff in the storm as long as my throbbing feet allowed and did not see any other movement around the cabin. Convinced there was no ambush afoot, I approached with my pistol at port arms. From the bottom step, I shouted instructions.

"Put your hands up where I can see them and tell me what you want!" I shouted.

The intruder's hands went up without pause. One empty; the other held a bulky briefcase. "My name is Mark Andrews. I'm looking for Marty Galloway."

Andrews turned toward me. He laughed when he saw me shivering and barefoot in the winter night. I went up the cement steps, twisted the knob, and shouldered my way inside. Andrews followed me inside and slammed the door shut against the blizzard.

"I'll tell you, Marty, you know where to go when you want to disappear for a while." Andrews smiled as he removed his dark blue trench coat and brushed ice off its epaulets. Underneath, he wore his bravo dress uniform; dark blue jacket and light blue shirt with a dark blue tie. At the bottom of each jacket sleeve were three bands of gold striping, two half-inch ribbons on either side of a quarter-inch stripe, signifying a lieutenant commander. He set down his government-issued black case and watched me drop the survival knife on an oak coffee table and unload the pistol.

"This for real? You go to DEFCON One on a regular basis?" he asked. "You're still getting death threats?"

"So you'd think I'm president."

He shook his ice-covered head in disbelief. "It's been more than five years. I figured the Discount Reich would have other enemies to fry by now."

"I try to avoid references to being burned. A minor anxiety."

He put a hand on his close-clipped hair. "Got an extra towel around here?"

"Sure, there's a least one unused bath towel in the restroom. Just down the hallway."

After fetching a towel and draping it over his head, Andrews warmed himself near the wood stove while I went for dry clothes, including heavy wool socks and leather moccasins. "Beer and snacks in the fridge; liquor in the cabinet above the dishwasher; ice in the freezer if you're not cold enough already," I called from the bedroom. "Help yourself to anything not past its expiration date." After toweling my hair, I pulled a bulky fisherman's sweater over my shoulders and tugged the shirt out at the neck and cuffs.

Continuing death threats were exactly why my paranoia meter peaked in the red zone so often despite the intervening time. A few years earlier, I went to Northern Michigan to investigate the disappearance of four Coast Guardsmen from a small boat found abandoned in Lake Superior. I found what the crew had already discovered — a pack of white supremacists smuggling automatic weapons via ocean-going freighters into Chicago and Detroit. They planned to ignite gang feuds and maybe a race war. In the end, their freighter sank, their would-be wizard died, and every racist in the country blamed me. It's nice to be popular; it's hell to be the rage.

When I returned from the bedroom, Andrews stood in the kitchen, holding an open beer and rummaging through packages of cheeses and deli meats in the crisper. "What, no Brie?" he asked with a chuckle. He loaded a few snacks on a plate and carried it back to the warmer front room, where a sofa and two cozy loungers faced a wide window and the wood stove. "This would make one sweet retirement cabin if it weren't for all the snow and cold."

"Part of its charm, sir; not many neighbors or visitors because of the weather," I explained. "Other than Coasties from Station Frankfort who live in the old keeper's quarters down at the light, I haven't see anyone around in days. I'm guessing these other houses are summer homes. For the snowbirds."

Andrews had stripped off his dress uniform jacket and loosened his tie. He slumped back on the sofa and took a passionate swig on an amber bottle, his eyes closed as he savored the taste. When he finished, he admired the bottle for a long moment. "I've always preferred German and Dutch, but Canadian could win me over. But after fighting this storm all the way from Traverse City, I could settle for something from Milwaukee or even Pittsburgh. Not that I'm that desperate. You'd think people would learn how to drive in it for as much snow as they get around here."

"Sir, with all the snow around here, the locals learn not to drive in it; they're all home in hiding. Any local out tonight may have stopped for a couple of drinks on the way home."

Andrews shrugged. "Still beats driving around L.A. What's the worst that could happen up here? A drive-by snowballing? Last year, I got home from work and found a bullet hole in my trunk." He glanced back at the weapons on the coffee table. "This is for real? People still remember Crisp Point after all this time?"

"What's the expression? Number one with a bullet?"

He shook his head in disbelief. "I finally saw that video tape about the whole thing. One of the agents brought it into a staff briefing. Amazing how they could twist every little detail about what actually happened to make it look like a big government conspiracy against innocent civilians."

The video, entitled "Attack on Crisp Point: the Federal Assault on the Second Amendment," claimed the Coast Guard and the Bureau of Alcohol, Tobacco and Firearms had conspired to murder an arms dealer because he was part of an innocuous group called God's True Patriots. Then the narrator suggested that law enforcement agencies fabricated an elaborate story about gun smuggling to cover up the murder. The video skipped a few key facts, like how the perpetrators kidnapped a Coast Guard boat crew. Or murdered one of the Coast Guardsman. Unimportant details if they don't match your chosen conspiracy theory, I suppose.

"Seems people believe anything they see on video these days." I said.

"Everyone loves a conspiracy. Helps if it improves their fundraising and membership," he said.

"I'm glad that they never found out your role in the investigation. Imagine how they'd play the race card on that: black officer denies citizens their right to bear arms."

Andrews chuckled. "Glad you're not bitter. I was concerned when the video kept referring to you as Irish Catholic. Thought you might take it as a personal threat."

As the lead investigator on the smuggling case, I became a target for particular venom. A "reporter" had discovered that I became a special agent because I was "unfit" to fly on Coast Guard aircraft and that I had been "denied custody" of my children during a divorce. A lawyer determined it unlikely that I could win a libel suit because innuendo and inference fall into a legal abyss.

"I want to know where they got all this personal information about you. How could they find out about your vision problem on the flight physical?" he asked.

I laughed aloud. "From the Coast Guard. The personnel office in

Cleveland received a Freedom of Information Act Request for anything and everything pertaining to Special Agent Martin L. Galloway. Some seaman in admin took it upon herself to photocopy my entire service jacket and put it in the mail."

Andrews' shock turned to astonishment. "Christ, what an idiot."

"Yeah, if she'd been a guy I would have kicked her butt. Put me through the wringer for two years. She gave the bastards everything they needed to tamper with my credit history, get me audited by the IRS, transfer a few thousand out of my savings. Good thing Brenda's new husband adopted Toby and Anne because these creeps haven't found them yet. Sometimes I wish they would come after me in a place like this." I motioned toward the Colt. "After Crisp Point, I think I could settle it pretty well."

"I'm sorry, Marty. I had no idea things have been so rough." He took another sip of beer and stared at the full clip next to the pistol. "Speaking as a Coast Guard officer, though, I have to warn you against doing anything stupid. If you go after one of these guys, the service will let you fry."

"Wait, you don't know the kicker yet. Because of the bad credit reports — they did things like renting a car at O'Hare and abandoning it in the projects, every stupid stunt you can imagine – the Coast Guard was ready to terminate my security clearance and pull my badge."

Finally, Andrews laughed at the situation, something I'd only been able to do after four frustrating years.

"You seem okay with it now. But let me know if there's anything I can do."

I twisted a leg up across my lap and rubbed the toes on my right foot until the feeling returned. "Short of creating a Federal Agent Protection Program, no, I don't think there's anything anyone can do. So far, there's only been one actual attempt out of, what? A hundred or more threats. To quote Indiana Jones, 'Besides, you know what a cautious fellow I am.' So what brings you all the way from California in winter?" I asked. When we last spoke, Andrews worked for the commander of the Pacific Area, the three-star admiral who oversees

Coast Guard operations along the West Coast and across the Pacific Ocean

Andrews looked at me in surprise. "I guess you haven't heard about the admirals' summit. Turns out after all the budget cuts to date, the money wonks in the White House want to cut another 12 percent from our operations funding during the next four years. So every admiral whose opinion is worth spit is up at the resort in Traverse City for a high-level conference. Whatever they decide will go to the Secretary of Transportation as the official blessed plan for downsizing the Coast Guard. Whatever the secretary approves goes to White House Office of Management and Budget." Andrews waved an empty beer bottle at me. "Can I get you anything on my next run?"

I pointed to the tumbler of whiskey next to my chair. "How about a couple of rocks." If Andrews intended to talk for a while, I needed to dilute my rising blood-alcohol mix.

"Where are you putting the dead soldiers of insobriety?" He waggled his empty bottle at me.

"There are cases in the back bedroom. Find the one that's got the empties." To chill the beer, I had stored the cases in the back bedroom, turned off the baseboard heater, opened the window two inches and closed the door. Every other day I restocked the refrigerator from the cold storage.

"You've got a helluva lot of beer back there," Andrews said when he returned to the kitchen. "You planning a polka party?"

What I planned was a week of sound slumber. Over the past few years, my sleep had grown marred by nightmares of failed rescues or senseless gunplay. My Coast Guard career began with two years at a small boat station whose primary clients were jumpers from the Golden Gate bridge. We called ourselves the "Bodysnatchers." Next came six years on rescue aircraft and seven years working as a Coast Guard Special Agent. These duties did not always create the happiest of outcomes. I keep any suggestion of my sleep deprivation or casual alcohol use as far from command attention as possible. The service now frowns on alcohol use, so the only time to become drunk is while on leave. With only two years before retirement, I do not want to face a medical board answering questions about my anxious days or restive nights. I am now as paranoid about the personnel hawks in the Coast Guard as I am the disciples of God's True Patriots.

Andrews returned to the room and handed me two ice cubes on a napkin. "I'm sorry to intrude like this, especially since it looks like I'll be staying overnight or longer. It all depends on the snow now."

"Well, at least I can offer you a challenging game of chess."

"I'd love a challenge. Is there someone else around here?" he asked.

The cabin's closet held a trove of board games, including a chess set in which both ranks suffered from attrition. Several empty thread bobbins replaced white pawns; a red rock served as a black rook. While Andrews set the plastic pieces in place, he described some of the proposals the admirals were considering for the future Coast Guard. I now massaged the toes on my left foot and didn't tell him that I anticipated retirement after those remaining years, as were many of my fellow chiefs.

"En garde," he challenged as he moved out his queen's knight.

I countered with the king's bishop pawn. "Should I drive over to Traverse City and solve the budget for the old boys? I've had a few ideas of my own on the subject for years."

"You wouldn't get past the commandant's aide. Not past security the way things are. You put twenty admirals in the same room, and you'd think the Joint Chiefs were having brunch."

Andrews brought out his other knight. I continued my pawn strategy.

"Which means our meeting here is not official business. Otherwise you would have arranged to have me summoned to Traverse City."

Andrews glared at me. "Yes. I'm here in an unofficial capacity. In fact, my boss would be upset if he knew why I was here. I want to hire you."

I liked Andrews and considered him among the finest Coast Guard officers I'd met, still I gave him the nastiest look in my repertoire and reached for the thick novel I'd been reading. "With all due respect, sir, I'm not Spenser for hire."

"Listen, Marty, I didn't mean anything by that. I know you've done certain favors which weren't job-related in the strictest sense." He perched forward on his seat, set the brown beer bottle on the coffee table, and fished a manila file folder from his briefcase. He held it open to where I could see the photo inside; a young African-American woman with small facial features and reddish-brown wavy hair cut in a tidy pageboy bob that fell below her ears. She wore a Coast Guard uniform with a set of silver bars on each collar.

"That's Lieutenant Janet Simms, a helicopter pilot at Air Station Kodiak. Extremely intelligent. Worked her way through college going to evening classes while she was a yeoman on the district staff in Boston," he explained.

After putting my readers back on, I took the file from him and flipped through it. The papers included her application for Officer Candidate School, commonly called OCS. Born in Indianapolis, Simms went into the Coast Guard weeks after high school. While assigned to the First Coast Guard District in Boston, she earned her bachelor's degree with credit from Harvard's extension program, holding a 3.9 grade-point average.

I glanced up at Andrews. "And now the rest of the story?"

"She's dead. Base Security said she went hiking around Buskin Lake on Kodiak, and someone found her body later that day." He spoke in a clipped tone people use to mask emotion.

"Cause of death?"

"The Alaska State Troopers said a bear mauled her to death." Andrews fished an oversized mailing envelope from his case, this one sealed and labeled: INVESTIGATION PHOTOS. "It's ugly," he warned as he handed it to me. He went to stare out the wide window behind me. The snowstorm still howled outside, and the wind groaned in the cabin's eaves.

I tore open the flap and sifted through three dozen black and white photos. Before becoming a special agent, I pulled flight pay as a rescue swimmer on a Coast Guard helicopter out of Air Station

Kodiak. As a result, I saw more corpses than anyone should ever encounter; many bodies that had suffered the awful indignity of exposure to ocean water. Still, I wasn't prepared for the graphic images of Lieutenant Simms in various states of dissection: the mutilated corpse on a surgical gurney; a few mangled organs laid across an examination table; her torn heart muscle resting on a steel tray; the empty abdominal cavity. Fighting the rising bile, I shuffled through the prints until I found close-up photos of her many individual wounds. Most of her torso had been ravaged. The meaty shanks of her thighs were also stripped away. A large chunk of scalp hung askew, exposing a massive head wound that looked like a huge bite mark. Her lovely face remained intact but appeared swollen. Upon closer inspection, the blush on her cheeks appeared to be petechial hemorrhaging.

The evisceration of Lieutenant Simms reminded me of an occasion when I found myself trapped by a Coast Guard warrant officer involved in that weapons smuggling operation on Lake Superior. He cornered me in his garage, leaving me armed with only an emergency flare gun. If you have ever witnessed a flare launch, you can imagine the consequences to a human body as I killed him.

Included in the envelope were a dozen color prints taken at the death scene by the investigating officer. According to the report, Base Security found her on the side of a small grassy hillock overlooking Bear Creek, her arms and legs tangled as though she had fallen and tumbled. The bear could have caused that as it wrestled meat from the corpse. Only the victim's boots remained intact; troopers surmised that the bear shredded the remainder of her clothing in the attack and they now hung in rags on her twisted limbs. The trooper had taken care to photograph the bear droppings near the body. Stapled to the official death certificate were copies of the investigation and witness statements.

I put the grisly photos away and listened to the blizzard outside. The London Symphony was long done, and I went to change the CD for a Chuck Mangione jazz collection. In time my nausea subsided.

"I'd like you to look into her death," Andrews said after a

respectful silence. He reclined on the sofa again, still sipping a Canadian beer. "Unofficially, of course."

"Sir, from what I see here, I don't see how there's anything to look into. The state troopers investigated and made their report. They're experts on Kodiak's bears. The AST deal with nuisance bears half the year; the rest of the year the bears are off sleeping. The AST have to decide when a bear must be put down if it causes a problem, especially around housing on the island. If the lieutenant died back in October, I'll bet they put that bear down five months ago."

He seemed puzzled, so I explained how a bear is territorial and follows the same routine for most of its adult life. Alaska State Troopers know the bears who come round the inhabited areas of Kodiak. If a bear becomes a nuisance — if it starts feeding on garbage or hangs around homes – the troopers know which bear it is and figure out a way to dissuade it from its naughty ways. It was, for the most part, because of the AST and the rangers from the wildlife refuge that a Kodiak brown bear hadn't killed anyone on the island in 50 or so years. Until this. The troopers would act fast to make certain it wouldn't happen again. Andrews sat through the lecture, gazing at me in disbelief.

"Friends in the AST when I was at Air Station Kodiak," I explained. "We used to fly the troopers out to the villages for criminal investigations if their aircraft wasn't available."

He nodded. "Okay, maybe there's nothing to it. I want you to double-check what they found. I need to know for certain."

"May I ask why the personal interest?"

"I recruited her," Andrews said. "She's my wife's sister." He corrected himself. "She was my wife's sister."

Andrews stood and wandered about the small cabin somewhat aimlessly. After several minutes, he returned to the same seat with a new lager. After a moment, he took a long swig of beer. "I recruited her and encouraged her to apply to OCS. I drove her to the recruiter's office, and I swore her in when she went to boot camp." Andrews rose and began pacing across the small room. "She was honor grad at Cape May. Number three at OCS, fifth at flight school.

Coast Guard's second black female pilot." He guzzled the last of his beer.

Andrews went into the kitchen. I heard ice cubes tumble in a glass. Studying the mismatched chess pieces, I realized the next two moves Andrews would make if the game resumed. By putting me in check with his knight, he would force the sacrifice of my queen. Given the arrangement of my pawns, I would have trouble countering his attack strategy. How had I missed his attack? Was I still cold? Already intoxicated? Out of practice? I hadn't played chess in three years or more. Of late, my recreational activities did not involve many other people.

Neither did my personal life. I rarely communicated with anyone outside of work except a supermarket clerk or a gas station attendant. My grandmother phoned every Sunday to describe my mother's progressive deterioration. My children weren't yet old enough to correspond without their mother's assistance and permission. Most of my friends had already retired before the Coast Guard's latest effort to cull the herd, a kind of "up or out" approach to personnel management. Others left early to start new careers. New friendships became unlikely as I came to trust fewer and fewer people after Crisp Point. And, I suspect, many people would like to avoid such a pariah as the guy who had an entire video devoted to his alleged sins and crimes at Crisp Point. Seemed the people most interested in making my acquaintance were other members of God's Own Patriots.

When Andrews returned, he carried a pint glass half-filled with whiskey and a green bottle of German beer. He sipped from the glass and slugged from the bottle. We didn't talk for a long time. We didn't play chess. We sat and drank in silence, him outdistancing my consumption by half again. But I had an early start. The wood stove roared along without notice of us.

"My wife blames me," he said at last. "She doesn't say it out loud. I know what she's thinking; that I recruited Janet and if I hadn't, then Janet would be alive now."

I went to add wood to the stove. "Your wife didn't want her sister to join up?" I asked.

"Angela seemed thrilled when Janet went to flight school. I think she envied her little sister. We married when I graduated from the Academy, so Angie never had as much chance to do anything after college. And here's her little sister learning to fly helicopters."

Andrews slumped deep on the sofa, his head resting against the wall. The hand holding his whiskey shook with a slight tremor. He brushed the back of his other hand across his cheek.

I stirred the embers in the wood stove with the poker, and the flame blazed up around the new wood. The small wood stove kept the room comfortable. "Sir, aren't you the one blaming yourself?"

"I may be responsible. I'm not certain."

"This falls in the act of God category. The only way you could have prevented a bear attack like that would have been to be hiking next to her with a 30.06 Winchester."

He sat forward and placed his glass next to the chessboard. "She called me. Two days before she died. She asked if there was anyone I knew in investigations that I trusted. She said she needed the name of a special agent."

I closed the iron furnace door and turned to watch Andrews' face. "What about the resident agents in Kodiak?"

"I don't know why she didn't go there first. She wouldn't tell me very much. Janet wasn't the paranoid type; she wouldn't get all secretive unless there was a good reason."

"And you think that call was somehow related to her death?"

Andrews stood and resumed pacing back and forth like the ducks in a carnival shooting gallery. "Well, it seems pretty odd that she'd call looking for help and then gets killed two days later. From what I understand, bear attacks are pretty rare, right? Even on Kodiak? Couldn't there be some connection?"

I stifled a laugh at the thought of a hit bear making a contract mauling. "I doubt it, but I'm curious what she was so concerned about. Did she mention any problems she was having up there?"

"I know it wasn't very easy for her there. The only female pilot at an Air Station. The only black officer on the whole Base. She wouldn't tell her sister or her mother about any of this, but I guess

Kodiak can be a hard place to fit into, and here she was a single, black woman, and a Coast Guard officer to boot."

"Not a lot of social invitations?" I observed, remembering how my ex-wife had hated Kodiak when we lived there.

"One good friend, and that was it. She took a lot of flak from the other pilots and flight crews. I told her to go to the C.O., but she didn't think the command would back her up at all."

Mulling over these disjointed facts, I went into the kitchen for a refill. Andrews followed and selected a different brand of beer, Dutch this time. I filled a fresh glass with Irish whiskey and ice.

"Must be something more than an allegation of harassment, that's something a C.O. can't ignore. And if the captain couldn't help her, there's nothing an enlisted agent could do. So what was on her mind when she called you?"

"That's what I want you to find out, Marty. I've been thinking about this for five months. There was a reason she called me. Even if it has nothing to do with her death, I want to know why she asked for help."

We settled on opposite sides of the wooden coffee table holding the chessboard. "I wish I could help, but I don't think I can get to Kodiak any time soon. This is the first leave I've had in the proverbial coon's age."

He smiled at me. "I talked with your boss about that. I saw him at Traverse City this afternoon. He said you could use up whatever leave you need, which I guess from the way he talked, is pretty extensive. Sounds like you need to get out more."

I nodded, stunned that my division officer would give me the leave time that was due. Our office in Cleveland was so strapped with work that I'd gone more than two years without a vacation. As a bonus, the Coast Guard cancels any leave beyond 90 days that you can't manage to use each fiscal year. Andrews saw my confusion.

"Your boss was a year behind me at the Academy," he explained. "We scrimmaged together. I was varsity fullback, and he was JV halfback."

"Small world, I guess."

He raised his beer in a toast and grinned at me. "I didn't need four extra years of kindergarten, but membership has its privileges." After another sip of whiskey followed by a slurp of beer, Andrews leveled his gaze at me again. "Back when we were dealing with those missing Coasties up in Lake Superior, I didn't understand why Admiral Thorne called for you in particular. I've done my homework since then." He opened a folder and read aloud. "Galloway, Martin, L. Born in Petaluma, California," he recited. "Fifth generation Coastie. Grandfather was one of the Coast Guard's first aviation mechanics. Your father is MIA since an Air Force bomber sank the *Point Manitou* off Vietnam. You enlisted after high school, earned the Air Medal and the Coast Guard Medal. Went into intelligence because medical problems removed you from flight duty. Distinguished career as a special agent. Wounded in the line of duty while assigned to a drug task force in Florida. Want me to continue?"

I laughed. "Sure, I'm vain."

"Cited for excessive use of force in apprehending a deserter. Relieved of duties in Juneau for assaulting an officer, who was later convicted of sexual assault of a minor. Avoided court-martial for pursuing a petty officer beyond Coast Guard jurisdiction. Still want me to go on?"

"Ah, no. But thanks for the memories."

"Look, Marty, I didn't come to you because your HR jacket is full of attaboys. You've spent a lot of your own time doing personal favors for people who couldn't fight back themselves. You've got a reputation as a hard case, and from what I've seen, you've worked very hard to deserve it."

Even as he stroked my ego like a chinchilla, I heard the punch line coming.

"If Janet were alive, I know you'd have gone up to help her." He stopped for a long moment, staring at his hands. "My admiral doesn't know about this, and he won't approve. He'd say I'm questioning the findings of the state troopers."

"But you are," I observed. "Why do I feel like I'm pulling scout duty at Little Big Horn?"

"Cause I'm asking you to do something you shouldn't. Nobody in Kodiak will be happy to see you. By asking questions, you could piss off a lot of people."

"I don't have to go to Kodiak to do that."

Andrews seemed to ignore my comment. "If you have trouble, I won't be able to help. A lowly lieutenant commander can't give you any sanction or official capacity. Not even in a court-martial."

"You'd never make it as a recruiter," I said as I finished my fourth whiskey of the evening, starting to feel the tingling of a buzz in my peripheral brain. "Sir, I don't think I've had any official sanction since I put on a badge."

"From what I've seen, that never stopped you before, either."

"I assume I can keep her record, the investigation report and the photos," I said. "I'll also need the name of that one good friend she had on the island."

Andrews returned to his briefcase and produced a third file folder. His perfect white teeth showed in a relieved grin. "You know, for a while there I wasn't certain you'd do this for me."

"That hint of a possible court-martial kinda won me over."

2

Andrews woke me in the dark, his rough palm across my mouth and a thumb holding my jaw tight.

"Marty, we have company. Two guys down on the road, checking out the place. Looks like they're carrying long guns."

I had dozed off in the chair, leaving a half shot of whiskey and an undefended queen at the mercy of his king's bishop. I needed a few moments to regain complete consciousness. Parts of my brain felt leaden, as though my temporal lobes had been surgically replaced with gravel.

From the corner of the large front window, I peered at the two intruders in the driveway. They did appear to carry some type of rifles, illuminated by their headlamps. "Go slow. Move down the hallway and turn right. I'll be right behind you," I instructed. "We want them to think there's only one person in the house." As Andrews walked across the room, I slipped to a four-point stance on the floor and crawled after him, pausing to reclaim the Colt on the coffee table. Once in the master bedroom, I opened my leather valise and dug into its side pockets.

"You okay to handle a weapon?" I asked.

At his grunt, I handed Andrews a Beretta .22 Auto and two loaded clips. I heard Andrews load and lock the Beretta, then the faint click of a safety being set and released to check its position. From another part of the bag, I passed a K-bar knife to him. Andrews chuckled.

"Well, you said you'd like them to come after you in a remote place like this," he observed.

"My grandpa used to say, 'Be careful what you ask for; you might get it good and hard,'" I observed. "If you spotted those guys down on the road, we have to assume they had time to surround the house. These guys train for this kinda stuff. They wouldn't show themselves until they were in position."

"You're the pro; you tell me what to do." The lieutenant commander showed surprising confidence by relinquishing tactical command to a chief petty officer. I wished I had a better strategy to deal with the situation. Or any strategy, at the least. "You have a plan?" he asked.

"Remember that scene at the end of *Butch Cassidy and the Sundance Kid* when Newman and Redford come out blazing?" I asked.

"Yeah. There were a thousand soldiers waiting for them. You have a better strategy than that?"

"So you have to trust me. Let me regroup for a minute." I led the way back to the living room, crouching as we went. I turned the back of the recliner against the couch and flipped all the cushions up into a thick hideout. "Stay behind this until you need to go out a back window." I peered out the lower corner of the big picture window. Two men came up the driveway at a modest pace, carrying rifles with scopes aimed at the sky, as deer hunters carry a weapon into the field. "I'm going to ask who they are. I don't know what time sunrise is here, but they could be deer hunters getting an early start."

"It's about 1 a.m., Marty. You zonked about midnight. They're not hunters."

"Okay, we can rule out legal hunters. But we can't assume they're trouble. If they shoot, I'll go for your car and lay down cover fire. You go for the driver's seat of the Jeep. Keys on the visor. Shotgun behind the seat and extra shells in the console. I'll get in the back if I can.

They don't seem to have vehicles in the driveway, so keep going. Hard left at the end of the drive. Any questions?"

"Are you nuts?" He stared at me. He held the Beretta barrel up with both hands wrapped around the stock. "Aren't we safer in here?"

"We have two pistols and a couple of knives. They're carrying long guns. You like those odds?" I took a deep breath. "They're after me. If I'm down, you need to hide out. They'll consider mission accomplished if they get me first. If we're in the Jeep, you keep driving. Don't stop to give me a Band-Aid."

"Thanks for your concern," Andrews said. "If you call me a coward again, I may shoot you myself."

"Fair enough." When I opened the door, two dark figures stood about five yards aft of the Grand Wagoneer's stern. "Hello," I called. "Can I help you, fellas?"

"Chief Galloway?" One of them yelled back. Both wore fluorescent orange float jackets with retroreflective tape on the arms and chest. The jackets were common among small boat crews.

"Yes. Come on up, guys." I opened the door wide and put my weapons on the coffee table. Andrews looked at me in surprise. "They're from the small boat station in Frankfort," I explained. "I guess they live down at the light."

After stomping their boots on the porch, the two men came in, wet and snow-covered. They turned off their headlamps and propped their long guns against the wall inside the front door. They remained on the square of linoleum around the entryway. I assumed it was their job to clean the carpet, along with their other maintenance duties around the cabin.

"BM1 Franks from Station Frankfort," the bigger man said. "This is GM3 Henderson." After taking off their gloves, we shook their hands as I introduced myself and Andrews. Their hands were cold despite their gloves, which I assumed had open palms for handling a weapon. They straightened to rigid attention when they heard Lieutenant Commander Andrews' rank. He acknowledged their respect and waved them off.

"Listen, we're sorry to disturb you or scare you," Franks said, nodding to our little array of weapons laid out on the table. "We live down at the lighthouse, and Chief McNulty asked us to keep an eye on the place while you're here. He told us what happened up on Lake Superior, and to his friend Senior Chief Drucker. He said there's been a lot of threats against you since that happened, so Phil got concerned when he saw that strange car in the driveway."

"I'ze taking the mutt out for one last whizz for the night," Henderson added.

"I appreciate you guys looking out for me," I said. "But next time wear some white hats so I know which side you're on."

"Well, we didn't know what we were getting into either," the bosun said. "Weren't sure if we'd meet up with you or whoever's after you."

"Hey, you guys want a beer?" I asked.

"Naw, we'd better get back." Franks checked his watch. "In about eight minutes, my wife is gonna call the sheriff, the state police and even the National Guard." The two Coasties started suiting up for the trudge back home.

"Hold up a minute before you go." I went back to the cold-storage bedroom and returned with a case of Holland's finest pilsner. "This will help you relax after all the excitement. And thanks again."

Franks stopped to speak while Henderson went out carrying the Grolsch carton on his shoulder. "You know, the chief says you're a real hero. I don't know if you ever met Chief McNulty, but he's old Guard. He wouldn't say that if you weren't rock solid, you know what I mean? It's been an honor to meet you, chief." He shook my hand again, then saluted Andrews. "Good evening, sir." He started down the porch steps behind Henderson. "Careful there," he called. "You have no idea what a case of that good stuff costs. That ain't Milwaukee sewer water."

When I turned from closing the door, Andrews looked pained. "Did you have to give them the Grolsch? There's plenty of German back there. Or Canadian."

"Sir, you don't understand. Right now those guys think I'm an average hero. By the time they finish off that case, I'll be a legend. How about you? Little nightcap to settle the nerves?"

"Not too little, now. You gave them a case of beer. Heck, I was the one holed up with America's most wanted, you know." He followed me to the fridge. "Why did you assume they were Coasties? You didn't ask for any ID."

"First, the way they carried their weapons, barrel up for safety, same way you did. If they were assassins, they'd have been ready to fire. Second, he called me, 'Chief.' Helps me. Threats are always addressed to agent or mister. If it doesn't say Chief or Special Agent, I know it's from somebody unfamiliar with the Coast Guard."

"Seems like you took a big chance."

"Yeah, but I had a secret weapon."

"Really? Please share."

"You, sir. Your ribbon bar has an E device on both your pistol and M-16. So I've got an Expert shot with me."

"And you? Sharpshooter or Expert?"

"Once upon a time, I was Expert on both. But I went to the range after having my shoulder dislocated up in the Soo. No longer have the same muzzle control as I had, even at basic training."

Andrews looked back at the weapons. "It's been a long time since I've handled a piece. Did I ever tell you about that fishing boat we boarded off Cuba carrying arms for the resistance? Almost another Bay of Pigs."

Then he told me about the incident in great detail, elaborating on all the coincidences and peculiarities that make law enforcement fascinating. We drank more, both of us off duty and far from the regimen of our respective commands. At times, our attention strayed back to the chessboard, but our disinterest and inebriation showed in the absurd moves that somehow put us both in check at once.

Finally, we held our own summit to reconfigure the Coast Guard. I suggested assigning all useful functions of Headquarters to a single admiral, five lieutenants and 50 yeomen with a master chief boatswain's mate to keep them all working. Tough times demand tough decisions, Andrews reminded me. So we agreed to terminate the silly-sounding ranks of "rear admiral, lower half" and "seaman apprentice."

"What does a seaman do that he needs an apprentice?" Andrews asked. "When I was an ensign, I was dumber than that end table. But I sure acted like I knew it all."

Before long, we'd fixed the Coast Guard and gone on to change the federal government. We could have stayed at that for days, but the liquor that made us so talkative and disrespectful, then finally made us both drowsy. When Andrews slumped on the sofa and began to snore, I staggered down the hall and curled up on the bed. I finally had one of those long, dreamless nights I pursued with reckless abandon.

3

When Andrews emerged from the shower the next morning, he found me at the dining room table, sipping a glass of orange juice while repacking various weapons into their designated compartments of the black valise I call my "little bag of tricks."

"What other weapons do you carry in that bag?" Andrews asked.

"As they say, I could tell you, sir, but then I'd have to kill you," I said. Been looking to use that line for years. Then on the small dining room table, I began to shuffle through the photographs from the investigation and autopsy of LT Janet Simms.

"Hey, I was looking for some coffee grounds for the pot on the stove. How'd you make chief without drinking coffee? Not part of your initiation?"

"You need caffeine, heat up some of that soda in there. Stir in a little milk and you won't notice the difference."

Andrews shook his head in disgust. "You're an evil bastard."

"So I've been told."

Breakfast was low cholesterol: bagels with marmalade, bananas, granola with milk and slices of strawberries. More orange juice. The compact disc machine played Native American flute music. Trying to rouse from his morning lethargy, Andrews opened a can of soda and went to rummage through the box of CDs for something more stimulating. He came back to the dining room disappointed.

"Too early for Wagner?" I asked.

"I never would have taken you for a classical music fan, Marty. You seem like an air guitar hero, who likes Slayer and Sir Lord Baltimore."

"Worries me you even know who those bands are."

Andrew wandered around the cabin, peering out at the snow from the prior night's storm. "Wow. Some pretty good drifts. Do you think they'll plow out the roads today?" He came back into the room where I stood. "So tell me, Marty. Do a lot of agents become anti-social? I could see how you'd start to look at everyone as a potential case file."

"No, sir, I hope I'm the exception. Most of the special agents I know are wonderful people, church-goers and teetotalers. Many have kids of their own, and they love everyone else's kids. I knew a fellow who raised five foster kids. I admire the hell out of them." I laid out the photographs he'd given me the night before on the dining room table so I could examine them with more care. "I can't tell people often enough to not judge all special agents by me."

"So what makes you so different?" He came to the doorway, but stopped when he saw the photographs spread across the tabletop. Turning on his heels, he returned to the kitchen.

"Sorry. I don't think I'm equipped to get into the whole nature versus nurture debate."

"And you spent years jumping out of perfectly good aircraft. On purpose," he added.

"Seemed like a fun idea at the time."

Moving from photo to photo, grouping and regrouping as I went, I studied both collections from the scene and the hospital examination, first apart, then mixed together. The state troopers took most of the photos before moving the body; they showed the corpse in the same position from various angles. I sorted out the close-ups and matched them with corresponding photos of the same limb or body part taken at the hospital in Kodiak. I reshuffled and compared types of injuries: a few bruises on her shoulders; the long slashes of bear claws; puncture marks of fangs and teeth, and then the catastrophic damage — the gaping wounds created by muscles stripped off limbs and organs ripped from the torso. Blood in her scalp corresponded in the photos to traces of blood and hair on a nearby rock, likely from a fall.

After repackaging the photos, I put on reading glasses to peruse the printed reports. The trooper listed the many mistakes Janet Simms had made. She wasn't armed, and she carried no noisemakers to scare off bears. She hiked along a hillside near Bear Creek when bear activity might be higher than normal because the bears were preparing for their annual hibernation and looking for a meal. Security police on the Coast Guard Base received reports of several bear sightings during the prior week. A special warning had appeared in the Base newsletter, alerting families to keep pets and children away from the Buskin River.

The autopsy report put the horror of the photographs into dull, clinical terminology that was no less horrific: multiple and serious contusions; extensive lacerations of the skin, subcutaneous tissue and muscle fascia; massive hemorrhage; uncontrolled blood loss; gross abdominal evisceration. The standard medical form did not allow for a thorough description of this type of total destruction of a human body. Petechial hemorrhages on her face suggested cardiac arrest or asphyxiation, but the condition of the heart prevented the coroner from making any determination. The coroner surmised the bear's weight had snapped most of her ribs. For the cause of death, the doctor penciled in the note, "Immediate cause unknown. General cause was blood loss and damage to internal organs caused by bear attack."

The phrase "immediate cause unknown" was neither surprising nor suspicious. Given the condition of the body, it would have been impossible for a medical expert to guess exactly which wound or injury caused death. Still, the coroner in Anchorage took his time to rule out the many customary signs of foul play. There were no indications of a gunshot wound, straight-edge laceration, blows from blunt objects or standard toxins. From the absence of dirt, fur, tissue, or blood under the fingernails, the physician concluded that she was unconscious soon after the onset of the attack.

For a fourth time, I went back through the gruesome pictures, now including the autopsy photos, examining each in relation to what the written reports explained about them. By then, I no longer saw the grotesque, only the minute details; a small discoloration on her neck, a patch of hives on the back of her left arm, a slight aniso-coria of her pupils, the swollen look of her face, a silver chain removed from her right wrist. Each was duly noted in the appropriate report.

When I emerged from the dining room an hour past noon, I found Andrews playing two sides of the chessboard. The plow had not come down the small road, and the big rented sedan Andrews drove wouldn't get far even if we could get it out of the driveway. The afternoon's soundtrack had shifted to the symphonies of Hayden.

"I would have beaten you if we had continued," Andrews gloated, pointing at the chess board.

"Sure, you've had that fancy education at the Boy's Academy on the Thames."

"Hold on now. The Coast Guard Academy taught me how to handle a three-masted sailing ship on the off chance Admiral Nelson attacks Pearl Harbor."

I chuckled to myself. My father graduated Officer Candidate School without the benefit of sailing on the Academy's barque *Eagle*, yet became skipper of a patrol boat patrolling the coast and rivers of South Vietnam.

"Tell me, do you have anything edible to eat?" he asked. "I'm not up for frozen."

"You can have anything you want out of the kitchen. It's all first-come; first-served."

"Great. But there's nothing edible in the kitchen."

"I can make you eggs. Any style you want."

Andrews considered this offering for a few minutes. "And toast?"

"Don't push your luck, sir." I headed into the kitchen to gather what cooking utensils I needed.

"Any cheese for scrambled eggs?"

I went back to the door into the main room. "Until yesterday. Sorry. I wasn't expecting guests."

"Understood. Look, I'll need to call the admiral by this evening. I asked for today off cause I figured the snow might get worse, but if I'm not back at the hotel this evening he may get annoyed. Not that he needs me. He's got this cute, chattering little j.g. who waits on him. She wants to apply for the astronaut program, so she needs every possible OER point she can get."

Talk of a lieutenant junior grade finagling a good officer evaluation report from her admiral seemed trivial after the stark images I had studied for hours. Yet, sometime in the past, Janet Simms had been a lieutenant junior grade herself, striving for solid evals, struggling for promotion, competing for selection to flight school. That was life as most people in the Coast Guard lived it: they talked about selection and promotion, re-enlistment and retirement, spouses and houses. They didn't study statements, depositions, criminal reports or autopsies. In a career, they might scoop a corpse or two from the briny sea. I had seen a hundred deaths, caused a few and lived through my own demise in such vivid detail that I often woke crouched on the floor, aiming an invisible weapon at unseen foes. The difference was nature, no doubt — the nature of my jobs and the various assignments and cases of my career. The only nurturing was my growing potential for insomnia, paranoia, and alcohol. If I wrote it up, experts might name a recurring traumatic stress disorder after me.

I fetched a beer out of the refrigerator. As a firm rule, I never touched the hard liquor before sunset, even on overcast days. I didn't want to become a drunk.

Andrews raised an eyebrow at the sight of the beer in my hand. I offered to fetch him one, but he declined. "They say the bottle's a cold mistress," he said, too solemnly for casual conversation.

"Only when properly chilled," I said.

He chuckled a bit and relaxed from full-on officer mode. "Marty, I've been wondering about last night. Twice you went to DEFCON One. Does that happen often? I imagine it would be pretty stressful to be on constant alert."

"No, I never worry at home, only when I travel to new places." Then I explained how I had reinvented my life in the past few years. A lawyer I knew put me in touch with his friend who worked in corporate law to help me create a new reality. Rather than using an assumed name, he created a phantom corporation that operates a series of subsidiaries. One anonymous subsidiary rents my current apartment west of Cleveland; another leases the cars I drive. My mail gets routed through a bogus post office box and then onto the lawyer. He charges me only a minimal yearly fee for the extra services because he enjoys the intrigue.

The same lawyer also played a fascinating shell game while moving my grandmother to a new, safer home where anyone angry about my adventure at Crisp Point would be unlikely to find her. While sending her on a series of connecting cruises and train rides across Europe, he had her furniture packed and hauled around the country: shipped from city to city; transferred between moving companies; and shuffled from warehouse to warehouse until only his secretary knew on any particular day where it sat. Finally, my grandmother's furniture returned to Ohio, ready to greet her upon her return to a new home, also purchased by another subsidiary of our bogus family corporation. Her new home is located about 20 miles from where her belongings began their transcontinental travels.

The process of disappearing into plain sight had consumed about 30 percent of the assets my grandmother and I held. To recoup the losses, the same lawyer suggested a safe, tax-shielded investment strategy that continues to astonish me when I receive the quarterly reports. Turning around the continuing decline of the capital left from two life insurance policies, he had made us first secure, then comfortable. No doubt our growing wealth would surprise and please my late father and grandfather if they knew.

Except for those times when I travel under my own name for the

Coast Guard, I feel completely safe. I never arrive at work the same
way twice in a week, but that prevents any commuter boredom.

"How long can you keep that up?" Andrews asked.

"About two years, sir. As soon as I retire, I plan to pack up my
mother and grandmother and then disappear without leaving a trail."

"And go where?" Andrews wondered. "If you panicked here in the
middle of nowhere during a snowstorm, where do you think you
could relax?"

"Maybe Canada. I know a Mountie in Ontario. Canadians don't
equate gun registration with castration. Or Ireland. We'd be three
more Galloways there." I smiled. "Imagine retiring to the Emerald
Island."

Andrew grinned at me. "Isn't that what they call Kodiak?"

The lingering snowfall ended in the afternoon. Bitter wind still
raised white caps on the big lake, and gray clouds hung low over the
trees. While waiting for the plow, Andrews and I finished packing up
and loading out. I put the boxes of empty bottles into the stern
compartment of the Jeep Grand Wagoneer. I closed the window in
that back cold storage room but left the thermostat off. I wrote a note
indicating that the remaining beer was to serve a party for the entire
crew at the small boat station in Frankfort. I knew that their busy
search and rescue season would start in a few weeks. So they might
enjoy an early celebration.

The county plow came over the hill and down to the driveway to
the lighthouse before turning around in a public parking area along
the lakefront. Andrews tried backing his sedan out of the driveway
but only seemed to dig it in deeper. GM3 Henderson returned, this
time driving his Jeep CJ5 with a winch mounted on the front bumper.
Andrews was free of the deep snow and on his way in about 20
minutes. Henderson offered to help me, but I assured him my Jeep
would be fine. But I brought him inside to show him what I was
leaving behind for a station party. He acted as if he'd never seen a
good deed. I feared he planned to hug me before I escaped.

The small boat station sat on Frankfort's waterfront. The village
stretches out along a natural harbor. The quaint shops and restau-

rants that line the main drag remain dormant after the winter season. I pulled up behind Andrews' car. He was already inside the station trying to report by phone to his admiral up in Traverse City. I went to return the key to the recreation cabin. I poked my head into Chief McNulty's office to thank him for having his guys look out for me. I also gave him a heads up about the beer stored at the cabin for a party. He, too, expressed surprise.

On the street outside the station, Andrews shook my hand and then stuffed a thick envelope into the open pocket of my leather jacket. "It's about ten thousand. I can give you more if you need it." When I protested, he cut me off. It was clear he wouldn't take it back without a physical scuffle, so I decided to get it back to him later. "Gloria, Janet's mom, usually goes to bed about nine. Even if you make good time in this weather, you won't have much time this evening. Why don't you visit her in the morning? That part of Indianapolis is a lot safer in broad daylight. Be gentle with her, please."

"Who, me? I'm the very model of discretion."

He gave me a worried look, then shrugged in resignation. "Listen, you can't call me. If you call work, the admiral may find out, and he won't be happy. If you call home, Angela will know. Won't make either one happy. I'll contact you when your boss tells me you're back in Cleveland."

I nodded. "Is this when you issue me a cyanide pill?"

"Yeah, it's kinda that bad." Andrews shook my hand before climbing back into the Buick sedan. He put down the driver's window and called, "Be careful. Good luck."

Four simple words I've heard throughout my Coast Guard career, as a rescue swimmer and then as a special agent. Nice happy thoughts from people staying behind: ashore, in the aircraft, in the office. Contradictory. If you're careful, you don't need luck. When luck runs out; all your care won't matter.

4

The shortest route from Michigan to Indianapolis took me down U.S. 31 South from Benton Harbor. I stopped over at a small motel near the state line. On the following morning, I drove through the northern corn fields into Carmel on the Northside of Indianapolis. From there, I continued down the Keystone Parkway past the well-manicured lawns, buildings, and homes. When I ran a scan on the radio, I picked up an FM station billing itself as the Voice of the Greyhounds of Carmel High School.

Gloria Simms lived in a duplex on the Northside of downtown Indianapolis, a neighborhood best described as past its prime. In the suburbs, a little street like hers is called a cul de sac; here, it is a simple Dead End. On either side of her building sat single-family homes boarded over and then spray-painted with an incomprehensible assortment of gang symbols. I wasn't playing on what I considered home turf. I wondered if the neighborhood high school also had its own radio station. Seemed more likely that the students shared the same textbooks that their parents once read a generation ago. Perhaps even their grandparents first studied from the books when new.

When I parked the Jeep in front of her home in the late afternoon, the boyz of the hood hanging out in front of an abandoned house nearby appeared to show deep concern about parking arrangements. They rose en masse and ambled over like schoolboys interested in the new kid on the playground. They trailed behind a tall, lanky kid, all of 19 or so, whose clothes were baggy enough to hold three boys with his belt size. He toyed with a set of nunchaku in a clumsy fashion.

I locked the Wagoneer and dropped the keys into an inside pocket of my leather jacket. I stopped to watch the Jets approach. After my encounter with the True Patriots, I had added a small can of pepper spray to the personal armament hidden inside my jacket. In addition to the Colt .45 in a shoulder holster, I carried a Beretta .25 strapped to my ankle, as well as an extending baton rigged on a strap in my jacket sleeve. As the gang of nine came toward me, I did the quick math of firepower. If simple intimidation failed, the situation would go badly unless I switched from offense to defense without delay.

"Nice wheels, dude," the lanky leader said as his backup crew fanned out around us. "How 'bout lettin' us take it for a little test drive?"

"Sorry. It ain't for sale."

Tall Boy laughed. "We wasn't thinkin' about buyin' it." They all laughed. He took another step closer to me, and the movement of the nunchaku became more coordinated. "So how 'bout those keys?"

I smiled and reached inside my jacket. "You're sure I can't talk you out of this?"

He slashed the air between us with the nunchaku sticks a half dozen times. His speed was good, but his form lacked any discipline or training. I wondered if he learned his technique watching old Bruce Lee movies. His associates twittered approval.

Their chuckles stopped when they saw the muzzle of my Colt pressed into Tall Boy's nostrils. Tall Boy himself dropped the nunchaku as if realizing that he was literally outgunned.

"If you like your face, ask your friends to give us a little space." I smiled. "Then you and I can negotiate."

When Tall Boy waved both arms in a backing motion, about half his group drew away. The others remained close enough to follow events. I watched to ensure I was not surrounded.

"So what's your name?"

"Bobby... Robert." He was looking for a way to sound innocent yet defiant.

"How about some ID, Robert?"

He fished a nylon wallet out of a back pocket in his saggy trousers. The name checked and the address corresponded to a nearby street I had passed on my way into the neighborhood.

"Robert, my name is Special Agent Galloway. My friends call me Marty. You'd like to be my friend, wouldn't you, Robert?"

Robert nodded tenderly because of the muzzle of steel resting on the tip of his nose. His crossed eyes searched for the exact location of the pistol's barrel.

"And friends trust each other, right? Robert, I'm going to trust you regarding my Jeep." After putting his wallet in my back pocket, I took the .45 away from his nose. "I need you to keep an eye on things for me while I conduct official business for the federal government." I flashed my badge and lowered the weapon to waist level. "Now, if I find something wrong when I come back, I'm not going to call the police, your parole officer or even the governor. I am going to come up to Kinnear Avenue and haul you out. And when I get done, even your sister won't recognize you. Understand?"

He nodded his head. He risked humiliation in front of his gang of peers, and it wasn't going to be easy to regain dominance after I left. For this gambit to work, I had to throw him a bone. I secured the .45 back in its holster.

"I've heard you're a go-to person in this neighborhood. Here's the deal. I need to talk to the woman who lives here for a few hours. Her daughter died up in Alaska, and I'm going to help her find out why. When I'm done..." I reached into an inside pocket and took four bills from the envelope Andrews had given me. "I will give you $200." I held the bills up where Tall Boy and crew could see them. Then I ripped the bills in half and handed four halves to him. "Remaining payment upon delivery. If everything's good, I'll also pass on to the local precinct that you cooperated. If there's a problem, I'll come to your home on Kinnear. All I'm asking is your patience while I'm here."

Finally, Tall Boy seemed to understand the terms of our little standoff. He crossed his arm and leaned against the Jeep's fender. "So go get it done," he said.

When I went up to the house, I found Gloria Simms inside her front door, watching events unfold on the street. She held a phone receiver in one hand. I flashed my badge at the window.

"I've been watching for you this morning," she said, opening the door wide enough for me to slip in sideways. "I figured you'd have trouble with those kids. They harass visitors, the mailman, even the cops; it doesn't matter to them. They call themselves 'gangstas.'" She led me into her small, crowded living room. The floral sofa and cherry furniture looked pushed to one side to make room for a large stack of brown shipping boxes.

"Those kids are wannabes, Missus Simms," I said, "Just white dopes on punk, as they say. But we've reached an understanding."

"Please, call me Gloria. Mark stands up to them, too, when he comes. But they scare me when they get drinking and doing their drugs." She motioned for me to sit on the sofa and settled into a well-worn recliner opposite me. Neither face nor figure betrayed her true age; she could have been 35 or 55. She wore a white uniform for either a nurse or cafeteria worker. "Some nights I can't sleep because of their music and partying out here."

"So are you planning to move?" I asked, motioning toward the shipping boxes.

"No, that's all Janet's stuff. The Coast Guard shipped it back from Kodiak a few months ago, and I don't know what to do with it."

"Do you mind if I look through the boxes?" I asked.

"If Mark thinks it'll help somehow. I haven't looked myself. Are you looking for something in particular?"

I shook my head. "No, I'm not sure what might be in the boxes. I'm afraid this is a case of 'I'll know it when I see it.'"

"And you'll show me anything you're going to take of hers, right?"

"Of course," I said. "I won't take anything without your approval. In fact, I'd like you to sit here with me while I open the boxes. It might help me understand any notes she made or whether anything was significant to her. Please let me know if something seems out of place."

We set to work on those boxes on top of the pile. After completing three, I checked the time. By the time on my chronograph and number of boxes remaining unopened, I could see this project would keep me busy longer than I could expect Tall Boy to persuade his followers to cooperate.

"Would you do me a favor? Call the best local pizza delivery place in the area. Order me five large pies of different assortments. But no veggies. I'll pay cash when they arrive."

"You must be hungry. That's a lot of pizza," Gloria said as she went off to the kitchen, looking for the phone book.

"No doubt. But a small price to pay if this works out." I sliced open the packing tape on the next box, careful not to injure the contents inside. The first three boxes were clothes, lots of sweatpants and sweatshirts with Coast Guard emblems. Some added the words or the logo of "Air Station Kodiak." Ironically, the patch featured a Kodiak bear on its rear legs, showing claws, fangs and red tongue.

Someone had taken special care to fold all the permutations of Janet's Coast Guard uniform: dress blue, work casual, and flight coveralls. Tucked into her uniforms, a smaller box contained all the uniform decorations she had accumulated: nametags; silver collar devices; gold aviator wings; and three rows of ribbons featuring a Coast Guard Commendation Medal, an Achievement Medal, a row of unit citations and her ribbons for sharpshooter with both a pistol and a rifle.

Boxes Five and Six contained shoes, a surprising number and variety of boots, sneakers, uniform shoes, and dress heels. I could only recall one or two places on Kodiak Island where it would be both fashionable and practical for a woman to wear strappy high heels. Although summer dried out enough to permit athletic shoes, most of the year was more suitable for rubber boots.

The pizza vehicle arrived and honked. Then the driver called the Simms house phone to announce his arrival. He informed Missus Simms that he wasn't planning to exit his vehicle regardless of the tip. So I walked out warily. Tall Boy maintained his position on the Jeep's front fender like the Queen's Guards outside Buckingham Palace. In the street, a group of five of his friends played footbag, expertly keeping a small leather cube in the air with just their feet. Three others sat on the porch of a nearby abandoned house. Could be more followers hidden somewhere close by, I mused, starting to doubt my strategy and sanity. Too late, I concluded. With Andrews' money, I paid the driver and tipped well, in case it was my last good deed. Then he passed five flat boxes through his open window before driving off in a hurry.

I walked the boxes of pizza over to Tall Boy. His head tilted in surprise. "I may be another hour, so I thought you and your friends might be getting hungry," I said. "Looks like they put napkins and plastic knives in the bag. You want me to ask if Missus Simms has any paper plates?"

He cast his eyes around his crew. "No, we good with this. We're not that fancy, usually. Think it's ok to use her picnic table?"

"I bet she'll be fine with it. Pile the boxes there when you're done."

"Sure thing."

As I went back to the Simms' front door with a hand on the butt of my Colt, I watched the expression on Gloria's face in the window for any sign of panic. She looked puzzled, as if she saw someone walk across hot coals for the first time. I felt safe, knowing that few things can hold a young man's attention like a pizza with all meat toppings.

Back inside the house, I opened the remaining packing boxes from Kodiak. One contained a large library of books intended to aid her career: leadership and management; personal styles of leadership; small-team leadership; leadership styles of great military men; leadership in conflict; and others in a similar vein. A somewhat smaller box contained her personal collection of fiction: a few current bestsellers; horror novels from big-name authors; three dog-eared volumes from the series about a boy wizard; and a well-worn copy of *Roots*, written by former Coast Guard photojournalist Alex Haley.

Gloria sat through my search in silence, only occasionally remarking about an item that I found; a particular book Janet had enjoyed, a shirt Gloria gave her daughter for a birthday, or the surprise of finding a naughty nightie. I once acted as funereal escort for a crewmate from the small boat station where I served who had committed suicide. During the reception after the funeral, I came to realize how little his family knew about the deceased.

Only in the very last box did I locate any personal paperwork such as correspondence, bills, or bank statements. I checked the time and looked out the window for confirmation. Twilight was fast approaching. I didn't want to rush combing through these materials, so I asked permission to take the entire box with me. Gloria Simms agreed.

"I suppose my Janet doesn't have any secrets now," she said.

I assured her I would be discrete. "Wish me luck getting out to I-70."

She gave me a broad smile and laughed. "You make it past the stop sign, you're home free."

The evening air was cool with just a faint odor of exhaust. I carried the box down to the curb. Tall Boy was back on duty, leaning again on the Jeep's fender. He jumped up and opened the rear door so that I could place the box inside. I noticed a small smear of marinara sauce at the corner of his mouth. He smiled when I gave him the remaining halves of the $50 bills.

"Pleasure doing business with you," I said. "I don't need a receipt."

He stuffed the bills into his jacket. His jeans were slung too low to reach the pockets. "If you need to come back, can we get Valeria's Taqueria? Up on Keystone Avenue."

As I opened the driver's door, I handed him another bill wrapped around his wallet. "Keep an eye on Missus Simms until I get back and I'll set you and the boys up with Valeria for a month. Deal?"

"You bet." Robert extended his hand to seal the deal, undoubtedly the first gentleman's agreement in his life thus far.

5

_____

With only a few pit stops along the way, I drove up to Chicago and checked into the Crowne Plaza near O'Hare Airport. Using years of loyalty points, I checked into a suite looking out toward the Chevalier Woods, a greenway in the midst of the city's asphalt, brick, concrete, and glass.

Before unpacking my luggage, I put the remaining bottles of Canadian beer in the room's refrigerator and opened the final moving box belonging to Janet Simms. The moment seemed a little like opening the Ark of the Covenant, and I felt unsure it was safe to look inside. If Janet had a secret she avoided sharing with anyone, the threat might lie hidden there.

Careful not to lose any loose papers, I removed the items one at a time and laid each on the suite's dining table. She had acquired a complete set of maps of Kodiak Island and surrounding minor islands; topographical maps of the ground, navigational maps of the surrounding waterways, and FAA maps of the relevant airfields and aviation hazards. Not one of the maps included any personal notation. The box contained a leather-bound personal daily planner. Janet had filled in the first few pages with the owner's personal information. She had added no entries in the address section, apart from phone numbers for her mother, sister, and brother-in-law. I wondered where to find personal details about other contacts. Without a list of her friends and acquaintances, my expedition to Kodiak would be like trolling without bait.

The section for Notes contained only bullet items to submit for her upcoming Officer Evaluation Report. Written in a tidy print, her planned submission consumed about 15 pages.

The daily planner's calendar remained mostly empty as well, apart from a few notations for birthdates and anniversaries or adjustments to the duty rotation. There were occasions listed when she had volunteered to cover someone else's duty. Either she was the most generous pilot in the Coast Guard, or her fellow officers owed her something in the proximity of two months of watch-standing.

The only data entry was a cryptic scrawl on the day of her death: "R-5678," written in pen. Followed by "8543," in pencil.

The most surprising find waited at the bottom of the box. Janet had collected all the course study materials for each of the enlisted aviation rates — all the crew who worked on any aspect of the helicopter she flew. Not content to know just how to fly, she also wanted to be the most informed person on the aircraft. I flipped through the study books, marveling at the detailed notes she printed in the margins. Then I packed it all back up to return to her mother.

I settled into the comfortable chair near the window to puzzle over a new mystery. Janet Simms enlisted and worked as a yeoman in the real property office of the First Coast Guard District in Boston. She finished a college degree with evening courses at Harvard. She excelled and attended Officer Candidate School, then qualified for flight school. She became a helicopter pilot, one of the few females in the specialty. Then she studied what the enlisted technicians on her aircraft would learn. How does a woman so focused, so prepared, walk so unprepared into the habitat of most predatory mammal on the continent?

Sometimes a thing makes no sense. You either accept that or force it to make sense. That's my job.

6

The overnight from Chicago to Anchorage by way of Seattle was far less restful than the travel agent who scheduled the flights led me to expect. A lot of business travelers on the flight, Melinda had assured me; after the second round of the beverage cart, they'd all be out like Sleeping Beasties. Somewhere over the Continental Divide, I decided to treat Melinda herself to the trip. Revenge is a dish best served with airline food.

Instead of business travelers, families herding packs of children like bleating lambs filled both overnight flights. Margaret, one of the veteran stewards on the first leg of my trip, explained this phenomenon. Parents like to believe that their little darlings will tire during the day and sleep overnight once they are in the air. What they forget, she said, was the excitement of the airport, the sounds of the airplane, the change of air pressure in their ears, misplacing Mister Snuggles, exploring the aircraft's funny bathroom. Instead of sleeping, children become restless as the flight goes on, with nothing to distract them in the dim cabin. Hence the squealing that no pacifier can alleviate and the endless chases in the aisles. With an understanding smile, Margaret offered me a pair of earplugs and kept a steady supply of Henry Weinhard's Private Reserve beers coming.

When the squabbling reached a fever pitch, she brought a Bailey's Irish Cream served with a plastic cup of ice, gratis.

Once the morning flight arrived in Anchorage, I decided to get a bagel rather than wade through those same families crowded around the luggage carousel. Children darted among the waiting passengers like salmon running upstream in Autumn. Even here, parents exerted no more control over their spawn than they had onboard the flight. When it appeared my bags were the only ones revolving on the baggage carousel, I claimed my luggage before the porters carted them off to the bowels of the airport. After retrieving my gear, I went the main terminal and claimed a seat opposite a towering polar bear, a remarkable feat of taxidermy. Eventually, the supply of taxis out front refilled. Finally, I emerged from the main terminal a little after 10 a.m.

Anchorage lies on a plain that appears tucked in the shadow of the Chugach Mountains at that time of the morning. To the West lies Cook Inlet, with Turnagain Arm to the South and Knik Arm to the North. These natural obstacles prevent the city's expansion, so the population expands North up Highway 1 toward Palmer and Wasilla. These natural barriers limit the city to a manageable size, keeping it attractive, mostly.

The taxi ride from the South end of Anchorage up to Elmendorf Air Base took less time than I expected. The driver seemed happy to talk to anyone coming to town for something other than fishing or hunting. When he learned I lived in Cleveland, he asked me about the upcoming Indians line-up with a surprising sports acumen, considering we were three time zones and a few thousand miles away. He expressed high hopes for Dwight Gooden, a recent trade from the Yankees to the Indians.

I headed to Elmendorf to see if I could catch a ride to Kodiak on the Red Tail Express, a Coast Guard C-130 that might be stopping through Anchorage on other business. The nickname comes from the distinctive paint on the C-130s' vertical tail. Usually, there are "morale flights" to give people a chance to get off Kodiak to visit the Air Force commissary and exchange or head to stores in downtown

Anchorage. Sometimes the Coast Guard sends patients from the tiny Base clinic on Kodiak over to the larger Air Force hospital. An Air Force base has all the amenities that the bases of other armed forces lack. An old joke suggests that after finishing construction of the "O" Club, gymnasium and golf course for a new Air Force base, the commanding officer returned to Congress for funds to build the hangars and runways.

The cabbie knew where to find the Space-A office, which arranged for active duty and retirees to fly in available space on military flights. I knew a retired commander who travelled around the world, courtesy of Space-A.

Shortly before noon, a C-130 appeared in the sky, coming from the South over Cook Inlet. The Lockheed was recognizable by its white paint job and orange stripe around its nose and across the upright tail. A 10,000-foot paved airstrip is no challenge for the Coast Guard C-130 pilots stationed on Kodiak who routinely fly into gravel strips out the Aleutians and along the Bering coast, like Cold Bay, Adak, Nome, St. Paul, and Point Barrow. Those muddy strips, often clouded in Alaska's ubiquitous fog, can test any pilot's skill and nerve. On the barren Weston Mountain of Attu Island lies the wreckage of a Coast Guard C-130 that later aviators see on approach to the island. It is a sobering sight.

The C-130 disembarked about 40 people in civilian clothing and another ten wearing uniforms, likely heading for one of the specialty care clinics at Elmendorf's hospital. I had made those rounds when I started having severe headaches while on flight duty at Air Station Kodiak. The rest of the folks were likely heading to do a little shopping; things can get quite expensive on Kodiak because everything is flown or shipped in. Anchorage also offers much greater variety.

When the pilots and crew headed into the Space-A office, I gave them a little time and space before introducing myself. I showed them my green military ID card rather than my badge; I wanted to hitch a ride back to Kodiak rather than initiate an investigation at Elmendorf. They seemed receptive to a transient Coastie on leave. I felt no hurry to raise any hackles before it became necessary. That would come soon enough.

With plenty of time before the C-130 returned to Kodiak, I strolled down Fighter Drive and spent a few hours at the USO during the long layover. The small mess offered only tea, no soda that looked good; however, the home-made chocolate chip cookies were delicious. From my big green carryall bag, I removed the novel about the American Revolution I first started back at Point Betsie. When I rejoined the book, rebel forces accepted the British surrender at Saratoga. The only other visitor in the USO that afternoon was an Air Force tech sergeant waiting for a flight to Mountain Home Air Force Base in Idaho. He stood about four inches taller than me and wore his hair longer than any other service would consider permissible. We played a few games of foosball to pass the time, then he went to the payphones and engaged in lengthy conversations with someone who might soon be an ex-, given how often he had to call back. I knew the process. Absence makes the heart grow fonder of someone else.

In the afternoon, I went back to the Space-A lounge. The C-130 remained on the tarmac, wooden chocks in place fore and aft of the wheels. The crew, dressed earlier that day in distinctive light blue flight suits, weren't in sight. During the afternoon, the terminal began to fill with women hauling foldable shopping carts loaded with paper bags from the commissary. One of the airmen returned and began to help the spouses load their purchases into the Hercules. The last preparation for departure was a homemade video of safety procedures for a C-130 played inside the terminal. No one seemed particularly interested in watching.

When the flight crew returned, they lowered the forward steps and the rear cargo ramp so the passengers could load while the pilots conducted pre-checks up on the flight deck. The transport bay of the Hercules contained pallets, each affixed with several rows of standard aircraft passenger seats. After 16 hours in a coach seat from Chicago to Anchorage, I settled into the canvas sling jump seat adjacent to the rear hatch. I'm not paranoid; I simply like to sit in the sections of an aircraft where nothing is likely to explode.

Elmendorf was sunny, and the winds were calm when we departed Anchorage. I sensed a bit of a crosswind when we passed from Cook Inlet over the Gulf of Alaska. The flight made good time; from the mainland to the island took the C-130 about two hours because the distance is approximately 250 nautical miles. Soon we descended into the clouds and fog that shroud Kodiak Island during most of the Winter and Spring, as well as Summer and Autumn.

Kodiak lies in the center of the Kodiak Archipelago, a cluster of sparsely populated islands occupied mostly by native Alaskans in remote villages. These islands lay south of the Alaskan Peninsula in the warm Pacific waters. In winter, the Pacific acts as a thermal blanket over the islands, keeping temperatures around a delightful 32 degrees, warmer than the mainland but perfect for producing a coating of ice over all exterior surfaces. The islands on the North-eastern edge have dense forests; however, the edge of the great boreal forest peters out farther Southwest on the main island until the land assumes the appearance of barren tundra.

Air Station Kodiak shares a runway with Kodiak's small civilian airport. Unfortunately, the runway sits on the waterfront, so the presence of seagulls and other birds is a constant risk. The FAA tries to frighten the birds off with noise cannons because a seagull, eagle or Canada goose can do remarkable damage to a jet's intake. The other hazard of landing a fixed-wing aircraft in Kodiak is that the longest runway aligns with the base of Barometer Mountain, a 2,500-foot pinnacle jutting up like the Rock of Gibraltar. In 1988, an Air Force F-15 struck the peak at the 2,200-foot level while flying from Elmendorf to King Salmon. The Air Force brought in explosives experts to ensure the site was safe for those of us in the rescue team because the fighter carried a full load of 20mm ordnance. Sadly, the pilot did not survive.

My flight back was an encore visit to Kodiak for me, identical to MacArthur's return to the Philippines but without the reporters, a marching band, or an army. I completed a tour at the Air Station as a

rescue swimmer earlier in my career before I developed a strange
affliction while in flight. I began to have a kind of migraine headache
somehow related to the increased pressure on my spinal fluid, or at
least that was one so-called educated medical guess. My ex-wife
thought I experienced a rational fear of leaving a functioning aircraft
while in flight. Subsequent commercial flights have taught me that
the cure for this curious syndrome is administering large doses of
Henry Weinhard Pale Ales augmented with an occasional whiskey
straight up. I failed to convince the Coast Guard command this was a
valid medical solution.

After punching through the white misty shroud, the C-130 made a
smooth landing, came to a stop abreast of the civilian airport, then
turned about to taxi West to the Coast Guard Base along a long paved
ramp. Traffic gates guarded where two streets cross the ramp to keep
vehicles from colliding with aircraft. I waited while the spouses and
children gathered their goods and made for the exits. If I took my
time, I'd miss the traffic rush, and the streets of the Base would be
safe to walk again. I didn't have too far to go. From the big blue
hangar, I hiked only a few hundred yards to the Base convenience
store, located, like many businesses in Alaska, in a corrugated steel
building. As I expected, inside the entrance, I found a bulletin board
full of file cards and scraps of paper highlighting items for sale.

Among the cards offering baby-sitting services, outgrown children's clothing, houseware parties, and used outdoor equipment, I
found a few vehicles for sale. I planned to purchase or rent something for the short time I would be on the island because car rental
companies can be a little prissy in Alaska. Rental contracts there
often contain language in bold red typeface forbidding things like
driving on gravel or off the pavement. That may make sense in corporate headquarters in Chicago where they paved the waterfront, but
Alaska is a very different driving experience, more like the Baja 1,000
than Miracle Mile. Another red-letter restriction prohibits trans-
porting dead fish or wildlife. Again, why go to Alaska if you're not
going to fish or hunt?

The streets and roads on the island have two different surfaces:

Pavement on Base Kodiak and in the town of Kodiak proper; packed gravel beyond that. The roads extend no more than about 50 miles in any direction from the Kodiak airport. Roads create an important distinction. Accessible areas are "on the road system." The rest is more remote, including the National Wildlife System Refuge, home to the distinctive Kodiak bears, *Ursus arctos middendororffi.* Any remaining lands are held by the native corporations.

In the Base convenience store, my good fortune surprised me. By chance, someone was selling a '93 Jeep Wrangler 4x4, with a five-speed transmission and a four-cylinder engine. I was familiar with the model because I'd owned one before. In fact, I had driven it up to Alaska from Elizabeth City and sailed over on the state ferry to Kodiak from Homer, while my wife flew up on Alaska Airlines and Mark Air. The only annoyance on the beautiful drive up the Alaska Highway turned out to be the giant recreational vehicles unable to maintain highway speeds through the Canadian Rockies. When we prepared to transfer off Kodiak after four years, I sold the Jeep to a newly arrived Coastie, a single guy who planned to jack it up with lifters and oversized mud tires. When I called the number on the card, I reached the quarterdeck on the Coast Guard Cutter *Storis*, moored at the Base pier. The watchstander promised to track down the seller and have him return my call. I explained my location and gave the phone number of the payphone inside the entrance to the convenience store.

Fifteen minutes later, a red Wrangler pulled up in front of the store. I recognized the Jeep on first sight. The driver was a skinny guy named Mark, the same kid I had sold the rig to years earlier. He wore a blue ballcap that advertised CGC *Storis*, WMEC-38, above a green military jacket and blue jeans. He laughed when he saw me. "This is a first for me. I never sold a rig back to the prior owner."

"A first for me, too. She looks great."

"She's the same as when you handed me the keys, not many more miles than when you left. So, what can I tell you about her?" he asked, lifting his ballcap and running his hand through hair longer than regulation. "I'm the second owner. First owner was a jerk but took pretty good care of her. One ding on the back tailgate. He claimed his wife put it there at the commissary. But you know airdales."

I decided not to bother clarifying that I no longer worked in the aviation field. "You never got around to the lifters?" I asked as I walked around the outside once. Considering it had spent the intervening years in Alaska, the Wrangler looked almost pristine. "You kept it in storage all this time?"

"Most of it. After I was on the Base for six months, I got transferred to the *Storis* and spent most of my time underway. Even in port, I had to stand rotating duty. So I bought a heavy protective cover for her."

"So why sell it now?" I asked, still in surprise that I had found my first Jeep again.

"I'm heading out next month for Class A school. Boatswain's mate course down in Yorktown. You want to take it for a test drive?"

"Sure. Did the clutch finally loosen up?" I asked as we climbed in. I didn't need to take the Wrangler far to know it was still in great shape. He explained that he did all the routine maintenance at the hobby auto shop on Base. I drove past the exchange and out the perimeter road around Nyman Peninsula, where the Coast Guard Base juts into Women's Bay. I stopped on the point facing Mary Island in the West. From my jacket pocket, I removed the envelope Lieutenant Andrews had given me and counted out $50 bills.

"I'm afraid it's impractical for me to buy it back right now because I'm stationed in Cleveland," I said. "But I need a rig for a couple of weeks that I may need to take off pavement. Would you rent it to me for a week or two week if I keep the For Sale signs in it?" I offered him a stack of bill.

He rifled through the cash and looked at me in shock, leaning away from me into the canvas window. "For five hundred a week? Are you serious?"

"I need to drive it on gravel," I admitted. "You know the rental companies don't like that."

"I heard about it. Couple guys in the barracks rented a car in

Anchorage and drove up the Denali Highway. Needed new shocks when they got it back. Cost them more than two thousand."

"Sounds about right. One other thing, can we keep this quiet? I don't want to advertise that I'm back on the island."

He gave me a look and a wink. "For that money, I can keep a lot of things quiet." He chuckled. "Anything else you don't want anyone to know?"

I figured I might as well start my investigation now. "Any chance you knew that female pilot at the Air Station, Lieutenant Simms? The one killed by a bear?"

He shook his head and shrugged. "Knew of, but didn't know her. Saw her at the Anchor Club a couple times, at the exchange a dozen times, pretty often at the gym. Not sure we said more than five words ever. But she seemed nice enough. For an officer."

"Uh oh. Sounds like a story."

"I had a roommate when I lived in the barracks. He played Santa one year for the air station's Santa to the Villages visits. In all the villages, the families gave the Santa cookies and treats for the reindeer. When they got back here, the pilot in charge took all the cookies and brownies home. My roomie never got even a cupcake out of it."

I shook my head, but decided to put on my best chief petty officer face. "I'm sure the pilot took the treats to the elementary school on base."

"You think?" He asked, incredulously. "Never met a pilot, huh?"

"At least I hope he did."

"Well, you can use the Jeep. We're going out on a patrol day after tomorrow. It'd be sitting the whole time I'm gone."

I thanked him. What he said made sense because, as an E-3 on a cutter, he'd have little opportunity to interact with an officer or a pilot, especially an airedale. "But you haven't heard any rumors about the lieutenant?"

"Me? No. But I'm sure if you asked around at the Air Station, but nothing I ever heard. Sorry."

On the way back up the peninsula, I dropped Mark where the *Storis* moored. I checked the time. Not even 1800, and I'd already secured a vehicle and interviewed my first witness. As I left the Base, I made a left on Cape Chiniak Road and skirted the Old Womens Mountain toward Bells Flats. The side of the mountain looked carved away to make room for the two-lane road, leaving a scar of gray gravel along the right-hand side of the road, opposite Womens Bay.

For commerce, Bells Flats offered exactly one bar with a cantina and a gas station complete with a convenience store and liquor store. For ambiance, the Flats was home to a lot of derelict fishing equipment: steel cages that once served as crabbing pots; pink and blue buoys to mark fishing nets or crabbing pots; miles of old hawser, fishing nets or anchor chains. Several gravel side roads led to private homes hidden in the dense trees. I pulled up to the pump and topped off the Jeep, then went inside to pay in the convenience store, followed by a quick stop next door for a six of Molson Canadian and a fifth of Jameson's Irish Whiskey. Then I headed toward the actual town of Kodiak, back past Womens Bay, the Coast Guard Base, the airport and around a big curve overlooking the dark waters of St. Paul Harbor. The road provided a panoramic view of the fishing fleet and the downtown buildings and houses of Kodiak spread along the base of Pillar Mountain. Fields of snow lingered on the mountain top, but most of the lower altitudes appeared green or gray.

I drove into town, made a left onto Thorsheim Street and pulled into the parking lot of the Baranof Lodge. The young woman working the front desk seemed very friendly, talking without hesitation about herself, the island, current events and many other topics. Her dark hair and eyes, together with her round face, suggested an Aleut heritage. She said she had grown up in a village on nearby Afognak Island but moved to the main island to attend Kodiak College, with plans to go to the University of Alaska in Anchorage. She hoped to go into medicine and return to work in her village. She wanted to help the village's elderly residents.

"Are you here for the launch facility?" she asked. "We've got a half dozen folks staying here already if you want a room near them."

"Sorry? Did you say launch facility?"

"Oh, you don't know? The state is building a rocket launch pad to put satellites into space. It's out at the end of the road by the bison ranch at Pasagshak."

This news completely baffled me — launching rockets from a remote island in Alaska? An island that a few years ago wouldn't even put fluoride in the water because people considered it too dangerous or even a Communist plot. "Why here?" I asked. I imagined a group of Kodiak bears with sunglasses and popcorn watching a rocket launch.

"The state said it's the perfect spot to put a satellite into orbit anywhere in the sky around the planet. And Juneau is always right, you know."

"You don't sound happy," I said. I detected a hint of tobacco smoke wafting up from the lounge off the lobby.

"They came in like they already knew everything, and they wrote up that there are two Alutiiq archeological sites out there. They never asked anyone how to protect the sites; just put in their big report that they exist." Her face had reddened, and she looked around to ensure no one else lingered in earshot. "We have archaeologists down at the Alutiiq museum who could tell them how to protect those sites, but not a word in the EASE about that."

"EIS?" I asked. "Environmental Impact Statement?" I imagined a group of Kodiak bears with sunglasses and popcorn watching a rocket launch.

"I guess. Sounds right. The library has a copy. If you ask for it, they put your name down. We're not supposed to ask questions."

"Like what?"

She leaned toward me and lowered her voice. "A lot of people make their livings on fishing. So these rockets will burn a lot of fuel over the best spawning streams in Alaska. A friend in Anchorage sent me an article about exhaust from the shuttle launches in Florida killing off the manatees."

I nodded in a vague, non-committal manner. "I hadn't heard about that."

"I heard they put it here because the other location they first considered on the mainland was too close to where our Congressman for Life lives."

I checked my chronograph. "Oh, look at the clock. I'm sorry, but I have a few calls to make before it gets too late back East. Looks like I've still got time to call Chicago." I thanked Lily for my room key and wished her good night.

She seemed like a nice girl, but I felt a little shy of following Lily down the rabbit hole. Seems there's always somebody handy with a conspiracy theory to peddle regardless of the evidence. A president assassinated by the mob, FBI, CIA, Cubans, or Russians. President's brother assassinated by the mob, FBI, CIA, Cubans, or Russians. The moon landing faked by NASA. Labor boss killed by the mob, unions, FBI, or CIA. A war in the Middle East started over stolen babies in incubators. A rocket launch facility on a remote island in the Pacific Ocean to destroy salmon fishing. What will *they* do next?

I spent the rest of the evening with my eyeglasses perched on my nose as I reviewed the notes I had scribbled two nights earlier in the Crowne Plaza while sorting through the box of Janet Simms' personal papers. I brought her appointment calendar with me so I could chat with the last people who may have spoken to her. Her calendar showed her duty roster. I popped the top on a Molson Canadian with the opener on my pocket knife. Next, I dug into my big carryall, hanging a few shirts and putting other clothes into drawers. Finally, I unpacked the locked carrier for my weapons. I reloaded clips emptied for the flights across three time zones. At last, I laid my personal armament on the small table and watched a television station out of Los Angeles while sipping a little Jameson's with ice from a hotel plastic cup. Finally, it was time for bed.

_____

7

My first order of business was breakfast at the King's Diner out on Mill Bay Road near Lily Lake. I ordered the reindeer sausage and eggs platter with hash browns and toast. Still as good as during my prior tour of duty on the island. The matronly waitress seemed to remember me, or she pretended to be nice. A clever act to get a larger gratuity?

Next on the agenda was a visit to the site where Lieutenant Simms met her tragic and brutal end. The report from the Alaska State Troopers included a photocopy of a topographical map of the Buskin River and Buskin Lake area, with an X marking a spot above Bear Creek opposite the base of Pyramid Mountain. I went West on Rezanof Drive through Kodiak's small downtown and back out to the civilian airport. There I turned right on a road labeled on the map as Kodiak Island Highway, which was a gross exaggeration of its physical condition. The pavement soon ended, and the road turned to gravel as it wound up toward a pair of tall radio towers belonging to the Coast Guard's Communications Station, the largest of the assorted buildings and homes in the wide valley between Barometer, Pillar, and Pyramid Mountains.

Once past the comms station, I stopped to put the Wrangler into

4x4, which required getting out to lock the hubs on the front wheels. Both turned without effort, and I moved the inside lever into 4 Wheel High. After a false start on a two-track that headed East toward Pillar Mountain, I found a dirt road that doubled back on itself and skirted the base of Pyramid Mountain. A flattened area in the brush still bore the shredded remainders of yellow crime scene tape hanging on wooden stakes. I parked the Jeep and waded another one hundred yards through the wildflowers blooming across the opening until I reached a location that matched the trooper's photos. Not far down the slope, Bear Creek, swollen by melting ice and snow on the neighboring slopes, rushed toward Buskin River.

With the AST's photos in hand, I stood in about the proximate location where the troopers found the body. Why did she come here? Her calendar for the day of her death had only a cryptic notation written in pen: "R-5678." On the same line was a scrawl in pencil: "8543." Were these local phone numbers that didn't require any area code and prefix? Locker combinations? Lottery numbers? Was she meeting someone here? Seemed like an uncomfortable place for either a business meeting or a romantic rendezvous. And dangerous in Autumn when Kodiak's big grizzlies are busy binging on any food available in preparation for winter hibernation. Despite its rather minor elevation, the site afforded a nice view of the Buskin River Valley, beyond the Communications Station and Coast Guard housing, all the way to Puffin Island in St. Paul Harbor. On that clear morning, I had an unobstructed view of the peak of Barometer Mountain.

Still, I worked my way through the gruesome photography, comparing the images to reality. The attack and the subsequent investigation appeared to have flattened the surrounding vegetation, leaving a rectangular opening in the flowers. I recognized irises, forget-me-nots, and fireweed in the field around me. Honeybees flitted between them. Where a photo suggested, I found a massive pile of bear scat that looked weathered by the past winter. I chose not to examine it up close because I could see hair, fur, and fish bones without effort. I felt very happy to leave any closer examination to scatologists trained for it.

After an exhaustive study of the site and the photos, I sat down to read through the AST report again. The trooper wrote a vivid, if graphic, account of what he observed when he arrived on the scene. No doubt he would be able to describe his observations in detail for years to come. One detail likely to haunt any witness was the amount of blood smeared across the surrounding ground and showing in the prints were the bear finally stalked away. After reviewing the autopsy notes, I put it all away and sat still on the ground amid the wildflowers. A mild North wind came down the valley from Anton Larson Bay. A white-tailed bumblebee landed on my left hand. For a brief moment, I worried about being bitten. After two prior gunshot wounds, the threat posed by a bee sting seemed mild. I assumed the bee and I were curious about each other. Finally, the bee flew off and landed on a blooming flower that looked like purple lupine.

When the morning warmed to afternoon, I stood and looked upstream along Bear Creek north to where it disappeared into a narrow cleft between Pillar Mountain and Pyramid Mountain. Whatever Janet Simms sought in this sea of flowers remained a mystery to me, and the AST as well.

Back in the Wrangler, I headed over to the Coast Guard Base. Although I was not on official business, I decided that informing the resident special agents on Base Kodiak would be a professional courtesy. Or a mistake.

8

The special agents in Kodiak occupied rooms in a former barracks converted to office space after the Coast Guard took over the Base from the Navy, which operated there from World War II onward. Few Americans appreciate that Alaska was a contested battleground then, with Japanese forces landing in the Aleutian Islands at Kiska, where they captured the Aleut population and interned them in Japan. In return, the U.S. interned other Aleuts in camps in Southeast Alaska. Major battlegrounds occurred at Dutch Harbor and Attu, where at least 2,300 Japanese soldiers died, sometimes in hand-to-hand combat. When the Japanese gave up their resistance, American troops explored the battlefield and found the enemy may have chosen suicide over surrender. While stationed on Kodiak, I hopped a C-130 making a resupply run to the Loran station on Attu and spent a few hours walking through the rusted military equipment abandoned by both sides after the battle.

When I went into the resident agent's office, a woman sitting at one of the two desks waved and pointed to the phone at her ear. I nodded in understanding, then went to look at the large, detailed map of Alaska spread across the wall while I waited. Colored pins pierced the map, indicating Coast Guard units located from the

Bering Sea and across the mainland down to Juneau in the Southeast peninsula.

After five minutes of listening to the phone receiver, she finally spoke into the mouthpiece. "I'm sorry, someone's come into the office," she said. She looked up at me and made a circular motion with her forefinger as if encouraging the party on the other end of the line to wrap things up. "Yes, I will look into this and call you as soon as I know something." She stood, still holding the phone at her ear. "Look, I must go now. Yes. I will. Good day."

Having dispensed with the caller, she turned her attention to me. She was a brunette of above-average height, no doubt a basketball player in high school. No make-up. No jewelry. All business. "I'm Special Agent Kathy Douglas. May I help you?"

"I hope not. At least I hope I won't need help."

Her expression was midway between bemused and confused.

"Let me explain," I said, removing my badge from a jacket pocket and handing it to her so she could inspect it and examine my green ID card. "I thought it would be best if you knew I was on the island. And I may spend some time on Base. Rather than have you find out from someone else that I'm hanging around." I held out my hand for my badge.

Special Agent Douglas gave me another look, then studied the ID again. She looked at me with doubt. "You're *the* Marty Galloway?"

"To my mother's eternal regret. Why?"

"Where are you stationed?" she asked.

"Cleveland. Why?" Now I grew suspicious. "Is there a problem?"

"I've heard a lot of stories. You know, agents gossip like my grandmother's bridge club. You don't look quite like what I pictured. After the stories I've heard."

"Expecting a cape? Sorry, but the tights chafe."

She laughed. "No, something more like Rambo carrying a rocket launcher. When you hear stories, you get a picture in your mind. You know what I mean?"

"So in your mind, do I drive an armored vehicle or an Aston Martin?"

"More like a Humvee, with an M-60 mounted on top. I hear they can be a bitch to lug around."

I laughed. "Yeah, and the recoil can be hell. "

"Are you here on a case? Frank didn't mention anything to me. Frank Anker is the special agent-in-charge. He's my boss. Well, you know that."

"I'm not here in any official capacity. The family of Lieutenant Simms asked me to look into her death."

"That pilot who died back in the fall?" Her complexion turned ashen. "That poor woman. Can you imagine?"

"I try not to. The family asked me to make certain that the investigation crossed all the t's." I walked behind Anker's desk to examine his "I love me" wall. In the center was a framed set of his full-sized medals that looked to include a full house from Commendation and Achievement Medals to Expert Rifle and Pistol.

Kathy sat back down at her desk. "The Alaska Troopers handled the whole investigation. Her remains went to Anchorage for autopsy. I went to her apartment to help her roommate pack her belongings. But otherwise, Frank and I sat that one out."

"So that was it?"

"We didn't launch an investigation at all. Left it to AST. But I talked to the kid from Base Security who was first on scene. He was pretty shook up." She stood and cleared the chair opposite her desk. "Sorry. We don't get many visitors."

"I'm sure. Were you called when it happened? Or Frank?"

"We weren't in the office. The CO granted everyone on Base sunshine liberty that day because we'd had a month of rain and fog. I was out at Pasagshak Bay, watching them build that new space port out there. Frank was out in Larsen Bay on his favorite salmon stream."

"With half the island's population."

She laughed at my comment for the first time. "So true. I used to love fishing, but here it's like sparring. You get yourself set up, but when the run starts you get shoved out of the way by the herd following the salmon run upstream."

I agreed. After my first year, when I came away with a black eye and a loose tooth, I stopped fishing on Kodiak. "When I was stationed here, I called it combat fishing."

Kathy laughed. "That's it exactly. So is there anything I can do for you?"

"No. I've got the AST report and the autopsy. I went over to the scene this morning. I'm going to talk to the lieutenant's roommate and a few other contacts if I can decipher her day planner. Then I'll be gone, day after tomorrow from what I can tell. Next day at the latest."

She offered a business card. "If you need anything, give me a call. Always happy to help a legend." She smiled, mischief showing around the corners of her mouth.

"You know it's always the sidekick or the partner who gets whacked."

"I'd rather be Catwoman than Robin anyway. Now that girl's got one hot-looking outfit."

9

The next visit on my list was Hannah Shangin, Lieutenant Simms' roommate for the past two years. I expected Hannah could tell me about Janet's social life and, more importantly, the lieutenant's demeanor in the weeks prior to her death. Special Agent Douglass indicated Hannah had packed Janet's personal belongings for shipping home to Indianapolis. If I got lucky, Hannah had heard Janet talking in her sleep.

The first item of business was removing the canvas windows from the half doors on the Wrangler. April felt warm enough that I could drive in the open air, protected only by my leather jacket. Repeated cleanings had removed most of the bloodstains earned during that brouhaha on Lake Superior a half dozen years earlier. I switched the radio to the local public radio station, KMXT-FM, which was covering national and state news.

As I came into town, I passed the Alaska Pacific Seafood cannery and the dozens of fishing boats in the harbor. The air had a faint scent of fish. I imagined the curse of working in either place, faced with purging that fragrance from your clothes and pores after work.

I followed Mill Bay Road East past the Alaska State Troopers Post and Kodiak Island Hospital before taking a right on Rezanof Drive

East, which took me around the Northern end of Kodiak Island and past the old World War II outpost, Fort Abercrombie. A few miles farther on, I found Three Sisters Way. A well-rusted Pathfinder sat in the driveway of the Shangin residence, so I walked up to the porch and knocked. Music played inside, which was a positive sign. I rapped on the inner wooden door several times before noticing the doorbell button. However, neither knock nor bell elicited any response from inside. I decided to try a side or back door.

When I opened a gate on the left side of the house, I came face to face with a big Malamute, one of the largest dogs I'd ever seen. Its huge brown head reached above my belt buckle. He seemed content to nuzzle me with his slobbery snout, leaving a swath of drool on my pants leg. After a moment, his curiosity and energy expended, he returned to a shaded area in the yard and sprawled on the ground. At that moment, I heard a woman's voice singing along to the music on the radio inside.

When I stepped around the corner of the house, I heard a woman shriek. "Who the fuck are you?" she screamed. She stood naked under an outdoor shower head. Suds covered her black hair and brown body.

I waved my badge. "Sorry. I'm here about Janet Simms. I would like to ask a few questions."

"Enjoying the show?" she asked. The terror in her voice had moderated to anger.

"Would you rather I lie?"

She laughed. "Go around to the front door. Stay there. I'll be there in a few."

The big dog raised his massive head to watch me walk back to the gate. He did not seem especially perturbed by an intruder or his owner's scream. After securing the gate behind me, I settled on a hand-painted wooden bench on the front porch. After five minutes, the homeowner emerged as promised, swathed in an oversized terry cloth robe.

"Do you have a name?" she asked. "And matching ID?" She seemed well-versed in the routine. Still standing half in the door, she inspected my green military ID and gold badge. Finally, she pushed the door open and motioned for me to enter. Then she waved at a neighbor. "That's Missus Stimpson across the street. With what happened to Janet, she keeps an eye out for me. I worked 20 minutes late at the cannery a few days ago, and I found the troopers camped out in my driveway when I got home, ready to start up a search." She motioned for me to sit on her big, plush sofa. The decor was classic Alaskan, with carved wooden motifs of salmon and bears on the wall and a framed topographic map of Kodiak Island. An old-fashioned milk can in the corner held a bouquet of colorful whale baleen.

"Sorry to bother you. Are you getting ready for work?" I asked. "I can come back another time."

"No, coming home now. I shower out there so I don't track the smell of dead fish into the house. In the winter, I strip in the mudroom and head straight for the inside shower."

"Sorry about surprising you, uh . . . ," I stuttered.

"Naked? Is that the word you mean?"

"Yes. Naked. Not how I usually start an interview. Thank you for talking to me anyway."

Hannah sat back in her chair and shrugged. "Not sure what else I could tell you I haven't gone over already. I've talked to the Kodiak police, the state troopers, Base Security, the captain from the Air Station, along with a chaplain who was planning to call her mother. And there was another guy with a badge that looked like yours. He spent most of his time hitting on me while he was here."

"Coast Guard special agent from the Base here?" Kathy Douglas had failed to mention Frank Anker's other proclivities included fishing for a different type of catch.

"I guess." She wrung out her dark hair with a towel. "Frank, something."

"I need to follow up on a few things. I went through Janet's belongings that the Coast Guard sent home to her mother. Things like her calendar. Did you pack all of that up for her?"

"Yeah, they offered to send packers, but I thought they might pack my things, too. I'm not planning to go anywhere, especially not to

Indiana, for sure. They did send a woman to help. She had a badge like yours, too. Nicer than the dude who works with her."

"Been on Kodiak long?" I asked as I fished my notebook out of my jacket pocket.

"All my life. My family is about half the population of Ouzinkie up on Spruce Island. I came to Kodiak for high school."

"Been at the cannery since?"

She leaned forward for a pack of cigarettes on the coffee table and lit one. "Why? That a problem for you? You feel sorry for someone stuck in fish guts all day long?"

"Me? I'd have no fingers left after the first week. I always keep an ice pack in my creel, but it's not for the fish."

She chuckled. "Lot of outsiders on the line that way. Come up for the quick money on a crabbing or fishing boat. Then end up at the cannery. I'm not saying it's not good money, but there are only so many boats now. And how many fish can they catch in a 24-hour opener? So they come into the cannery for work because they want to stay up here. I don't blame them. But they're no better with knives than chopsticks."

Starting in the late 1970s, the government began to impose individual fish quotas, or IFQs, and limited time periods, called openers, to restrict fishing to enforce several quotas. The goal was to give the fisheries a chance to recover from what many believed was overfishing by foreign vessels before the signing of the Magnuson-Stevens Act that established American waters out to 200 miles.

"None of my business why you stay here. If I had to guess, I'd say it's because of your family in Ouzinkie. Parents getting older. Grandparents still alive. So you look out for them, and you see they get out of the village safe when they need medical help. Close?"

"You guess peoples' weight at carnivals?" she asked. She stubbed out her smoke with determination, then lit another.

"No. I looked at the pictures on your walls. Sorry if I upset you."

"Oh, I thought you were investigating me."

I raised my hands in front of me. "No, my apologies. I should have called before I showed up and intruded."

She exhaled a long trail of smoke and laughed. "I have nothing to hide. You go up to Ouzinkie, you could learn anything. Hell, you've already seen me naked. A little late to be shy."

"I am sorry for bursting in. You have no reason for embarrassment."

"So you did enjoy the show." Then she laughed. "Nice to know." Putting her cigarette to rest in the ashtray, she stood and went into the kitchen. Did she add a sway to her hips as she went? In a moment, I heard a back door open. "Anton," she called. "Anton, dinner time."

Without warning, I was face-to-face with the dog's white snout and brown eyes. He greeted me with a low "woo-woo" noise deep in its throat then did an about-face when he heard kibble clattering into a steel bowl. In a moment, Hannah returned carrying two open bottles of Moosehead Beer. She handed me one then returned to her seat and cigarette. "I hate to drink alone."

"I'm always glad to be of service." I raised my bottle in a salute. "Do you mind answering a few more questions?"

"Sure, I'll try to help, but I've already answered every question imaginable," Hannah said, resting back in the chair.

"Was Janet dating anyone?"

"Not that I knew. But she could because I've been going home on some weekends to help with my grandmother. She broke her leg when the snowmobile rolled over while she was out gathering firewood."

"Tough stock," I said.

"Not as tough as she like to think. So, yeah, Janet could have had a few dates then. No Coasties, I don't think. What's the thing you guys have? Anti-fraternity?"

"Fraternization?"

"Yeah. She was kind of paranoid about it. Me? If I don't date guys from work, the pickings get slim. Not a lot of guys walk in while I'm naked."

"Their loss."

"Well said." She crossed her legs, so a trim calf peeked through her robe.

I smiled and tried not to stare or become distracted. "On her day planner, I found a note for the day she died. R-5678. Then 8543. Any idea what she may have meant by either?"

Having finished his dinner, Anton lumbered into the room, still licking his jowls with a long tongue. With effort, he climbed up onto the loveseat opposite us.

Hannah reached onto an end table and picked up a pencil and pad of paper. "Give me the numbers again." As I did, she wrote them out in large script. "In one, the numbers go up and in the other the numbers go down. 5-6-7-8 and 8-5-4-3. We could mix it up to get phone numbers on the island, using the prefix either 486 in town or 487 on the Base or out in Bells Flats. Live here long enough you know those."

"But then we're left with any combination of four numbers for the number. Might take me a while to dial something like ten thousand possible phone numbers. More if I have to dial both prefixes."

"Don't get huffy with me," she said, tossing her notepad aside. "You intrude on my shower and expect me to solve your algebra problem?" She fired a third cigarette. I never intended to be a bad influence on her health.

I waved my empty beer bottle at her. "May I?"

"Go on. Bring me one, too."

With a beer run for cover, I headed into the kitchen. Kitchens can reveal a lot of information. Stainless steel cooking utensils covered the walls, some of which I could not identify. After retrieving the beers, I searched the refrigerator for a bottle opener affixed to the door with a magnet. Instead, I noticed a business card for a local real estate agent. I opened the bottles with my pocket knife and headed back to the living room.

"Are you looking to buy a house on Kodiak Island?" I asked. "Not going home to Ouzinkie?"

Hannah looked up at me in surprise. "No, I'm not planning to go anywhere. I renewed the lease here not long ago. You wouldn't believe how expensive rentals have gotten since they started building that damn space port thing."

"There's a business card for a real estate agent on the side of the refrigerator."

"Really?" She sounded surprised. "I can't imagine Janet put it up there. She was up to rotate out this summer if I understood right. Sorry. I'm not sure how it got there."

"Anton looking for a bigger yard?"

She laughed. Looking at the malamute sprawled across her loveseat cushions, she nodded. "Wouldn't put it past him."

With a new Moosehead in hand, I toured Janet's vacant room. The bed was bare, and all the drawers sat empty. Two dozen plastic hangers remained in the closet, along with four wooden suit hangers and a collection of wire hangers. These last no doubt held her uniform components after dry cleaning. Easier to maintain a uniform when they hang well. I didn't recall seeing the typical mover's box in Missus Simms' house in which clothes can travel on hangers. Irrelevant to my questions; I dismissed it.

Anton performed his own rounds of the lieutenant's room, sniffing at each item of furniture. He nosed his way through the room as if expecting to find Janet waiting with a treat. He went out before me, saying lowly that deep "woo-woo."

I thanked Hannah for her time, knowledge and beer. She invited me to return if I needed more information about Kodiak. Or Janet. I was not yet past the embarrassment of surprising her naked in the outdoor shower. I wondered if she would forgive me.

10
───────

I left Hannah's house with a real estate agent's business card and a pants' leg now trimmed with the drool and fur of an Alaskan Malamute. I decided it was too late in the afternoon to call the real estate office. So I stopped at a news box and purchased the most recent Kodiak Daily Mirror. At the bottom of the box, I found editions for three previous days. I put a few singles in the stack where the old issues began, then took two back days. Even old local news would be more interesting than the television news from Los Angeles.

Back at the Baranof Lodge, I found the lobby crowded with an interesting mix of men. Half the crowd appeared to be Coasties, identified by short back and sides haircuts. They wore the Coast Guard logo on hats and jackets above blue jeans and black work boots below. The others seemed like they would be comfortable working as roadies for a concert tour, wearing gaudy satin jackets. I didn't see a bus in the parking lot, so I couldn't guess who was convening in the lobby. I weaved my way through the crowd and headed for my room.

"Mister Galloway," a voice called from the front desk. "Marty! I have a message for you."

I went back to the desk and accepted from Lily a pink slip of paper. I thanked her and turned to head back across the lobby. A tall, lanky man with a dark mullet and bushy goatee blocked my path up to the rooms.

"You're Marty Galloway?" he asked. "With the Coast Guard?" He wore a deerskin leather jacket with fringe on the chest and sleeves.

My hackles went up, but I thought the lobby was too crowded with witnesses for this to be dangerous. I resisted my natural inclination to reach for the Colt inside my jacket. "Yes. Sorry, I don't recall that we've met."

"You don't know him?" the closest Coastie asked. "He's Travis Pike. He had that big hit, 'My Girl is a Five Whiskey Girl.'"

Another Coastie jostled his friend aside. "No, no. His bigger hit was, 'Tequila Time Tonight.'"

"Wasn't your biggest one about driving your tank in Desert Storm?" the first man asked the tall man in the fringe jacket.

"You were tank corps in Iraq?" I asked the musician. "I've heard it was a challenge to keep the tanks operational in the sand."

"No, that was a song." Travis Pike spoke with a tenor of contempt for military service that surprised me coming in front of a group of enlisted guys who risk their lives serving in Alaska's wilds. "I got no time for that Elvis thing."

"Come on, Travis, we've got a reservation for dinner," a voice called. "They asked us to be on time because there's so many of us."

The whole group left together, but I wondered if any Coasties were among those invited to dine with Mister Pike. As I headed up the hallway to my room, I wondered how Travis Pike knew my name. I didn't recognize either his name or his tunes, but I don't squander a lot of time listening to the radio, partly so I never heard music like "My Girl is a Five Whiskey Girl." "That Elvis thing," I thought, sounded pretty snotty. Say what you want about the King; when the Army called his number, he took his place in the ranks.

The phone message slip read the 487 phone exchange for the Base and a four-digit extension with the name Frank. No doubt Kathy had informed her boss, Frank Anker, of a special agent visiting

Kodiak. I assumed he would be unhappy with my stopover. Special agents can be a little territorial.

Before settling in, I took a Molson out of the mini-fridge. I would visit Frank in the morning, then call upon Marilyn Solverson, the real estate agent. Unless bowled over by a herd of new witnesses, I expected to be on my way back to Cleveland even sooner than I planned. I debated staying an extra day or two on Kodiak, stocking up on fishing gear at Big Ray's Outfitters downtown and then hiking into one or two of the lakes on the Road System for trout, pike, or Dolly Varden. With the ice melting off the inland lakes, fish gobble up any flies drifting in front of them.

With an open beer in hand, I glanced through the *Daily Mirror*, a black and white tabloid on newsprint. The front page above the fold: Coast Guard rescues an employee suffering an apparent heart attack from a fish processing ship in the Bering Sea north of Akutan. Below the fold featured a progress report on the space port construction at Pasagshak. The crime report on page 2 accumulated the mundane from the island: pack of dogs loose; pack of teens lose; warnings of threatened knife fight at the high school; stolen halibut traps and buoys; stolen vehicle taken for a joyride through McDonald's drive-thru then abandoned by the Main Elementary. The issue of fluoride in drinking water resurfaced in the Letters to the Editor because someone had found out that the Coast Guard Base added fluoride to its water system. This caused a bit of outrage because the Base water supply served an elementary school on Base as well as the airport, the FAA, the Fish and Wildlife Service, and NOAA. The letter writer described the evils of fluoride, dangers exceeded by only the introduction of pool tables in River City. A century ago, people believed that telephones were the work of the devil.

The classified ads featured what you might expect in a community with a closed economy; other than one grocery store with a section for household goods, most merchandise was sold and resold through For Sale ads, Garage Sales, and Yard Sales. The sole car dealership on the island maintained an inventory of about a half dozen new models, leaving plenty of opportunity in the future trade of used cars back and forth for years to come. I had no doubt the Wrangler would see many happy new owners in its future on Kodiak.

A small note on Page 6 announced a celebrity sighting on the island. A musician of some note, Travis Pike, intended to lay over a few days in Kodiak waiting for the weather to clear enough to fly a charter into Larsen Bay on the Northwest side of Kodiak Island for a bear hunt. My ignorance about country music aside, Mister Pike must be doing well enough in Nashville to spend at least $10,000 on a professional bear guide. Non-residents must hire guides in Alaska; the guides are well-qualified locals who deal with hunters from Outside possessing a range of skills. Hunting big game has become like mountain climbing; with enough money you can hire a guide or sherpa to ensure your success, no matter how little you deserve such a prize. Two years ago, these boutique expeditions ended in tragedy on the slopes of Mount Everest.

How did Travis Pike know my name? I wondered. And why was my first reaction to think about putting a .45 caliber slug into him? In the years since my episode involving the missing Coast Guard crew on Lake Superior, various groups targeted me for vile and lethal threats. Some of which defied both biology and physics. Generally speaking, the human body only experiences death once. The recurring vitriol made me paranoid. And a little panicky.

My schedule for the following day appeared straightforward and brief. The only question seemed to be whether I would get any fishing done on this visit to the island.

11

Not long into the night, I woke in relief to see that the room was not afire. I sat up to shake off a dream of an H-3 lowering me onto the bow of a burning trawler in the Gulf of Alaska's twilight. When none of the crew greeted me, I unhooked from the hoist cable and went aft, past the empty wheelhouse. On the fantail, I found a young woman working hard to keep a pump running and the end of a hose over the side to draw water from the ocean for those below fighting the engine room fire. She pointed me toward an open hatch where I could find the skipper.

With some effort, I climbed down the ladder to the lower deck. Two men handled the nozzle of a water hose connected to a foam canister. They laid down a layer of foam over the flames coming up from the bilge. Another crewman used an extinguisher on the electrical panel. A fourth man staggered toward me. His hair, beard, and eyebrows smoldered from what must have been a flash fire that did not singe his skin. I led that man topside and radioed for a hoist.

The helo lowered a basket to a hover over the fantail. I prepared the injured man for rescue and then waved for the basket to be hoisted away. In minutes, the basket dropped back onto the deck.

After grounding it on the deck, I leaned into the engine room and signaled with my flashlight at the three remaining crew. The man trying to subdue the sparking electrical board tossed his extinguisher aside and came toward me. I motioned him to climb up to the main-deck and helped him into the basket. With him safely away toward the helo's open door, something in the vessel's bowels erupted. The trawler rolled hard to starboard, pitching the young woman over the gunwale. I tossed a lifering after her then peered through the open hatch. One crewman appeared motionless on the grated deck below; his shipmate stood over him, hosing him down with water. With a renewed sense of urgency, I went back down the ladder and motioned for the man standing to go topside and flag for a basket drop. Then I pulled the prone, burned mate over my shoulder. With luck, the exit up to the main deck was a set of steel steps rather than a vertical rung ladder.

By the time we were back topside, the helo's basket rested on the fantail, sliding with the vessel's roll. I debated how to position the crewman so the steel cage did not exacerbate his burns. I motioned frantically for the helo to hoist away, hoping the cable and basket did not snag on the trawler's superstructure. Once the basket was hoisted away yet again, I staggered to the starboard rail, searching the churning seas for any sign of the young woman or the lifering. Seeing a flash of silver retro-reflective tape, I went over the side.

As I thrashed in the ocean, the HH-60 banked off and travelled away from my location. As the fishing vessel's waterline continued to disappear into the ocean, I rode the wave crests, searching for the young woman's blonde hair with my flashlight. A pale hand waved in the surf. I marked the location in my mind and swam toward her. She fought me at first, perhaps afraid I might pull her down. Then she calmed and even cooperated, as I rolled over so she could rest with her back against my chest. Together we floated for more than 25 minutes until the helo returned from the clinic in Dutch Harbor. As we waited, I felt her body shudder against me as she sobbed.

When I woke, I climbed out of bed and put a finger of Irish

whiskey into a plastic cup. Then I sat on the desk chair, sipping. How had my alcohol consumption fallen so short this evening? Since leaving Michigan, I failed several nights to accomplish my goal of a good night's sleep without the usual unrest and disruptions of my personal work history.

12

I chose to think that Frank Anker wanted to get together in the spirit of special agent esprit de corps. At the least, I intended to invite him to breakfast at the Buskin River Inn. He appeared to have a different intention, five degrees this side of gunpoint.

"Why the hell are you here?" he asked while we were still in the parking lot outside his office. He'd come out to meet me upon my arrival. He wore an oversized arctic parka, so I worried what weapons lay hidden within.

"Good fishing, I hear," I said. "I can get you brochures about it."

"I don't need Super Agent getting up in my business. I heard all about Boston and you ratting out some yeoman." Frank struck a pose like someone entering a dojo. The stance didn't look especially threatening on a guy with a salt and pepper brush cut. "The AST determined a bear killed the lieutenant. Done. End of story. No contraband machine guns." With his staccato pattern of speaking, Frank would have done well as a drill instructor at basic training if he failed to make the cut as a special agent.

I put my hands in the air in mock surrender. "OK. No question from me. I'm here because the family wants closure."

"What more could they ask?" he asked with stress in his voice. "I walked that whole area with the chief of Base Security. Nothing. Wasn't nothing there." From a parka pocket, he withdrew a cigarette that he lighted using a silver flip-top lighter.

I ignored the double negative. "That's all I've found so far. And that's what I'll likely tell her mother that I found," I explained. "The only difference? I'm going to be sitting in her living room. Looking her straight in the eye. No phone calls. No distractions, just the sad truth."

Frank looked at me. Then he checked his watch. "OK. We can still eat on Base. But the Buskin Inn is much better if you're still offering."

"Sure. I'm never one to renege on an offer."

"OK, but you gotta tell me the real story about getting the *Mackinaw* to ram a freighter. Were you crazy?"

For the first time in my career as a special agent, I could explain that the crazy part wasn't my idea. The skipper of the icebreaker made the decision, and he wasn't even relieved of command for it, perhaps due to the intervention of Admiral Thorne. The Commandant of the Coast Guard can be quite persuasive. For me, well, I kept my badge, but I've become a target of many unhappy people. For the moment, I was too far away from Michigan to worry about them.

13

Marilyn Solverson ran her real estate business out of her home on the Northeast corner of Kodiak Island. The tall, elegant house stood on the waterside of Cliffside Road, with a dramatic view of Mill Bay. I parked in the wide driveway behind a Range Rover. Individual lights illuminated as I progressed around the house on a cobblestone walk. The door alarm sensed my presence on the porch and sounded without any physical contact.

Real estate is a very good business on this late end of the supply chain. The original owners, the Aleuts, lost possession of Kodiak and the Aleutian Chain when the Russian fur traders and missionaries arrived. When the Americans bought Alaska from the Russians for about two cents per acre in 1867, pundits dubbed the purchase a folly. In comparison, the Louisiana Territory cost about four cents per acre about sixty years earlier. Try buying an acre in Alaska for pennies today.

A servant or staffer invited me into the front foyer, which would have been a mudroom in any other home on Kodiak, except the average mudroom lacks the crystal chandelier and brass busts resting on waist-high Doric columns in each corner. Not a mounted deer head in sight. David pointed to a brass sign requesting visitors remove their shoes before entering. There was an elegant wooden bench to assist in that chore. Brass coat racks stood guard on either side of the interior door. I declined his invitation to hang my leather jacket, concerned David might react badly to my holstered Colt .45.

David led me into the main room of the house. Where I expected a paneled great room, I found instead a room straight out of a Fifth Avenue mansion of New York City's Gilded Age. The floor appeared to be granite, covered with a beautifully intricate Persian rug. A field-stone fireplace with a massive mahogany mantelpiece consumed most of a wall facing the entrance. Another wall held bookcases, floor to ceiling, with a ladder on rollers to help reach the upper shelves. What the entry way lacked in mounted animal heads, this room compensated for with an astonishing collection of domestic and foreign wildlife trophies. I recognized those species native to North America but relied on the engraved brass plates to help identify certain exotic heads. What little I knew of the trade suggested that someone had invested at least several million dollars on African safari hunts to acquire a leopard, a lion, and a rhinoceros, among others. An empty mount held a brass plate engraved "Siberian Ibex." A wall dedicated to eight bear mounts included both a polar bear and a Kodiak bear, as well as three exotics, likely from Asia. Perhaps mounting a panda bear would be considered déclassé. On the way through town, I observed three building sites promoting the work of Hans Solverson Construction and Contracting. Clearly the family business were operating well into the black.

David didn't leave me alone in the great hall for long, as if out of fear that my motive was to case the place. He escorted me into a side room about as big as my apartment in Ohio that appeared to serve as an office. The furniture included an oak desk the size of a double bed, a meeting table able to seat a dozen visitors, and a drafting table. The reddish hue of the upholstery on the leather seats complemented the desk. David motioned for me to sit at one of the chairs facing the massive desk. He promised my host would arrive soon. The wait provided an opportunity to study the intricate carving on the face of the desk — a nature tableau with a Kodiak bear at its center. In the corner stood a 10-foot carved wooden totem pole. From a distance, it looked to be genuine.

Marilyn Solverson swept into the office like a runway model. She wore a black cashmere sweater and white silk pants with matching ballet slippers. The styling of her auburn hair looked like a significant project for any hairdresser. Discrete pearl earrings and necklace. Though tasteful, her mascara and eyeliner stood out because most other women on Kodiak went sans make-up. Rouge highlighted her high cheekbones. I stood to meet her, and she extended her hand, knuckles up as one might expect her ring kissed. I shook her hand in a more businesslike manner.

"Thank you for agreeing to see me, Missus Solverson." I displayed my badge. "I'll try to take but a few minutes of your time."

"Please have a seat." Rather than sit behind the big desk, she sat next to me in the chairs facing it. This put us rather close, and she could put a hand on my wrist or knee without effort. "Your job must be so interesting, Mister Galloway. Investigating crime and apprehending wrong-doers. My husband and I enjoy that show, *JAG*."

I chuckled. "Well, I assure you my job is nothing like that. I spend a lot of time on security clearances. Some fraudulent enlistments. An occasional desertion."

She leaned forward and put her hand above my knee. "Tell me, do you carry a weapon?"

"Sometimes. Now I have a simple question for you. Do you know why Lieutenant Simms had one of your business cards on her refrigerator when she died?" I sat back in the chair, removing myself from her reach. I could not afford the distraction during the interrogation of a beautiful woman's hand on my thigh. As a precaution, I never discuss any weapons I might carry.

"That young woman whom the bear mauled last year?"

"Yes. Your name isn't in her day planner. Nothing in any of her paperwork. She was due to transfer out this summer, so no reason she'd be buying property except as an investment."

She stood and walked behind her desk, then tapped the intercom on her phone. "David, could you find my appointment calendar from last year and bring it to me?"

"Thank you. I didn't mean to put you out," I said.

"No trouble, but they say memory is the first thing to go. My husband and I have a great deal of business going on. He's a builder and contractor. I imagine you saw two or three of his projects driving out from town."

I wasn't certain how to respond to that information. At that moment, David came in carrying a large binder that he placed on the desk before her. He left immediately. She flipped to the back pages. "I don't have her name in my list of contacts. Do you have a time when she would have contacted me?"

"No, I'm sorry. No notes on the business card."

"OK, we'll do it the hard way — day by day from January to December. Can David get you anything?"

Despite my curiosity about her reaction if I requested a beer before noon, I declined. No doubt her kitchen appliances included an imported Italian cappuccino machine. And a wine cooler set to 55°.

Marilyn searched through each week with due diligence, a pair of elegant reading glasses perched on her nose. The forefinger of her right hand guided her eyes to track her progress. After announcing her arrival at July in her calendar, she called for David to bring her a glass of Perrier water, straight from the fridge, with no ice. "So apart from my business card, did you find any indication that the lieutenant contacted me?" she asked.

"No, I can't say with any certainty that she did attempt to contact you," I said. "I'm sure we all have business cards that we picked up along the way."

David delivered a water goblet accompanied by a green bottle that he set on a leather coaster and then retreated. After filling her glass, Marilyn continued scanning pages, sipping from time to time. "Here we go," she announced, turning the book to face me. I stood and glanced over a page at the end of September, two weeks before Lieutenant Simms died.

In an elegant hand, Marilyn had written, "Lt. Simms, $/ac."

"Do you recall speaking with her?" I asked. "Or meeting with her?"

Marilyn sat back in her stately executive chair. "I apologize. Now I do recall her. She called me with a question about property values on Kodiak. I'm sorry I didn't remember sooner because we did meet once. We met at one of the old Army surveillance turrets up at Fort Abercrombie. She seemed afraid someone might follow her. She asked me to estimate how much an acre of land on Kodiak is worth."

I wished now I had requested a beer earlier when Marilyn offered — this might take some time to unravel this new information. "Did she say why? Was she planning to invest in property for the future?"

"I'm afraid we didn't get into that much detail. I could not give her a direct answer because values fluctuate so much. Is the property on the coast? In town? Have an ocean view? All property is valuable here because the island doesn't have much private property available. There's the Coast Guard Base, the Wildlife Refuge, and the land owned by the native corporation. I'm afraid there's not a lot of land left for private ownership."

"And you now recall all this?" I asked, immediately sorry for how accusatory that sounded.

"Yes, this year has been insane. With the space port coming in and lots of residential and business property in town getting big offers," she said as she shook her head. "And in the middle of it, I received a suggestion that I should run for the state legislature. All too much to keep straight." She took a long sip of her French spring water.

I suspected Marilyn Solverson had little trouble keeping her business affairs straight and could even manage the operations of the United Nations on the side. "Did she ever contact you again? About a particular land purchase?"

Marilyn fanned through the remaining pages of her calendar. "No, I'm afraid I have no record of that. And I do not recall any other conversation with her. If I remember, her accident took place only weeks after we met in person."

"When you did meet, how did she seem? Calm? Nervous? Afraid?"

"As I said, she seemed afraid somebody had followed her. Or me. In some ways, the meeting was a waste of time."

"How so?"

"Well, I didn't know beforehand what she wanted to know. I assumed she wanted to put a bid on a property without anyone else knowing she was in the running. A lot of people get anxious because they don't want the price run up by the owners through proxies. But I couldn't answer her question because the value of an acre swings so much. I'd have to see the acre in question, and then I'd have David gather a set of comps." She gave me an inquisitive look. "Are you familiar with how we price real estate? We look at similar properties that have sold recently. They're called comparable sales, or comps. Then we find an average value. Next we add or subtract for the unique features on a property. For example, a house with a pool or a garage is going to be worth more than a house without any amenities."

"I see. And Janet didn't give you any idea of the location of this hypothetical acre she had in mind?"

"Not a clue. I'm not even sure why she called me. I don't advertise."

Something suggested that Marilyn didn't have to advertise. Husband handles construction jobs on the island. They live in an opulent mansion on the water. Somebody wants her to run for political office. How many people drive a Range Rover on Kodiak?

"A couple of other questions, if I may. Did she give you any indication she would follow up with you?"

"No, she didn't ask."

"Did she give you anything? Like a map? A document to review?"

"No, nothing. I left empty-handed."

I thanked Marilyn for her time. I asked permission to stop back if I learned anything more about Janet's mysterious acre. Then I, too, left my meeting with Marilyn Solverson empty-handed.

14

In April, Alaska's days begin to stretch daylight in ways most people find confounding. While stationed on Kodiak, I played in a softball league that scheduled July games for 1 a.m. because it was still light enough and nobody slept with daylight streaming through the bedroom windows. So I decided to take advantage of the long evening and headed up Monashka Bay Road. When I reached Hannah Shangin's house, the old Pathfinder was back in its parking place. I decided to ask about the only real clue I had to work with — an acre of Kodiak.

"You?" Hannah asked when she opened the door. "I thought we finished yesterday."

"I've got some questions for Anton," I said.

"OK, but you make sure he understands his rights first."

I followed her inside, and we sat in the same places.

"Another beer?" She wore a silk blouse over blue jeans, so I guessed she had plans for the night other than answering my questions. I caught a fragrance about her other than eau de halibut.

"I'm not a man to turn down a Molson," I said.

"Good. That's all I have at the moment." She brought two open long-neck bottles back into the living room. "So how can I help the Coast Guard tonight?"

"No Anton this evening?" I asked.

Hannah laughed. "Listen, the dog has an alibi, OK? Besides Janet kept a distance from him. She didn't like how he shed on her uniform all the time."

"So here's something that came up today. Janet asked that real estate agent how much it cost to buy an acre of land on Kodiak now. Did she ever mention that she wanted to buy property here?"

"Janet? Like I said before, I thought she was transferring off Kodiak this summer. She sure sounded like she couldn't wait to get out of here."

"Yes, that's my understanding as well," I said. "But she met with the real estate agent to ask only that question. Nothing else."

At that moment, Anton lumbered into the living room. He stood in front of me and gazed into my eyes before sitting his enormous girth at my feet, where he continued to gaze up at me. I looked at Hannah for direction.

"He wants a taste of your beer," she said.

"What?" I asked. "The dog drinks beer?"

"Only when someone shares," she explained. "I don't put it in his bowl, and so far as I know he can't open the fridge or use a bottle opener."

"Too bad, he could be on David Letterman's Stupid Pet Tricks bit."

"I heard about that show, but it wouldn't be on TV here until well after my bedtime."

"That'd be well past Anton's bed time," I said.

I lowered the bottle and tipped the lip in front of the big dog's snout. He lapped at the emerging stream with his wide red tongue. A small amount ran down his jowls and saturated the fur on his neck. When I took the bottle away, Anton twisted his head in disappointment.

"Ignore him," Hannah said. "That horse could finish a case if I let him. Listen, you have any other questions for me? I've got plans this evening. Someone's stopping by, and we're going out. And why am I telling you my life story?"

"Sorry. This is how I get confessions." I twisted the top of the bottle in my shirt front to clean it. But I hesitated before I took a final sip.

"OK then, I confess I'd like you to leave. If you have any other questions, you can call me."

I stood and stepped over Anton's big carcass. "I don't have your number."

She laughed as she went to a side table. "Now that's a sly way to ask a woman for her phone number."

"That obvious, huh?"

"You'd better work on it," she said, as she handed me a note with a phone number scrawled on it.

15

W hen I returned to the Baranof Lodge, I replaced the window panels in the Wrangler's half doors then bought two Heinekens in the lounge to take up to my room. I gave Lily a quick wave as I passed the front desk then followed an elderly couple up the hallway. He carried their expedition-quantity luggage as she read aloud from a guidebook. From the nature of their discussion, it seemed clear that their travel agent had included Kodiak on their itinerary without explaining the island's many natural charms. Their conversation made clear neither fished nor hunted. They had no interest in Alutiiq or Russian history. Of Kodiak's remaining attractions, I met few people who enjoyed the fish cannery experience.

Back in my room, I spread across the bed the few bits of actual evidence I had regarding Lieutenant Janet Simms' untimely death: her daily planner; a business card; the Alaska State Trooper's report; a topographical map; and an autopsy report by a state coroner over in Anchorage. So far in my time on the case, I'd spoken with the victim's mother, a Kodiak roommate, a recent personal contact, and an unhappy Coast Guard resident special agent. As a bonus, I had met the Nashville sensation Travis Pike. If only I'd gotten an autograph, I would have something to show for the whole trip.

In all this, I had not met one person who believed this was something more than a terrible act of nature; a human standing too close to where a massive carnivore was feeding before hibernating from the winter. Even Lieutenant Commander Andrews had no knowledge or evidence that pointed to anything more sinister. He wanted something called closure. In surveillance agencies, they called my task a mop-up operation.

But for:

R-5678.

8543

I stared at the two sets of numbers until I finished the second beer. What prompted Lieutenant Simms to record those numbers in her calendar? If I couldn't answer that question to my own satisfaction, could I call quits on this case? Tell Andrews that I came up short? Face Gloria Simms?

I thought about my father, commanding officer of a Coast Guard patrol boat off Viet Nam when an Air Force fighter strafed the *Point Manitou*. After ordering his crew to abandon ship, he returned to the bridge and tried in desperation to communicate to the Air Force that the *Point Manitou* was American. As skipper, he disappeared with his ship.

I decided a little fresh air might help me focus my brain on this. I finished the last of my glass of Jameson's then put on my leather jacket. I tucked my Colt into the holster under my arm, my Beretta into the holster on my left ankle, and my extending baton into a retaining clip on my left wrist where it was accessible.

The Kodiak evening was bright but cool as I walked down Thorsheim and across to Center Avenue. From there I could see the masts of fishing vessels anchored in St. Paul Harbor as well as the vacant state ferry dock. Ferry service wouldn't begin for a week or two. A bank of fog rolled toward Kodiak over the water, coming on those proverbial cat feet, smelling as if the kitty had finished gobbling down a dinner of fresh salmon.

Kodiak is a town of simple architectural tastes, dominated by corrugated steel. An occasional Quonset hut does not look out of place. A tsunami levelled most of the downtown following an earthquake measuring 8.4 on the Richter scale that struck South-central Alaska in 1964.

Kodiak's downtown remained unchanged from my prior tour at the Air Station. Around the square sat a handful of businesses: a trinket trap for tourists; a diner; two lounges facing off across the asphalt parking lot; and an office goods store specializing in boxing and shipping overnight packages. This was an especially useful service to visiting hunters and anglers who could bring in their haul for packing in dry ice for the long trip home.

I walked down Marine Way and went into the open door of a bar facing the inner anchorage. The lights were dim except over the bar and the red spotlights on the stage. A young blonde woman stood onstage, singing a karaoke version of "Where Have all the Cowboys Gone," a beat behind as she waited for the bouncing ball on the screen. I settled at the bar and asked the bartender what beers he served. He pointed to a shelf above the big mirror behind the bar. Two dozen beer bottles and cans lined the shelf, including most American and Canadian brands I knew along with a few European brews. I ordered a Red Stripe, wondering whether it came from the original Jamaican brewery or the Heineken brewery in the Netherlands after their recent merger. To my disappointment, it arrived in a green bottle rather than the traditional fat brown bottle from Jamaica. I assumed the Netherlands won out.

The song ended to tepid applause. The singer appeared two seats down from me and took a thick stack of cocktail napkins from the rack. She proceeded to wipe her face and neck. With a second supply of napkins in hand, she raised first one arm, then the other, and wiped her arm pits with the napkins.

"It's hotter under those lights than you'd think," she said.

For a moment, I didn't realize she had spoken to me. "I'm sure it is. You watch a concert, and they have headbands, wristbands, and towels to catch the sweat."

"I'm in a band," she offered. "Down in Seattle. We don't play this Top 40 crap. We played the Fenix Underground a few times. Once we opened for the Scud Mountain Boys."

I nodded, a little lost. Sometimes I can fake my way through a conversation by reading a few magazines every month. Seattle's post-grunge music scene was a decade too far for me. "Are you the band's singer?"

"Singer, flute, sax, manager, and roadie. What, you never saw a girl with an empty glass before?"

I motioned for the bartender. I ordered a refill for her and switched to a Heineken. If I was going to drink an export of Holland, it might as well be the real thing.

When the drinks arrived, she moved into the vacant seat next to me. "We've got a gig next weekend, if my bass player gets straight in time. I swear it was easier to handle her on smack than oxy."

"Has she gone to rehab often?" I asked.

"More often than I get my teeth cleaned." She fished the garnish out of her drink and ate the cherry. Then she looked at the empty stage. "Maybe I can get the ball rolling. Watch my drink." She returned to the stage and flipped through a binder looking for a particular song. "Hi. I'm Sage. Here's one of my favorite classics."

A sparse arrangement of a bass line and finger snaps came up. Her sultry alto hit the intro on time:

"Never know how much I love you
Never know how much I care..."

Everyone looked as surprised as I when the petite woman with big round eyes chose an old Peggy Lee jazz ballad. By the second stanza, all eyes in the room focused on the slight woman crooning into the microphone. Wispy blonde hair framed her face. When she finished, she returned to the chair next to me, stopping on the way by a few tables to accept compliments.

"You haven't got a clean handkerchief, by chance?" she asked.

I handed her my white kerchief and watched in dismay as she reached under her shirt to towel down with it. I waved it off when she offered to return it.

"I love that song," she said. "May I have another?" She held up her empty glass.

I motioned toward the barkeep. "So when do you go back to Seattle?" I asked. "For your next gig?"

"In a couple days. I've been working to raise some money for the band. Went on a crabber to the Bering back in January. Worked on a fish processor in Bristol Bay for two months. Been at the cannery this month. Banking 50K right now. Thought I'd relax a little before I go home."

"Oh? Maybe you should be buying the drinks," I said.

"You look like the kind of guy who thinks he should be buying. 'Cause you think you have a chance with me if I get drunk enough."

When a man gets to a time in life when a younger woman hints at a sexual liaison if she's fully intoxicated, he needs to consider the realities. Was she far more inebriated than she seemed? Would it be easier to hand over cash and credit cards without suffering bodily injury? How many accomplices waited in ambush? I excused myself and headed for the men's room. There I concealed the 1911 Colt in my belt rather than its more obvious shoulder harness. I hoped to avoid the paperwork of a missing weapon with both the Alaska State Troopers and the Coast Guard.

Back at the bar, I found my Seattle singer still waiting for her next turn on stage. She splayed her fingers across the bar while she repainted her chipped nails candy apple red. Despite the growing crowd, she managed the manicure without getting jostled and smearing fingernail polish up her wrist.

She extended her right hand. "I'm Sage."

"I'm Marty." I pointed at her wet nail polish. "Sage is interesting."

"Oh, yeah." She shook her hands in a rapid motion to air dry her nails. "My parents were hippies. Even joined a commune for a while, until the bashwan running the place started telling them to practice with machine guns. Then my family escaped, and we snuck off to Seattle. My dad is a fishmonger at Pike Place."

"They support your band?"

"More than selling drugs or turning tricks, I suppose," she said before taking a gulp of the anonymous concoction in her cocktail glass. "But last time home, I got the grandkids lecture for the first time."

"No interest?"

"You ever see a successful band carting a kid around? Besides, it's easier to get kids after you get a guy first."

"Some of those groupies look pretty young. Prospective babysitters?"

She laughed. "Hey, careful. I followed Pearl Jam for my junior year of high school."

"Good thing your folks were hippies."

"What could a couple of Deadheads say to me?"

I finished my beer and ordered another for her. I gave the tip to the barkeep so it didn't go astray. Then I wished her good night and good luck with her bass player.

"Hey, I'm almost up. You're not going to stay for my next song?"

I begged off and headed for the door and out of the hazy blue air. Unlike many states, Alaskans still puffed on whatever cigarette they could afford in restaurants and bars. I thought the cost of good liquor on the Final Frontier was prohibitive enough without adding tobacco taxes.

The night air was cool, and the sky still light. A mist hung over the harbor, now obscuring the masts of the fishing boats moored there. After dinner on an evening like this just a few years earlier, I would watch my son play tee-ball on the field near his school. Those memories are no easier than my dreams of rescues gone awry. I walked back to the Baranof. Fortunately I managed to tune in a West Coast baseball game just in its third inning. Without even knowing the teams playing during the first three at-bats, I listened until I drifted to sleep sometime after the seventh inning stretch.

16

After another breakfast of reindeer sausage and eggs at the diner by Lily Lake, I headed back out to the Coast Guard Base, lying between Old Womens Mountain shrouded in mist and the calm blue Pacific Ocean. I returned to the old barracks building on the hillside overlooking a small calm bay. I went back to the office that housed the resident special agent. Kathy Douglass was on duty. She said Frank was over in Anchorage at the Marine Safety Office there.

"Just as well," I said. "I got the sense when we met that he would prefer I wasn't here."

"That's an understatement. I was sitting here when he called the District Office in Juneau. But as long as you are on leave and don't interfere with any official investigation, you're free to do as you wish."

"But I'm wasting my time?"

"You're free to do that, too." Her grin was a little too dismissive.

"OK. Am I permitted to ask you a question?"

She settled back in her office chair and nodded. "So you need my help after all? Of course, I may refuse to answer."

"Well, with that understanding, here's my problem. In the lieutenant's day planner, I found two four-digit numbers. R-5-6-7-8 and 8-5-4-3. Could one or both be phone extensions on Base?"

She scribbled both numbers on her desk blotter. "I don't recognize an extension starting with a 5. An 8 could be a possibility though."

I lifted the receiver on Frank's desk. "May I? I'll leave a quarter." I dialed the extension number; the phone rang. The other end picked up immediately.

"Lieutenant, j.g. Holland. May I help you?"

"Sorry, sir, I dialed a wrong number." I hung up.

Kathy gave me a curious look. "Not much of an interrogation."

"No, I'm not ready for that yet. Who is a j.g. named Holland?"

"He works over in the Base office. Kind of jack-of-all-trades. He oversees the morale and welfare program; Base Security; public affairs; and anything else the command needs doing. Nice guy. Prior service as an Army first sergeant, then Coast Guard officer candidate school."

"Know anything about his personal details?"

"Let's think," she paused. "Fitness nut who spends lunch at the swimming pool. Hour a day at the gym. Hear him two nights a week as a DJ on the public radio station in town. Plays jazz, deep tracks."

"You've noticed him, then?"

Kathy gestured toward me with a particular finger. "Yeah. He's good looking, OK? Works out. And he's single. He drives a classic Monte Carlo with a sound system you could hear in Homer. In case you didn't get the memo, they stopped blinding married women years ago."

I settled into Frank's desk seat, flipping back through my notebook to see if the name Holland had popped up earlier. No joy. I thought about an approach I could use to question the lieutenant without raising suspicions or worse. "What's his first name?" I asked.

"Sir."

"Apart from that."

She took a moment to search down the one-page phone directory for the Base. "First initial is r. So maybe Ron. Or Ronald. That help?"

"Kind of. There's an R before 5678, but not with 8543."

"Don't look for zebras," she said.

"Sorry, what?"

Kathy laughed as she placed the laminated phone directory back into the clutch of books on her desk. "My bad. Let me explain. My husband is a doctor over at the Base clinic. One of his professors in med school gave his class a piece of advice: 'If you hear hoof beats, don't look for zebras. Most likely you're going to see a horse.' What he meant was, if someone has a fever, don't assume they have dengue fever. So, if you see the initial R and you find someone named Ronald, it's a more likely match than looking for somebody named Roderick."

"Sure. But besides the Base, there's an Air Station, the Communications Station, the *Storis* and other cutters that come and go, plus the rest of the Base staff. Could be a lot of other guys named Rick, Richard, Reggie, or Roland."

"Roland?" She stood and began pulling on a windbreaker. "OK, then here's how you can screen them. She was a junior officer, so enlisted guys and married men are off limits under the UCMJ. Maybe she'd date a pilot, but only a C-130 or Jayhawk. She can't date a fellow H-65 pilot because they might end up on the same flight rotation together sometime. Now I'm going to lunch with my husband up at the Anchor Club. When I get back, you can tell me how many zebras you found." She picked up her purse and headed for the door but paused before opening it. She looked back at me. "You know, I expected a super-agent to have super detective skills."

"They're in the shop for a tune-up," I said.

Kathy went out, directing a particular finger toward me again.

17

While debating the merits of lunch, I scribbled some thoughts in my notebook. While I liked Kathy's theory, I saw a minor flaw. How did I know that Janet was dating someone? Neither her mother nor roommate thought she was. A mother a few thousand miles away might be kept in the dark, but a roommate tends to have eyewitness information. I wondered if young Lieutenant j.g. Holland could explain why Lieutenant Simms had written his phone extension in her day planner.

I thought about how to interview Holland without raising his suspicions or attracting unwanted attention. Walking into his space in the big square building that housed Base Kodiak's administrative offices might not be the least conspicuous move. Or the smoothest. I tried a little of that detective work that Kathy Douglas thought I lacked. Using the local phone book, I found the phone number for the island's public radio station.

"KMXT-FM, how may I help you?" a chipper voice asked.

"Hello. I have an odd question for you. I'm on the island for a few days, but I heard that you have a great local jazz show a couple evenings a week. Can you tell me when that airs? I'd like to catch it before I leave."

"Sure. You must mean Ron Holland's program. I love it. It's on tonight from 6 to 8. You can also catch the same show Sunday morning from 10 to noon."

"That's great. I'll try to catch it tonight."

The young lady seized an opportunity. "If you like it, you can support our spring membership drive. We have several levels to choose among."

While I appreciated her enthusiasm, I wasn't ready to commit cash. "Tell you what. Let me listen tonight, then I'll decide how much to contribute. I'll call you tomorrow."

She thanked me, disappointment clear in her voice. By standards in the lower 48 states, or the "Outside" as Alaskans call it, she caved much too early. In other states, the pitch for a donation or sale doesn't end until the caller surrenders a credit card number. Smart people don't answer their phone between noon and midnight to avoid the conmen, grifters, and swindlers, or worse, the home improvement salesmen.

Having a few hours to kill and an appetite for lunch, I headed out to the Wrangler. A young African American male already waited there, wiping the hood with a soft rag. He wore a dark blue jumpsuit. He glanced up when I approached but continue working.

"You're Galloway, right?" he asked without pausing his work. "Please act like you hired me to clean your car."

"Hey, thanks for getting me into your work schedule," I said. "Is this lunch time for you?"

"Yes, I'm only going to do the hood. Don't have time for the rest and lunch, too. I sell this waterless cleaner; a spray bottle and a soft cloth are all you need to wash your vehicle."

I examined the shine on the hood where he had finished. "Thanks for what you've done already."

"I work at the Air Station. I've heard some guys talking about making you disappear. Like forever. I heard somebody in town recognized you from something that happened years ago. Like back before Waco."

"Nice of you to let me know."

"I came because of Lieutenant Simms."

"Oh? You think she wasn't killed by a rogue bear?"

"Talk to everyone. See what you'll see." He stopped wiping the Jeep's hood and climbed into a Chevy sedan. In a moment, he was gone.

Even if his warning didn't pan out, the Jeep's bonnet looked clean and shiny. If I were planning to keep the Wrangler, I would purchase a few spray bottles from him. With another minute or two, I would have gotten his name. I felt grateful that he had shared the nefarious threat against me which he had heard on the wind. Word about me had spread through the Air Station hangar. Why wasn't anyone ever happy to see me?

18

The evening was cool, and I sat with the Wrangler's canvas windows removed and stowed in the back. KMXT played on the Jeep's radio. After the 7 p.m. newscast from National Public Radio, DJ Holland aired a jazz classic, the 1962 collaboration between Duke Ellington and John Coltrane, a performance some critics still consider one of the finest jazz albums of all time.

Shortly before 8 p.m., a well-rusted Toyota Land Cruiser pulled up outside the radio station. A trim woman with long blonde hair climbed out and went inside without giving me any notice. When the radio news played again, I started watching for Holland.

The j.g. emerged from the radio station about 8:15, wearing jeans, a flannel shirt, and a Colorado Rockies ball cap. He headed toward a well-maintained 1976 Chevy Monte Carlo with fancy rims. Myself, I would hesitate to risk such a nice ride on Kodiak's gravel roads. Every man to himself. I started the Wrangler and drove up next to the driver's door of the Chevy. He gave me a suspicious look.

"Good evening, sir. My name is Marty Galloway. I'm a special agent." I showed him my badge and green military ID card. "Lieutenant Simms' family asked me to look into her death. Can we talk for a few minutes?"

He opened his car door and put a foot inside in preparation to leave. "No point. I don't know anything about her. Tragedy though," he said as an afterthought.

"Well, sir, can you tell me why she wrote your desk extension in her day planner?"

"She did?" Mister Holland sounded surprised, whether because she wrote it down, or I found it, was unclear.

"Yes, sir, on the date that she died." I paused to watch his reactions. "I'm afraid some people on the island know who I am, so it might be better to talk someplace a little more private. Why don't you hop in?"

He walked around the Jeep and climbed into the passenger side. We went east and then made our way up the steep climb to the top of Pillar Mountain. A purple twilight rested upon the western horizon.

"So, what do you want to know?" he asked.

"What kind of a relationship did you have with Lieutenant Simms?"

He removed his ballcap and brushed his hair away from his forehead. "We were friends. That's all. We weren't dating. And we were never involved." He paused. "Nothing physical. Ever. We talked. Sometimes we spotted for each other working out. She could bench 250."

"Impressive. What else?"

"Sometimes she'd help me select music for my show. The station has a pretty good jazz collection. She had a real talent for helping me put together musical themes in a show. She'd help Alice program the evening classical show as well. I've never met anyone with Janet's knowledge of music, across all forms."

"Sir, there's a reason I'm here. In the weeks before she died, Lieutenant Simms asked her brother-in-law for help investigating something, but she didn't tell him what it was. Do you have any idea what she would have wanted to look into?"

He shook his head even as he paused to consider this. "No, she never mentioned anything like that to me. Nothing that she said needed investigating."

"Well, she didn't tell her mother or brother-in-law, either." I twisted in my seat so I could watch his reaction. "Did she ever mention the numbers 5-6-7-8 to you? In any reference?"

Holland looked at me, not letting his eyes drift furtively in any direction. I wondered if he spent a lot of time learning techniques to frustrate interrogations by watching true-crime shows.

"Nothing I recall. She used a lock combination at the Base pool? Or on a locker at Ready Crew Berthing when she was on flight duty? The aircrews stay overnight so they can launch faster if there's a distress."

I nodded. "I know. I was a rescue swimmer here before I went into CGI."

"Well, you would know about that better than me then. Sorry, I don't know what those numbers indicate. Did she write those down in her day planner as well?"

When a witness begins asking questions, you have to decide whether it is a sense of natural curiosity or something more nefarious. I err on the side of caution. "Thank you for answering my questions. I am not here in any official manner, so I'm grateful. Let me get you back to your car." Twilight faded into night, and the air on the top of the mountain cooled.

Mister Holland remained quiet as we worked our way back down the steep mountain road into Kodiak. He spoke only once. "So do you think there was something odd about her death?"

"I don't know what to think. The family asked me to come make certain the t's were crossed and i's dotted. Everything looks pretty straightforward so far. But if you think of something, please call Frank Anker. He'll get a message to me."

"Sure, anything I can do to help," he said as we drove into the parking lot at KMXT.

"Oh, one last thing," I said. "Did the lieutenant ever mention to you an interest in buying land on Kodiak Island?"

"Good Lord, no. She hated it here." Holland hoisted himself out of the Jeep seat by gripping the roll bar and lowering himself onto the pavement. "Her dream billet was Air Station Traverse City. Up in

Northern Michigan. Or the air station near Detroit. Put her close to her mother in Indianapolis."

"Thank you for your time," I called as he closed the door. "Good night, sir."

He waved and climbed into his Chevy. After a moment the classic Monte Carlo's engine roared to life. The deep roar from a modified exhaust system scattered the seagulls roaming the lot.

19

The following morning, I drove out East Bay Road and stopped opposite Lilly Lake at the Alaska State Troopers' post. This was the only appointment I had scheduled before boarding planes in Chicago for Anchorage. I thought I had a better chance of talking with Corporal William Montgomery if I arranged an interview in advance. Catching an AST with spare time to chat is as likely as reeling in a record King Salmon. Alaska's state best is a mere 97 pounds.

This isn't to suggest that the officer was ready to talk or pleased to see me that morning, even with a scheduled time. In the thick fog between town and the airport on Rezanof Drive, a car had collided with a pick-up truck heading in the opposite direction. His study of the accident scene determined that neither driver was at fault; it turned out to be another instance of Alaska weather getting the best of people. Both drivers were dead, but the car had three survivors, children who watched their mother die. Not a fun investigation to catch, and his poor disposition showed when he came out to the waiting area to find me. On the other hand, he may have been uncomfortable in a uniform about four sizes too small for his massive frame, the physique of professional boxer.

"First time I saw a person killed by a bear," he admitted, turning to my inquiry. "I've dealt with moose-vehicle collisions back in Anchorage. When an RV hits a big game animal, the damage to both can be catastrophic. But even after responding to a few of those accidents, I wasn't ready for this scene." He pulled a thick file folder from a bottom desk drawer. "I thought the Coast Guard was ready to close the case on this."

"I'm following up on behalf of the family," I said.

"An insurance thing? Doesn't matter, I guess." Montgomery opened the file and spread it out in front of me. "Hell of a scene. I felt even Base Security was less than enthusiastic when they saw me. Sure didn't look like there was anything anyone could do; it was an act of nature."

The file at that moment lay open to a photo of Lieutenant Simms' corpse in situ, as the forensic experts say. On the opposite side of the folder, a topographical map showed the exact location on the West shore of Bear Creek. The report Andrews gave me had a black and white, photocopied version of the chart. Immediately, I noticed a difference between my version and the AST's original map. Across Buskin Lake, yellow marker highlighted four sections of the Coast Guard reservation to the West of the death site. The highlight would not appear on a photocopy. Sections are squares of land within a township that surveyors use to describe individual parcels. Each section includes one square mile or 640 acres. The yellow highlight outlined four sections in the Northwest corner of the township. Counterclockwise from Buskin Lake, the four numbered 5, 6, 7, and 8.

"Tell me what you think of this," I said, turning the file back toward him. "She died here," I explained, pointing to the X on the map between Buskin Lake and Bear Creek. "So why are these highlighted? Did you find something there?"

His thick forefinger landed in the middle of the four sections. "I have no idea, other than the victim highlighted the four sections in marker on her map. No other notes or marks on the map. I didn't see any reason to go up there. I copied them onto my map just to keep track, in case I can see some connection later. Fish and Wildlife helped identify the suspect bear and we put it down before hibernation. I'm ready to close the case out."

At the back of his thick file, I found a white envelope labeled "Photos." I unclipped it. "May I?" I asked, holding up the envelope.

"Sure. Nothing critical. I take a lot of pictures because you never know what might be important until later. I had a sergeant who always said film is cheap, but evidence is irreplaceable. I get a lot of extraneous photos that stay in the case folder to rot."

I began to shuffle through the photos but stopped. "Did you find that she had a camera with her?"

"No. Nothing but her car keys. I did a grid search with Base Security. I thought it was weird. She carried nothing. If someone doesn't have fishing gear, you'd expect to find a camera, binoculars, a hiking stick, or a rock pick. She had literally nothing. No compass, whistle or bells, bear spray, not even her wallet. Found that in her car."

I looked back at the photos and continued sorting through them. Halfway through the stack came a surprise — the image of a classic Monte Carlo. I held it up for the trooper to see.

"Nice, huh?" Montgomery asked. "I saw it over by Buskin Lake. I've got a thing for an old Chevy. Not related to the case that I could see. Somebody fishing in the lake probably. Listen, are we almost done? Something came up this morning. I've got to fly over to Afognak for an assault case. Might turn into a sex assault when I get a chance to talk to the vic."

I thanked Trooper Montgomery and headed out to the Wrangler, now carrying two distinct mysteries. First, why had Lieutenant Simms gone into bear territory without any protection? Nor did she carry any basic outdoor gear, such as a compass. She would have learned the basics of bear safety during the Air Station's survival training for aircrews. I still recall a bit of wisdom shared by the master chief who taught the course. In the event of an aircraft crash landing on land in Alaska, your first action should be to drag any corpses away from the crash site to distract any nearby bears from the survivors.

I needed to revisit Lieutenant j.g. Holland to ask why he failed to mention being at Buskin Lake that day, within a mile of where a Kodiak bear brutally attacked Lieutenant Simms. Had he heard a scream? Did he notice Alaska State Troopers and Base Security arrive to investigate? Did a passing bear chase off Holland's curiosity? First responders don't like lookie-loos, but a natural curiosity is, well, natural.

Now I had an idea of what Miss Simms meant when she scribbled 5-6-7-8 in her day planner. As a result, I had to revisit all my earlier interviews to ask whether anyone recalled the lieutenant expressing interest in four sections of Coast Guard property. She had asked real estate agent Marilyn Solverson the value of an acre. The value of 2,400 acres would be much greater.

I knew from prior investigations that you couldn't buy or sell government property, anything from tools to vehicles to vessels. Sometimes people try. I remembered a case in which another District Office invited me to play the bogus buyer in an undercover sting operation. A chief boatswain's mate running a small boat station in the Northwest had a side business ordering extra government equipment to be sent to his house. His garage could have supplied several small boat stations with everything from foul-weather gear to outboard motors. He kept an overflow of materials crated in his backyard, covered with tarps. I heard a final inventory put the value at a quarter million dollars, not including anything he sold before CGI became involved.

After leaving the trooper post, I drove out to Buskin Lake with Simms' topographical map as my guide. First, I went around the lake on a gravel road that encircles the lake, crossing the feeder stream on the Northside and Buskin River, where it left the lake for the Pacific. Next, I toured the remainder of Sections 5 and 6 accessible by road. The ground there levelled off, unusual for Kodiak. The topography of Sections 7 and 8, on the other hand, rose in a steep slope up the lower elevation on the Northside of Barometer and Erskine Mountains. While one road took a minor loop through the Northeast corner of Section 8, the remainder of 8 and all of 7 were inaccessible by vehicle. Nothing suggested Lieutenant Simms' interest in the sections on her map, which appeared to be two miles, as a seagull flies, from where Base Security found her body.

Parking the Jeep at the highest point I could drive up Barometer, I set the parking brake and climbed out. Although I did not anticipate meeting a bear at that elevation, I took a can of pepper spray from the back seat. The surrounding vegetation initially reached over my head as I started climbing toward the peak. With a copy of the lieutenant's topographical map as a guide, I went to what I estimated to be the upper perimeter of Section 8. The view North through the pass toward Anton Larsen Bay looked impressive. Three years earlier, a chartered Piper Saratoga bringing three Coasties back from a hunting trip across the island to Karluk struck the side of fog-shrouded Pyramid Mountain, killing all aboard.

While in the neighborhood, I drove over to the Base proper and checked in at the security gate. Unfortunately, the special agents had left the office for the day, so I went back across the taxiway to the Base convenience store for a six-pack of Samuel Adams Boston Lager. Not seeing anyone I recognized on Base, I returned to the Baranof Lodge to review the day's crop of fresh facts and new confusions.

20

B ack at the Lodge, I once again spread all the evidence I possessed across the second queen bed in my room. I walked down to the front desk to borrow a roll of tape from Lily so that I could display a couple of maps on the wall. Key photos I posted to the mirror. When I returned the tape, Lily was busy checking in other guests, so I left the dispenser where she could see it, relieved that I wasn't destined for a rant about that time conspirators shot the President and replaced him with an actor.

Finishing a big burger I had picked up at the drive-thru on the way back into town, I read through my hand-scrawled notes while verifying facts against the evidence in front of me. At times, I have found my handwritten notes as impenetrable as the case on which I'm working. I blame the nuns who made second-grade penmanship a form of corporal punishment that I did my best to avoid.

On a clean sheet of paper taped on the mirror, I listed evidence trails yet to follow. Did Hannah Shangin know if her roommate went hiking often? Did she go prepared for the Alaska wilds? Did Janet even own the proper gear? If so, why wasn't it returned to her mother? Why had Lieutenant j.g. Holland failed to mention he was near the remote location where Lieutenant Simms died? Did Janet

Simms approach any real estate agents on the island other than Marilyn Solverson? Assuming that the lieutenant's service member's life insurance went to her mother, would anyone else might benefit from her death? If so, how could that effect an act of nature.

Despite the beer, I began to get a headache. My brain does not have the operational capacity of the old WANG desk anchors the Coast Guard first adopted as some cutting-edge technological advance a dozen years ago. Even the most tech-savvy yeomen I knew kept their old IBM Selectric II typewriters on their desks to get the necessary paperwork done for those times when the computer systems failed to cooperate. So, I gathered all the new evidence back into the proper folders and secured them in the locking case where I store my weapons. Donning my leather jacket, I stowed my weapons into their appropriate holsters before heading out. I finished my beer as I walked down the hallway and dropped the empty bottle in the garbage at the end of the hallway.

The Kodiak evening remained bright and warm, oddly clear for a second straight day on an island celebrated for its International Fog Festival, which runs from January 1 to December 31. I decided to walk down to the same lounge on the mall to see if Sage was performing karaoke for a second night. At least I needed to say a proper thanks for her help after my conversation with the sidewalk.

As I crossed the parking lot, a voice called my name. When I turned, I saw Travis Pike striding toward me, swinging a Louisville Slugger like the next batter warming up on deck. "Martin L. Galloway, right?"

One of the first things you learn in law enforcement training at Glynco, Georgia, is threat assessment. One man with a bat looked bad but manageable. I put a hand inside my leather jacket to grip my Colt. At that moment, I felt the round barrel of a weapon press into the back of my neck, no doubt a long gun to give the carrier safety of distance. Before I could work through a response, a blow glanced off the back of my head. Instant sleep.

21

I woke in darkness, bound up in a heavy canvas sarcophagus. Hands tethered behind my back. Legs cinched tight. Duct tape ear to ear. As my claustrophobia began to emerge, I focused on this snare. I wasn't going anywhere until my captors decided.

Judging by the sounds around me, I did not seem headed anywhere nearby. I heard the distinctive sound of a de Havilland Beaver cranking, the whorl of the engine with rhythmic drumming as cylinders burst to life. In a moment, the drone of the Beaver's Pratt & Whitney engine smoothed out. Next, I felt the aircraft moving forward as the engine powered up, and the craft angled skyward with elevation.

My canvas shroud permitted no answers to the questions that filled my brain. Was this flight in twilight or dawn? I had no way to calculate whether I had remained unconscious for one hour or six. Were we destined for the mainland or another Kodiak location? Was inflight cocktail service available? In my darkness, I couldn't track how long we had been in the air. I decided not to ask my pilot many questions. Not that the duct tape permitted either questions or complaints.

Why Travis Pike?

What possible connection did an obscure country singer have to a Coast Guard pilot stationed on a remote island in Alaska? Unlikely she had criticized his music from 4,000 miles away. His only hit song chronicled a tank commander in Desert Storm? Again, no obvious nexus.

Then I recalled meeting Travis Pike in the lobby of the Baranof Lodge. While his entourage surrounded him, he took the time to greet me. How did he know my name? What grievance did he hold toward me? What connection...

God's True Patriots?

With all the propaganda, fear-mongering and conspiracy theories floating around, I thought it likely that Travis recognized me when Lily called my name. He knew my full name, including middle initial. Pike came to tag a bear and bagged me instead. Literally. No doubt, taking down the *Galloway sapien* came with better bragging rights. But a lousy shoulder mount.

The flight ended with a steep descent and a water landing, evidenced by the slight splash of the pontoons hitting the surface. The Beaver taxied a short distance before seeming to beach on the shoreline. After a short wait, my deboarding bore all the elegance of a bale of hay dropped from a barn loft. With a bit of good luck, I landed in shallow water and muck rather than rocks. Two male voices squabbled for a minute about what to do with me. One advocated adding a few dozen stones to my canvas cocoon, then shoving me into deeper water. The other insisted that they adhere to Mister Pike's original instructions or they might not be paid. Those instructions specified taking the canvas back so I didn't have any shelter. I did not get a vote.

They dragged me farther up an embankment before one of them took charge of their crime. "Take the gun and get back in case he tries something when he gets free of the bag," one of the two men said. "If he moves, shoot him."

"Pike said no bullets. No evidence of foul play."

"We can cut the slugs out."

Not comforted by their debate over my demise, I inhaled through my nose when the canvas opened to reveal a thick fog with a low ceiling. A dozen feet away stood a short man with an AR-15 aimed straight at my torso. He wore camo from hat to boot. Dark hair brushed back from his face, almost touching his collar. His partner stood by my feet, rolling up the canvas he then pitched through the rear door aft of the Beaver's wing strut. He wore blue jeans and an off-tan Carhartt jacket. His hat advertised Federal Shotshell. Heavy beard gone gray. I memorized the aircraft's tail number, but I assumed that whatever they had in mind did not involve my return to Kodiak proper alive.

Waving my survival knife, the man closest spoke to me. "I'll leave this for you." He pitched it further up the embankment. "In case you want to open your wrists."

"Come on, let's go. Don't get all sentimental on him." The shorter one said. "I've got a charter this morning." So, he was the pilot.

"You've got another job in this soup? Couldn't pay me to fly again today."

"Thank God for IFR," the pilot said.

He referred to Instrument Flight Rules that allowed a pilot trained on a properly equipped aircraft to fly in poor weather conditions, like clouds, fog, or rain. That information might help me find him again if I ever got back to civilization. Not great odds on that, but I bore that in mind as the primary objective.

Wasting no time on niceties, they climbed into the Beaver, and I heard the Pratt & Whitney engine crank over. After a moment, all nine cylinders in its rotary engine came alive. With a bit of maneuvering on the lake surface, the big engine surged, and the aircraft sailed over the lake before ascending into the fog. In less than a minute, I could hear the Beaver overhead but no longer see it disappear into the mist. Soon there was no trace of it, sight or sound.

Alone in Alaska's wilds, I thought back to the survival training I endured while on flight duty at Air Station Kodiak. Those sessions were so rote that the crews called them "sermonars." Year after year, we heard the same themes: Stay near the downed aircraft; rescuers will find it first. Coast Guard aircraft are painted white and international orange, and they carry an electronic location transmitter. The aircraft fuselage could provide shelter; however, we then practiced constructing primitive shelters with natural materials. The instructors stressed purifying water from lakes and streams because most Alaskan waterways contain beaver fever, an illness caused by a parasite named giardiasis that is characterized by severe abdominal distress. If you're lost in the wilderness, cramps and diarrhea are among the last things you want to add to your experience.

Our training taught us to recognize the bright red berries that grow on Kodiak as baneberries; a handful will kill an adult.

First order of business: retrieve my knife and cut my way out of bondage. With my wrists and ankles bound, I couldn't hoist myself up. Instead, I pushed with my feet, sliding forward on my shoulders. Probably did not enhance my leather jacket. I kept my hands up and hips elevated to reduce any drag. Each launch with my heels propelled me about a foot.

Never having practiced crawling on my back, this process took some time to master. I felt the neck of my shirt filling with dirt, pebbles and twigs, making the whole effort as uncomfortable as possible. I smiled, thinking this situation couldn't worsen; until a cold, light rain began to fall. This precipitation reminded me of Murphy's Law: If anything can go wrong, it will — at the most inopportune moment possible. I continued slithering up the bank, stopping twice to crane my neck to keep track of the knife's location.

With a half dozen shoves forward, I halved the distance. At that point, the soil turned from mud to sand. Near the top of the embankment grew thick grasses. Once I reached that edge, I maneuvered to my right to get my hands on the knife. Pulling it out from its sheath, I wedged the wooden handle between my palms so I could saw at the wide tape binding around my wrist behind me. In time, my arms broke loose. Then a pair of quick hacks with the blade freed my knees and ankles. Finally the delicate, yet painful, process of peeling the tape from my face. No need to shave for a few days.

I first checked to see what remained in my arsenal. The holster under my arm was empty — someone had removed my Colt. They took the extending baton and my chronometer from my right wrist.

When I checked my opposite arm, I discovered they had also taken my MIA bracelet. To my surprise, the little Beretta remained snug in its holster on my calf. Travis' crew wasn't as thorough as I would have expected. His boys also missed a flat flint and steel set hidden within a zippered compartment in my belt — one of those ideas I picked up after my adventure to Michigan's Upper Peninsula. The belt also contained a set of traveler checks, which might help start a fire. My abductors kindly left me with the ultimate all-purpose tool –– duct tape. I wrapped the strips they used to bind me around my waist. Inventory complete, I rolled into a kneeling position, then crawled to the top of the bank to see if I could determine my location.

Not far off, I made my first discovery: a low camo-colored tent covered with a netting festooned with moss and dry roots intended to make it undetectable from the air. Getting to my feet, I stumbled toward the enclosure, holding my Beretta in front of me. No one hid inside; I found only a generator and a freezer. Beyond the tent, I saw an aluminum frame, standing ten feet high, staked into the ground with guy lines on four corners. Given the straps hanging at each corner, the frame seemed like an easy manner to suspend game — especially a large grizzly bear. There was no other animal on the entire island that large. The local Sitka deer are relative runts compared to other deer, half the height of the Western mule deer.

At first, I assumed I had stumbled into a rudimentary bear hunting camp, one operated by the owner of the blue de Havilland. Then I saw something that convinced me I was wrong. Two dozen yards away, I saw a pile of bear corpses stripped of their furs, beheaded, and the paws hacked off. The distance spared me from experiencing the likely stench. These carcasses seemed like an improbable haul for legal hunters who may take only one bear in a four-year period. The Spring bear season begins April 1, so killing a half dozen bears in three weeks within the law seemed impossible. But it occurred to me that the poachers placed the dissected bodies where they did so the odor would attract new bears near their camp to become the next victims.

With an added incentive of reporting this probable poaching

operation, I turned my attention back to reaching the road system. Kodiak's topography exhibits a monotonous sameness, with long mountainous ridges running primarily North to South. Distinguishable landmarks are based in your memory. Off the road system, the only signs are animal scat, which can be notoriously unreliable for navigation.

The lake below me where the Beaver landed looked elbow-shaped, which I thought I recognized from flying over the island as a rescue swimmer years ago. Terror Lake angled Northwest from my location toward the Gulf of Alaska.

Although I don't possess a photographic memory, I had a pretty clear image of the island's map in my mind. Terror Lake lies about ten miles from Bells Flats, the closest civilization as the eagle flies. That distance did not include the up and down of seven or eight mountainous ridges to cross. An island created by tectonic shifts bore many valleys and deep crevasses where water ran into the Pacific for thousands of years. This time of year, steelhead salmon would be spawning in a few of those streams. These would attract the late-emerging bears looking for a feast after their long winter hiatus. I really, really wanted not to become anyone's feast.

Lingering near the tent, I took a few moments to assess my new situation. In the plus column, I had my Beretta, survival knife, fire-starter tools, leather jacket, and boots. On the other side of the balance sheet, I had no food, no drinking water, no water purification system, no rain gear, no sleeping bag, no tent, no map, and no compass. The poacher's tent contained nothing useful in my situation, especially no radio. I felt lucky about my current location; although several streams emptied into Terror Lake, I saw no bears fishing in their outlets. On the far Northwest corner of the lake, Terror River flowed out on a Northwesterly course toward Terror Bay.

The time of day eluded me. My assailants grabbed me in the early evening; then I remained unconscious for some undetermined length of time. I awoke in the canvas shroud, still unable to determine the time. Now, the fog prevented me from observing the sun's position in the sky. Or the moon's. Yet, I had enough visibility to walk without falling or tumbling down an embankment. The thin mist did reduce the likelihood of becoming snow blind from the reflection of sunlight on the snow-covered terrain. I needed to keep moving as long as I had light during Kodiak's lengthening days. More dangerous than poison berries, contaminated waters, or marauding bears was the danger of a late April ice storm making the hike out of the wild nearly impossible. And hypothermia would become all the more likely the longer I stood still.

Facing toward the direction I presumed to be East, I climbed a gentle slope through a waist-high thicket. Aware that I might stumble upon a Kodiak bear or a bear cub with concerned Mom nearby, I recited aloud lyrics to songs I knew well. I did not sing to conserve my breath for the climbs. Also, the nuns designated me a "listener" back in third grade, and I haven't sang aloud since. I went through the best of Sam Cooke before jumping to Leonard Cohen.

After a gentle hike, I entered a wide, flat valley on all sides of a small lake. Hills rose to the left and right toward snow-capped crests. Ahead, a gentle incline rose toward a snow-covered ridge. From that elevation, I might identify a landmark with which to set my course, such as the aerial beacon at Kodiak airport. So, I took a bead on a col between two prominent heights on the ridge above me and began climbing. Soon, I left the grassy field and began an ascent into a tundra-like area covered by clumps of grasses and flattened trees. Ahead lay a wide rock wall that would be challenging to climb without any technical gear. I veered toward my left, farther toward the Northeast, aiming for what appeared to be a gap through the long ridge. Of course, I had no way of knowing where that pass would lead me. As I approached the higher elevation, I came into deeper ice and snow that slowed me down. Worse, my lower pants legs became wet and began to freeze.

As I struggled up the slope, I pondered how I had arrived there. Travis Pike recognized me in the lobby or the Baranof Lodge. A coincidence I couldn't attribute to anything else. The young man wiping down the Jeep warned me that word around the Air Station indicated trouble in my future. After my meeting with Pike outside the

Baranof Lodge, somebody landed a blow on my skull; then a seaplane owner and an accomplice flew me deep into the wildlife refuge, home to the world's largest bears, a particularly voracious carnivore. All with the goal that I die in the wilds of exposure, exhaustion, or emaciation. Maybe consumption by a Kodiak bear. Leaving no Travis Pike fingerprints on my corpse. Or any connection to God's True Patriots.

The most prevalent danger in Alaska is hypothermia because the frequent weather changes challenge the body to regulate its warmth. A little exertion climbing a hill might cause perspiration that chills the body, and soon the body begins to lose heat. A visitor doesn't have to travel far from their vehicle to get into trouble. Add a little dehydration, and soon you have a search and rescue case. Or a corpse.

An obvious solution for thirst is the plentiful snow and ice. A clear drawback to eating snow or ice is the loss of body heat, no matter how minimal. When a body's temperature begins to drop, the effects tend to snowball. First comes the shivering, followed by exhaustion, confusion and loss of coordination. Curiously shivering is a good sign, because it's when your body stops shivering that you are in serious trouble.

Of course, I could not ignore the danger of Kodiak bears. In April, they were emerging from hibernation and grazing in the berry bushes and grasses. The most dangerous are sows with new cubs born over winter. Cubs are defenseless against male bears and other predators like the red fox, and sows are especially territorial and dangerous in their efforts to protect their young.

I adjusted my course toward the presumptive East, through snow-covered mountainsides above the streams and greening shrubbery. I remained below the ice fields hugging the crests of the mountain peaks and ridges. I intended to walk as long as possible before fatigue, hunger or thirst overtook me. The closer I reached to the Coast Guard Air Station and Kodiak airport, the more likely a signal fire might attract a pilot's attention. Back on Terror Lake, I knew the most likely spotter was another floatplane headed for a remote hunting camp. I could wait a long time for that rescue. The trick was to recognize the limit of my endurance in order to signal for help while I still had strength left.

As I hiked, the stream below me began to drop into a deep crevasse, and both sides of the valley steepened. In the thick fog, I could not see the contours of the valley ahead. If I got too far into an arroyo, I would have trouble getting back out. Scaling icy rocks with bare hands seemed a bad idea. So I backed out of the valley by following my prior footsteps. When the wall on my left became a more gentle slope, I started up the incline. In a few hours, I reached the snow-covered crest of a ridge several hundred feet high. I found a rock ledge with a view in the direction I assumed was Northeast and settled down to calculate my next course.

For several years as a rescue swimmer, I flew medical evacuations, or MEDEVACs, to the small Native villages around Kodiak Island. From those HH-3 helicopter flights, I recalled the two large bays carved into the island's Northeast corner. The Northern-most was Kizhuyak Bay, uninhabited for miles until Port Lions, near where Kizhuyak flowed into the larger Marmot Bay.

Located somewhere to the East of me was Chiniak Bay, from which three smaller bays protruded into the island like fingers: Women's Bay, Middle Bay, and Kalsin Bay. The main road system wrapped along the Western shoreline of Chiniak Bay. Getting to a road meant finding a way to town and, if lucky, even a ride.

The immediate decision facing me: choosing the right stream to follow down to a bay where I could find help. If I chose poorly, I would wander along an unoccupied waterfront for days. I took a chance and continued on what I believed was an Eastward course. With an eye on a promontory on the high ridge across the next valley, I set off down a slope covered with thickets of alder and shrubs ripe with salmonberries. I moved with caution, talking aloud to myself so I did not surprise a bear, and I made occasional stops when I found patches of salmonberries already ripe earlier than usual. At the bottom of the slope lay a thread of a stream that I stepped across with ease. The water flowed diagonal to my path, which I took for North-east, so I continued along my original course. Soon, the elevation began to rise toward another round knob. As I came up to a height where I could see down the long valley toward what I believed was North lay a long, wide body of water. If my memory of Kodiak's geography remained accurate, Kizhuyak Bay lay about five miles down that valley, creating a false trail out to civilization. In the lower 48, the common advice for the lost was to follow water downstream to eventually reach some outpost of civilization. In Alaska, that strategy could just as easily lead the lost to a place my very Irish grandmother called Mag Mell, from which no one ever returned.

All shrubs and grasses disappeared when I reached the bald slope at the end of the ridge. Green lichen grew close to the ground, littered with dead wooden roots, like on a tundra. Beyond the ridge I crossed, I could see behind me the upper arm of Terror Lake, indicating I had covered little more than four miles. Still, I felt tired, no doubt, because I had not recently been hiking in such rugged terrain. The darkening sky indicated the long Alaska day was ending, so I found a rock outcropping where I could have a little protection from the prevailing winds. The peak of the ridge rose at least 400 feet above me. Then I set about gathering dead wooden roots and limbs, as well as dried, brittle lichen for kindling. With two of the longer branches, I wedged dried lichen into one end to create torches if I needed to fend off any predators. Then I settled against the stone face and watched the sky to gauge the arrival of sunset. I recalled that late April days on Kodiak lasted almost 13 hours, with an hour of twilight on either end. When the Eastern sky began to darken, I started working to build a fire. With the flint and steel from my belt, I struck sparks until flame lighted the lichen, then fed in the smallest shards of roots and branches. My back against the rocky outcropping, I soon felt some warmth generated by the blaze. The night air felt cool, not cold, with a mist on the breeze. Typical for Kodiak in Spring because of the Pacific air stream. From a distant valley, I heard the yipping of a red fox. Apart from the fox, I heard no other noise on that ridge top apart from the whisper of wind.

At that altitude, I thought a chance encounter with a bear unlikely, especially if I kept the fire burning in front of me. Still, I laid the improvised torches on either side of me; the knife and Beretta a few inches in front of me. Of course, at best, a .22 caliber pistol could only annoy a Kodiak bear. Each week I spend time practicing on the shooting range, but I placed no faith in my ability to shoot out a bear's eye, likely the only kill shot with such a small-caliber weapon on such a large animal. History and mythology describe frontiersmen who killed bears with only a knife; I am no Daniel Boone or Hugh Glass.

Situated between the fire and rock wall, I leaned back and dozed through the dark hours. As the night wore on, the stone face radiated some heat back toward me. In the darkest hour, the fog blew off, exposing a stunning view of the Milky Way with a vast number of shimmering stars like a Van Gogh canvas. A glow on the horizon encouraged me, suggesting the light came from the swath of civilization from Bells Flats up to Kodiak village. Above the white light pollution, several red aerials marked the broadcast antennae of the Coast Guard Communications Station and the commercial radio towers atop Pillar Mountain. The white beam of the bright beacon at the civilian airport flashed across the sky. With the clearing night, the temperature fell. I scavenged out as far as the firelight permitted to gather more ancient roots with which I created a pyre intended to generate warmth. If a pilot happened to spot it, so much the better.

Unable to sleep and now too sore from the chilly air to doze, I stretched and sat closer to the fire. To keep my fingers moving, I field stripped and reassembled the Beretta. Twice. This distracted me from hunger after 24 hours without anything to eat but salmonberries or drink except snow. I thought it improbable that snow carried dysentery.

Although I wasn't ready to give up, dying on Kodiak didn't seem so far-fetched. In 1912, the island experienced a mass extinction event when the Novarupta volcano erupted on the Alaskan Peninsula. The largest volcanic explosion in the 20th Century lasted three days, covering Kodiak Island with sulfur dioxide gas and a foot of volcanic ash. Blinded by the ash, the bears starved along with many other mammals. Birds overcome by the ash and gases fell from the sky.

Ash-filled streams killed the salmon. The volcano exterminated even the mosquito population.

Without the thick fog, I watched the Eastern sky brighten from black to light blue. The shadow of a waxing moon emerged toward dawn; Mercury glimmered just over the horizon. Knowing air traffic in and out of Kodiak would begin about then, I added all the remaining wood I had gathered into the fire. Soon the sky would be too bright for the fire to be a useful beacon. By then, false dawn showed the terrain well enough that I could get moving on my hike. After stretching my stiff muscles, I kicked the fire apart and stamped out the embers, scraping some snow onto the fire with my boot. Minus a shovel or water, I could not extinguish the coals to Smokey Bear's standards, but nothing smoldered when I finally set off down the ice-covered slope.

The colder temperature overnight froze a thin crust over the snow. The shell was not thick enough to support my weight, so I broke through with each step. The crust then scraped my shin, making progress rather painful. After 300 feet, I stopped to cut my handkerchief with my knife and then ripped it into two equal pieces. I wrapped these around my ankles as bandages, which I held in place with strips of the duct tape that once bound my wrists and ankles.

Despite these poor-man gaiters, the ice and added pain slowed me down, and I still navigated the ice with cautious steps on the downslope when I heard an engine echoing in a nearby valley — the lovely, familiar sound of a Sikorsky MH-60. I turned back in time to see the beautiful orange face and black snout of a Jayhawk rise over the ridge where I had spent the night. The bulbous proboscis on its front housed its navigation equipment. I waved my arms to indicate distress; I didn't want them to think I was out for a morning stroll amongst my bear friends. As it approached, the helo's aspect turned so I could see its open cabin door. Inside the helo, the crew prepared to deploy a hoist basket.

The helo maintained its distance until they were ready to effect a hoist. I've been under many prop-wash downdrafts, so I appreciated their restraint at not swooping in too eagerly. When they were ready, the crewman at the winch lowered the basket so that it made contact with the ground before they approached me. This prevented me from getting a sharp electric shock upon touching the basket. It's surprising how much static a helo's rotors and cable can generate before a litter reaches the ground.

When the big basket settled on the ice- and lichen-covered ground, I let it sit for a count of ten before I touched it. The wind remained calm when I rode up to the helo's door on the hoist cable; then, the crewman swung me inside the cabin. I settled myself on a sling seat against the back wall, as I had demonstrated to many people I had assisted while a rescue swimmer. I sat on the web seating of the helo, drinking a bottle of water. One of the crew passed me a headphone with a mic attached to the helo's IC.

"What the hell you doing out in the middle of the bear refuge?" one of the pilots asked me. "This some kind of tryout for your own reality show?"

I pressed the plunger on my IC's cable. "I don't think they could pay me enough for that. No, I got left behind."

The rescue swimmer slapped my arm. "Seriously?" he asked. "You need some new friends."

I tapped into the IC. "Then I'm buying up at the Anchor Club when you guys get done with this rotation. You too, sirs," I added to the pilots.

"How do you know about the Anchor Club on Base?" one asked.

"I was stationed in Kodiak years ago," I said. I didn't want to give them too much information because my new car detailer indicated at least someone at the Air Station talked about my likely disappearance. I looked down on the rugged terrain below that would have been necessary to cross before reaching the road system.

One of the crew waved me over to the starboard window. "Look who was waiting for you," he said.

I peered down and spotted an enormous grizzly bear standing on its rear paws in the middle of a thicket not far from my intended direction down the slope. Had our paths crossed, my only defense would be a little .22 caliber Beretta. Hurling stones may have been more effective.

"How did you happen to find me out in the middle of nowhere?" I asked, comparing the immediate danger a little way down the slope and the long distance remaining before I reached civilization.

"The pilot on the morning FEDEX flight coming into Kodiak called in a signal fire," the co-pilot explained. "We were in the middle of crew change, so it took us a little longer to get in the air. We had some fog toward Pasagshak, but it was clear through to Anton Larsen Bay, so we went up around the North end of the island and came down Kizhuyak Bay."

"You need an ambulance to take you down to the island hospital to get checked out?" the rescue swimmer asked. "Think you might have frostbite or any signs of hypothermia?"

I shook my head. "No, I'm good. I'll help you fill out the SAR report when we get back to Base."

"Thanks. Only downside of a SAR is the paperwork."

The pilot spoke up for the first time. "Oh, stop your whining, Owens. You don't have half the paperwork we do. Especially when you go jumping into the water. You know how much paperwork pilots have after a swimmer deployment?"

Paperwork, complaints, and good-natured feuding between pilots and crew. Nothing had changed much since I last jumped out of a perfectly good helicopter.

22

Back at the big blue hangar on the Coast Guard Base, I went into the operations office to provide all the basic information they needed to complete their reports. Only when they asked for my ID did I realize that my wallet was missing. This was a problem: my wallet contained my badge as well as my Coast Guard identification, which could provide access to the Base here in Kodiak or any Coast Guard facility nationwide. Taking my badge struck me as egregious as lifting my MIA bracelet engraved with my father's name. I asked if I could use an office for a private phone call. The operations officer left earlier on a C-130 for the LORAN station on St. Paul Island in the Bering Sea. He wouldn't be back for ten hours. His yeoman ensured I would see no sensitive material on the commander's desk and let me use the phone there. She closed the door behind her.

Frank Anker answered on the second ring.

"Hi, Frank. You have some time to help a fellow agent?" I asked.

"Might depend upon what you have in mind. I plan to retire in three years. Are you going to screw that up?"

I paused to consider what could happen in the next week. "Not my intention, no. I'd say odds are pretty good that you'll make it."

"I guess a guarantee is too much to ask. OK, what can I do to help?"

"Thanks. First, can you come get me? I'm sitting in the Operations Officer's office at the Air Sta."

"I'll bet that'll be a story."

"The first of many."

"See you in 15."

I hung up, then fished through the Kodiak phone book because my notebook was back in my hotel room at the Baranof. "Trooper Montgomery, please."

"I'm sorry," the AST dispatcher said. "He's dealing with a nuisance bear out on Monashka Bay this morning."

"Understood. When he returns, please ask him to call Frank Anker's desk out on the Coast Guard Base."

"Will do. Have a nice Alaska day."

After hanging up, I thanked the yeoman on my way out and headed down to the parking lot. I took off my jacket to inspect the damage from my ordeal. Mud streaked down the shoulders and back from when I wriggled about on the shores of Terror Lake. Getting the leather cleaned without shipping it to Anchorage seemed unlikely. I needed something to wear in the interim. Within a few minutes, Frank drove up in a gray, four-door Chrysler K-car. When I climbed into the passenger seat, he raised a hand, palm-out, to silence me. "Don't say it. Last thing that Base operations had to assign when I got here."

"Good thing you don't have high-speed chases on the island. There's no place to go. Listen, could we make a quick stop over at the exchange? I need to buy a new jacket."

Off we went with Frank driving a little faster than the Base speed limit. "So how did you come to get yourself rescued this morning?" he asked.

I told him, including pertinent detail and excluding the irrelevant. I finished as we drove into the parking area in front of the exchange/commissary building.

"You ever go anywhere and not cause a problem?" he asked.

"Not that I recall," I said. "Do you mind coming with me? I don't have my ID card."

"Where's your ID? You don't keep it in your wallet?"

"Didn't I mention they kidnapped me? They took my wallet, weapon, and badge."

"Crap. You don't have any money or credit cards? Are you also expecting me to pay, too?"

"No, don't worry. I have money." Once we got inside, I removed my belt and unzipped the hidden security panel. In addition to the fire-making tools, the belt contained ten $200 traveler's checks.

"Interesting piggy bank," Frank said.

"My grandmother taught me to always have emergency funds."

"Your grandma was Civil Defense back in the day? Come on, I don't know what kind of selection you'll find here. If you get desperate, I'll try to finagle you a flight jacket from the Air Station."

I headed for the men's clothing section of the exchange. While Frank's offer was practical, I wanted to avoid the appearance that my presence on Kodiak was in any manner official in nature. That would cause problems for me and Andrews. Better to fly under the radar as best I could, although rescue by a Coast Guard HH-60 didn't help on that score. I found a nice rack of brand-name leather jackets that would serve as a good replacement. The clerk busy folding shirts for a display nearby unlocked the cable snaked through the sleeves of the jackets on the rack.

"You get a lot of shoplifting?" I asked Frank.

"Some. But never a repeat offender. The commanding officers don't let offenders slide with petty theft. Come to mast on shoplifting charges here, and your C.O. is going to be certain the other C.O.'s don't hear your name again. Same if there's any trouble downtown."

The same clerk checked me out once I made my selection. I wondered if the staff earned commissions because she seemed happy with the final price I paid. I felt relieved to have a few checks left from my belt safe.

"Lot of petty crime with folks partying downtown these days?" I asked as I cut various tags off the jacket with my knife as he drove.

Frank laughed. "Hardly any. I've been here four years now. I tracked down a deserter for the District Office once. The rest of the time has been National Agency Checks for security clearances. One time, Kathy had a domestic abuse case — and we handed it off to Kodiak PD because the family wasn't living on Base."

"Don't sound too disappointed."

"Well, that case might have given us something to do at least, and we could have kept a lot of the details out of the local newspaper. We didn't need that added to an already bad situation."

We drove over to the old barracks that housed his office. I pushed open the door. When we entered his office, Kathy was not at her desk. "She's catching the Red Tail to Elmendorf; she wants to spend a day shopping in Anchorage," Frank explained.

I pointed toward a large whiteboard on wheels in the corner. "May I? I need to lay out two different cases to enlist your help in each."

He nodded yes, so I rolled the board between the two old steel desks in the office — the same steel furniture that may have seen service in WWII. I drew a straight line down the middle. On the left-hand side, I scrawled "Janet Simms." On the line below, I wrote, "5678." On the opposite side, I wrote out Pike. "Let's start on the left. We'll need Trooper Montgomery to help us on the other side."

From there I proceeded to explain my investigation on Kodiak to Anker. His eyes widened when I told him that young Lieutenant j.g. Holland omitted certain information from our prior conversation. I cautioned him about jumping to conclusions, especially with an officer involved. Besides, I explained, we weren't even investigating a crime. At least not yet. First, we had to solve the riddle of 5678. I added "Holland" below those numbers on the white board.

"Why are these numbers special?" he asked.

"I found them on the page of her planner for the day of her death. And those are section numbers for an area on her topographical map she had when she died."

From a desk drawer, Frank removed a topographical map of Base Kodiak and surrounding areas. "She died in one of these sections?"

"No. These sections are on the base of Barometer. She was found about two miles from there." I pointed to the sections in question and then at the X marking the spot someone had drawn on his map indicating an area along Bear Creek. "I'm not sure why these four sections are significant."

"Does it matter?" Frank asked. "Maybe she wanted to go looking for cloudberry. Do you think it's connected to her death somehow? Do you have any reason to think her death was anything but an act of God?"

"Well, you get a lot of ideas pop in your head when you're half dozing out on the tundra overnight. What if she was already dead when the bear arrived? What cause of death could slip past a medical examiner if a body was mutilated?"

Frank opened his desk drawer and removed a pencil with which he doodled on his blotter. After a moment, I saw that he was drawing a crude representation of a coroner's illustration of an autopsy.

"That bear inflicted damage that would disguise a lot of sins," he said. "But the AST ran a toxicology report that was clean. There was no sign of gunshot wounds. No sign of sex or sexual assault."

"The autopsy mentioned petechial hemorrhaging. Would her neck wound obliterate any sign of strangulation?"

"That bear did terrible damage to her head and neck. As I understood from Fish and Wildlife, bears attack their victim's head first."

I added that possibility to our list. "Do you feel comfortable interviewing Mister Holland with me? It's not an official investigation. For now."

"My good sense is telling me to call down to Juneau to check in with the Regional Office. But I'm also smart enough to know what answer I'll get if I do. Especially if I mention your name."

Before I could reply, his desk phone rang. After answering, Frank put the caller on speaker phone. "Thanks for calling. He's right here in the office with me. You're on speaker now."

"Good morning, gentlemen," Trooper Montgomery said. "I'm afraid I have no new information regarding your lieutenant's death, and I'm getting pressure to close out the case and move on."

"Understood. We have a few more details to run down before we close out the file ourselves," I explained. "We'll share any new information that we learn. But now I need to report a different crime. Two nights ago, I was abducted outside the Baranof Lodge. I was flown on a Beaver out to Terror Lake and left to fend for myself, likely to freeze to death in the mountains or have a run-in with a hungry bear."

"Do you make enemies everywhere you go?" Frank asked in a quiet tone.

"Any idea who's responsible?" the trooper asked.

"You bet. I'll give you the tail number of the de Havilland that took me to Terror Lake." I then recited the alpha-numeric combination for him. "But the person behind the whole thing is Travis Pike. He accosted me, then somebody hit me from behind. And the guys in the Beaver mentioned his name out at Terror Lake."

"Do you want to press charges?" Montgomery asked.

"As many as we can come up with. I'm thinking assault, kidnapping, theft, attempted murder. And that's just the state charges. Frank, I'd like you to talk with Juneau about federal charges of abducting a federal agent. Along with theft of my weapon, federal ID and badge. And any outstanding warrants somewhere. I want to know if Pike's got unpaid parking tickets anywhere. Same with all his accomplices."

The trooper laughed at my laundry list of felonies and misdemeanors. "Before any arrests, can we establish Pike's motives? What's some one-hit wonder got against a Coast Guard LE agent?"

"Marty's got a way with people," Frank said. "How many people did you kill up in Michigan? Ten in a week?"

"I broke a weapons smuggling ring on Lake Superior with ties to a white supremacist," I explained to Montgomery, leaning on Frank's desk to talk into the speaker phone. "So now I'm famous on the church-burning circuit."

"Be honest," Frank interjected. "Infamous."

"I get regular death threats from certain groups. Pike accosted me in the lobby of the Baranof a few nights ago so I know he recognized me. Then he stopped me outside the Lodge while somebody whacked the back of my head. I woke up on a Beaver flying to the wilderness with my arms and ankles bound. I want Pike's next tour to include Alaska's correctional facilities before he moves on to a federal prison."

"Careful now," Frank cautioned. "*Folsom Prison Blues* put Johnny Cash on the map."

The trooper's laugh echoed on the phone line. "From what I've heard, Travis Pike is no Johnny Cash. But I've also heard Pike got both his bear and a bison, so he's probably leaving tomorrow, if he gets a break in the weather."

Frank looked at his watch. "We'll meet you at the Baranof in fifteen minutes. If you're not there in thirty, we'll proceed under the federal statutes."

"Sounds good," Montgomery agreed.

"Remind me to check that Pike had a permit for the bear he took. Might be nice to invite state game boys to play," Frank said.

His comment jogged my memory. "Speaking of which, someone involved in abducting me is also running a bear poaching operation out in the refuge. Near where they dumped me, I found a crude camp with a frame for field dressing a bear. Not far off was a dump of bear carcasses. There's a camo tent with a freezer."

"A freezer?" Frank asked. "In the middle of the refuge?"

"That's what I saw."

"Would have shocked me if you didn't find a freezer," Montgomery said. "Attached to a generator, right? They have to freeze the gallbladders for shipping to Asia. Other parts go on the open market in the lower 48. You cannot believe how much a bear's gallbladder is worth in Korea."

"I don't think I want to know," Frank said. "Can we meet at the Baranof in fifteen minutes? You can deal with the poaching later."

Frank's K-car surprised me with its pep and agility as we cruised into Kodiak, around the big curve overlooking St. Paul Harbor. We pulled into the parking lot of the Baranof at the same time as the AST's big Ford SUV.

23

Young Lily was working the front desk when Frank Anker and I entered the lobby. Trooper Montgomery watched the rear entrance to the lodge in case anyone tried to make a fast exit. By the young woman's smile and pleasant greeting, I assumed she had nothing to do with my unscheduled visit to the Kodiak Wildlife Refuge. I approached the desk and leaned as far forward as I could.

"Tell me, Lily, do you know if Travis Pike is in his room this morning?" I asked.

"Oh, no. There's a big publicity shoot up at Fort Abercrombie. You know, the old Army base on the North end of the island. They flew in a whole photo crew from Seattle yesterday. Make-up, lights, photographer, the works."

"Any of his local fans invited?" Frank asked.

"Oh, no. They closed the whole park for the day. Some security guys from Anchorage. Kind of jerks, if you ask me."

"Thanks." I said, sliding toward her some cash left from exchanging the traveler's checks. "Please don't mention to anyone that I asked you about it."

"You bet, Marty," she said, slipping the bills into the pocket of her frock. I assumed I had doubled her weekly salary.

"What do you want to do now?" Frank asked as we headed out to the parking lot.

"Let's go talk to the trooper. We're going to need him to get past Pike's new security detail. Unless you're up to doing it the hard way."

He stopped without warning and gave me a curious look. "You are insane, aren't you? You want to take on Pike's hired muscle?"

I took his arm and led him back to the AST rig. "Come on. I'm kidding. We don't need the hassle of the extra paperwork."

When we approached him, Montgomery seemed pleased with the opportunity to chase off a few rental cops. Frank and I followed the AST vehicle North through the village up to Fort Abercrombie State Park. A muscular man clothed in a tight shirt manned the entrance; he offered no resistance when Montgomery drove up. Frank put down his window, flashed his badge, then said to the guard, "We're with the trooper."

Finding Pike and his entourage wasn't difficult. They had several vehicles and a herd of ten workers. Pike himself stood in the middle of a well-rusted weapon mount from one of the eight-inch coastal defense guns installed during World War II. The gun's actual barrel lay across two concrete mounts a short distance away.

Pike wore an alligator skin jacket and black jeans shellacked to his legs. His Fender guitar featured a pearl inlay of his initials. The Stars and Stripes decorated his cowboy boots. Small turquoise eggs encircled his cowboy hat on an engraved silver band.

As we approached, the photographer instructed two assistants holding large white cards to move into different positions while he tested and retested with a light meter near Pike's face. I asked Montgomery to give me a few minutes alone with Mister Nashville. I promised not to take long. With the trooper's permission, I stepped over the barrier surrounding the old gun carillon. I motioned for the photographer and assistants to give us privacy. Pike recognized me and began to back away.

"You touch me, I'll have your badge," Pike threatened. He held the body of his guitar with one hand and the neck with the other. He aimed the guitar's head toward me like holding an AR-15.

"You already have my badge. Along with my ID and my gun. Leaves me in the clear to do what I want." I drew my Beretta from my jacket pocket. "But your boys missed this." I palmed the pistol so only he could see it, and I kept my voice low so only he could hear me. "So how about a song?" I turned to face his people gathered around in curiosity. "Wouldn't we all like to hear Travis Pike sing for us?" I asked, raising my voice. I turned back to face Pike, raising the Beretta across my chest without pointing the weapon directly at him. "So how about a rendition of that Patsy Cline classic, 'Who's Sorry Now?'"

"Go to hell!" Pike yelled at me.

"Very likely. But you and me, we're stuck for now. So, sing or strip. Your choice."

"Galloway!" I heard Frank call. "Get him in cuffs and let's go."

"Agreed," Montgomery said. "Make the arrest and be done." He then read aloud the Miranda warning for Pike's benefit.

"OK. You're getting off easy," I told Pike. "Put down the Fender, turn around and put your hands behind your back. Looks like Trooper Montgomery will do the strip search when he locks you up." I turned toward Frank. "Do you have a set of matching bracelets for today's lucky winner?"

"Here," Frank called as he tossed a set of handcuffs. "Make' em' tight so they don't fall off his scrawny wrists."

"Careful," Montgomery said as I stepped next to him. "We don't want to compromise the case with a tainted arrest. He's got a lot of witnesses."

"All hired, according to the young woman working the front desk at the Baranof. The photo crew out of Seattle; security out of Anchorage. You can't hire loyalty." I turned to look up at Montgomery. "I assumed his photo team would film everything, so I kept my voice down."

"Are you some kind of prosecutor's nightmare?" the trooper asked. "Am I going to regret getting involved in all this?"

I thought about that for a few moments rather than responding with a misleading denial. "Let me say that the U.S. Attorney in Anchorage might still remember my name. I'm memorable, but not in a good way."

"He's cursed," Frank said as he pushed a hand-cuffed Travis Pike past us. "You want me to put Mister Pike in our car for the ride into town?"

"Sure. Can you give me a head start so I can explain things to the boss?" Montgomery asked.

"You want me to come along?" I asked. "Provide a statement?"

"Hell no," Montgomery said, swearing for the first time since I'd met him. "If you talk to my boss first, I'll be re-assigned to Nome or the Pribilofs."

"Come on, Marty," Frank Anker called from the K-car. "Give the officer a chance to save his career without you butting in."

One of Pike's security details stopped me as I started toward the sedan. "Should we wait here for Mister Pike to come back out to finish the shoot?" he asked.

I glanced over the crowd of waiting photographers and assistants, as well as the make-up artists, hair stylists, and personal assistants. "No, I wouldn't wait here. He may be tied-up for a while. I'm guessing 15 to 20." I smiled and lowered myself into the gray Coast Guard sedan alongside Frank. Travis Pike sat behind us, hand-cuffed and spewing angry, racist bile that likely never made it into his concerts.

24

Frank Anker and I spent the afternoon at the Alaska State Trooper post assisting Montgomery in typing up the complaint regarding Travis Pike's various nefarious activities. With a single call, Montgomery managed to identify by its tail number the owner and pilot of the de Havilland Beaver that took me to Kodiak's interior. Montgomery learned Joseph "Joey" Cross would return soon from dropping a pair of anglers out in Akhiok, an Alutiiq village on the far South end of Kodiak Island. Frank volunteered to go greet him when the aircraft returned. Montgomery seemed hesitant at first, but his workload won out. He decided to process Pike before a horde of lawyers arrived from Anchorage or Nashville. They both concluded that my involvement might complicate future prosecutions. Or that's what they said.

Back at the Baranof Lodge, Lily provided me with a new room key. The afternoon stretched into the evening as I waited sprawled on my bed for Montgomery to arrive with a search warrant for Pike's room that would allow me to recover my personal items: badge, Colt, wallet and, most importantly, my black POW/MIA bracelet. Anker arrived first, excited to tell me — over a cold Molson – that Joey Cross was all kinds of eager to spill on Pike in exchange for any possible deal that might keep him out of prison. Frank said Joey expressed considerable anxiety about male intimacy behind bars. I had the sense that Frank enjoyed toying with Joey the way an angler teases a salmon with a yellow bomber fly. About the time the trooper arrived, Frank decided he needed to head home for dinner.

Montgomery declined my offer of a beer because he was on duty and in uniform. He settled onto the desk chair and took out his notebook to share what he learned by interviewing Travis Pike. Nothing he said came as much of a surprise. "Ever have a suspect who was his own worst enemy? I reminded him of his rights, and he said he wanted to remain silent. Then he spent an hour telling me every reason he wanted to remain silent. He was giving me a headache with his gibberish. And of course, I couldn't ask him anything because he said he wanted to remain silent."

"Fun evening?" I asked.

Montgomery unfastened the golden badge over his left shirt pocket. "OK, give me one of those Molson muscles. Let's toast to stupidity. In the course of remaining silent, Pike told me that he knows all about God's True Patriots. He knows all about you and the gun ring in Michigan. He's upset about Waco; happy about Oklahoma City."

"You didn't explain the meaning of 'silent'?" I asked. "If he keeps going, we could learn about a lot of conspiracies. Like who was on the grassy knoll?"

"No, I didn't try to calm him down. Are you kidding? He was just getting started. He wants to do a benefit concert for the Patriots, even dedicate a CD."

I sat up and put down my beer. "And you stopped the interview to come here? Doesn't everything he said count as an excited utterance? The U.S. Attorney could get it all admitted. He was Mirandized and still talked."

"Oh, he talked and talked and talked," the trooper added. "But he's got the best shysters money can buy coming up from Seattle overnight. They'll be here tomorrow. First thing they'll do is get everything he said excluded."

"May I make a suggestion then? Are you up for some three-card monte?"

He shook his head. "I'm not much of a gambler."

"Well, hear me out first. Right now, we have Travis Pike and Joey Cross jailed together. But we don't want them to coordinate their stories. Let's transfer Pike up to federal detention in Anchorage."

"You don't think that will upset Pike's attorneys when they get here in the morning?"

I rested my chin on my fist. "So how much does that matter to me?" I asked. "Alex, I'll take 'None at all' for five hundred."

He laughed then slugged back the remainder of his Molson. He pinned his badge back on his uniform shirt. "Let's execute a warrant in his room, then I'll call my boss. I may be taking the late flight up to Anchorage."

25

Some people are born into a life of crime. They can con a dog out of its fur. Travis Pike is not one of those people. When Montgomery and I went into Pike's room at the Baranof, we found my badge and weapons together in plain sight on top of the dresser. My wallet was in the top drawer, along with the balance of the cash Andrews had given me in a bank envelope with Andrews' name from a credit union in Alameda, California. Montgomery whipped out his little camera and snapped two dozen photographs before letting me move anything. In another drawer, I located my POW/MIA bracelet.

"I wonder if Travis had the same idea as your partner Frank about a prison album like Johnny Cash to kickstart a career," the trooper said as he did a quick sweep of the room. "Pike sure looks like he wants to be performing *Jail House Rock*."

"You have enough to support a charge of kidnapping. Think your boss will let you take him to Anchorage?"

He stopped his search to stare at me. "He'll be OK with it tonight, but he might be pissed in the morning when Pike's suits arrive. I'd feel better if I can tell him what we're planning to do."

I nodded in agreement. "Understood. We have nothing to hide.

Kidnapping a federal agent is a federal offense. You can cite chapter and verse if he asks. 18 USC something. We don't want Pike conspiring with Joey Cross and mucking up the cases against them."

"You only gave me chapter, no verse."

"That's why you're talking to the U.S. attorney. Make them do a little legwork."

"Yes, I guess I should go on up to Anchorage anyway, so I can talk to the prosecutor. I'll need to get a warrant for Pike's phone records while he was staying here. We'll need to know who else may have been in on this whole thing."

I picked up Pike's day planner and flipped through the pages. "We know we're missing Joey's accomplice. If we can get a warrant to search Joey's float plane, we may be able to figure out who helped him." I stopped and laughed. "Do you think Joey put me on his manifest for the flight to Terror Lake?"

Montgomery chuckled. "I know it's a legal requirement, but that's the least of his crimes. If I mention it to my boss now, he'll laugh at me."

I waved the thought away. "No, Joey's in enough trouble. But something that the prosecutor might want to put on the charge sheet to help with any type of plea deal."

"I'd better talk with the boss. And go pack for Anchorage."

I returned my Colt to its shoulder holster and clipped my badge to my belt. The wallet, cash, and baton went into my trouser pockets. When Montgomery was ready to close up the room, I headed back to my own, with a black bracelet back on my wrist.

26

B ack in my room at the lodge with a white bag of dinner in foam containers, I settled on the desk chair to think. Passing up a beer, I settled with a half glass of Jameson's mixed with a Coca-Cola from the vending machine. With Montgomery and Anker focused on my sojourn to Terror Lake, I needed to direct my immediate attention back to Janet Simms. Why did a young woman with little prior interest in outdoor adventures, and unequipped for such excursions, put her life at risk?

Glancing at the alarm clock, I realized Mister Holland's jazz show would be wrapping up soon. I swilled the last of my drink, unwilling to waste good Jameson's. I put on my new jacket and headed into the hallway. At the exit to the parking lot, I stopped to scan for any suspicious characters loitering outside. I walked out and climbed into the Wrangler. I didn't intend to spend much time walking around Kodiak during the remainder of my stay on the island, possibly still wearing a target for unknown hostiles.

I drove back up to the public radio station and parked, passing the time for the young officer to emerge by watching the flock of white sea pigeons as they explored any tidbit of litter on the asphalt. Seagulls are a danger to aircraft coming or going over at Kodiak airport because it sits on the water's edge. The FAA fires off an air cannon in their daily war to keep birds from crashing through an aircraft's windscreen or being sucked into a jet turbine.

Shortly before 8 p.m., the same rusty Landcruiser rolled into the lot. The engine continued to rumble after the driver climbed out, belching a thick cloud of black smoke when it finally stopped. By then, the driver was already unlocking the station's door. On the Jeep's radio, I heard Holland sign off for the night. Next, the national news played on the hour. A young woman took over to read the weather forecast for Kodiak, along with the maritime forecast for surrounding waters. Holland emerged from the station, still pulling on a nylon jacket.

He looked disappointed when I pulled up in front of him. Opening the Wrangler's door, he leaned in. "I don't know what more I can say than what we've already talked about."

Waving my hand, I motioned for him to climb into the Jeep. Once the door closed and his seatbelt fastened, I started, accelerating hard and shifting up fast. I didn't speak to let him stew in his own curiosity. He didn't know what I intended to ask. Better that way.

We rolled into Hannah's driveway on the North end of the island. I parked behind her Pathfinder. Climbing out of the Jeep, I asked Holland to wait for me. When I rang the doorbell, Hannah answered with only a brief delay. The big Malamute pressed its snout against the screen door and sniffed at me. She wore a silky robe over flannel pajamas; the dog wore drool.

"You?" Hannah said. "I heard you went to sleep with the bears." I admit "sleep with the bears" is both an original threat and geographically apropos, too.

"You could have given me a heads up."

"And deprive the bears? You're kind of beefy. With a little tenderizer...."

"You've given this too much thought. So how did you know about my time in the refuge?"

"On Kodiak? I could tell you all kinds of things. Helps to have two brothers on the Kodiak PD. And my cousin works the front desk at the Baranof."

"Lily?"

"She said Travis Pike asked a lot of questions about you. Then you disappeared. And one of the maids noticed your badge and ID in his room."

"It's OK to warn me, you know."

"I don't have your number," she said, echoing my comment to her just days earlier.

"Look, I need a favor. Can you have a look at my Jeep and tell me if you recognize the passenger? Did he ever come around here to see Janet or turn up after she died?"

Hannah gave quite a performance, pretending to restrain the Malamute in a manner that allowed her to press her face against the screen door. After a fast glance, she pressed a hand on the dog's rear end to settle it and shook her head. "Never saw him. Before or after Janet died. You want me and Anton to question him?"

"No, thanks. He's on active duty, so I can't violate the Geneva Convention."

"OK, call me if you want Anton's help." She shoved the dog away with her knee so she could close the door.

Back in the Wrangler, I decided it was time to interrogate Holland a little more. "Sir, I need to remind you that I am not here in any official capacity. You do not have to answer my questions. However, if you tell me something that may impact the investigation by AST or CGI into Lieutenant Simms' death, I will have to share it."

"So I should keep my mouth shut?" he asked.

I started the Jeep and backed out of Hannah's driveway. Across the street, Missus Stimpson peered out of her front window. We drove back toward Holland's car at the radio station.

"I thought the state trooper covered everything," he said. "We talked for two hours, and he showed me some horrible photos." Holland's mention of photography reminded me of Montgomery's snapshot of the lieutenant's Monte Carlo. We pulled up alongside his Chevy in the parking lot outside KMXT.

"Sir, why didn't you tell anyone you were near Buskin Lake on the day Lieutenant Simms died? Montgomery has a photo of your car. There's only one like it on the island."

Holland's complexion turned from red to gray. "I tried to tell Montgomery," he stammered. "And Anker, too."

"Try me. And try harder."

"Yes, she asked me to meet her and another friend. I thought she meant by the lake, but I guess she went over to the creek."

"What did she want to talk about out there?"

"To be honest, I have no idea. Yes, I knew her, and we got along. But she never explained what she wanted. Said it would be clear when we met."

"OK, if you hear from the trooper or Anker, be direct with them about meeting her out there."

"Funny thing is, whenever I got something from her, it was usually suggestions for my show. She had an incredible knowledge of classic jazz. We're talking Monk, Coltrane, Corea. I think I told you before that Janet had an encyclopedic knowledge of music. Jazz, classical, rock, she knew it all. Well, I guess maybe not country-western."

I was not sure where to take our conversation next. "Do you recall what she sent you for her last suggestion?" I asked.

"Yeah, hang on." He climbed out of the Jeep and opened the trunk of his Chevy. He returned a moment later with a brown expandable folder used for larger collections of documents, addressed to LT j.g. Holland on its flap. "She usually sent me playlists and homemade mix tapes sometimes. This stuff didn't make sense to me at all."

Inside the thick, heavy envelope, I found pages removed from real estate guides, the classified listings from several issues of the *Kodiak Daily Mirror*, and articles about the future Kodiak space port. As I showed these to Holland in turn, he denied any knowledge of their significance to Lieutenant Simms. Finally, after showing him about 25 pages from Janet's file, I abandoned this line of questioning. I didn't know what more to pursue, and Holland seemed exhausted. I decided to go easy because he had put in eight hours at work, two on the radio, and probably snuck in a work-out. I took the four-inch file and left him in peace.

I made a quick run to the grocery store on the North end of the village to get dinner and a six-pack of Moosehead. On my way out, I noticed a few racks containing publications with real estate listings. I picked up a copy of each issue and returned to the Lodge. I put a bowl of fried rice from the grocer's deli into the microwave. While waiting for dinner to cook, I settled at the desk and removed the paperwork from the envelope. The stack looked to be more than 200 pages deep. This would take some time. I fished out my reading glasses and opened a beer.

The top 20 pages were real estate advertisements. Most were homes in Kodiak, with a couple of downtown business properties. Single-family homes, apartment buildings, storefronts, office build-ings, vacant land, remote hunting cabins, and vacant property. If there was a theme in common, I could not decipher it. I doubted that Janet Simms had an interest in that many types of property. I did learn that Marilyn Solverson was the top-selling real estate agent on the island.

The next pages clipped together were photocopies of articles from the *Anchorage Daily News* and the *Kodiak Daily Mirror*. The common subject was the space port, especially the economic impact on Kodiak and greater Alaska. A reporter on the Anchorage paper named Stephanie, with an unpronounceable Russian surname, had written a series of scathing articles in the Anchorage paper about the process the State of Alaska had taken to site the launch pad on Kodiak Island. As Lily suggested when I first arrived, an important factor appeared to have been keeping the space port away from a Congressman's home near Fairbanks. A flier promoting Marilyn's real estate business fell from the pages when I flipped into *Daily Mirror* stories. The local stories were generally more favorable toward the idea of a space port, quoting Marilyn Solverson and others engaged in the real estate business. If my memory of the area around the proposed site was accurate, the Air Force once operated a radar tracking station there as part of the NORAD system.

Below the news articles, I found a draft of the Environmental Impact Statement prepared for the space port. I struggled to understand the connection that prompted Lieutenant Simms to request a copy. But it made no more sense to me than the next document in the stack: The Alaska Native Claims Settlement Act of 1971. The Act resolved the Native Alaskan claims over lands in Alaska, clarifying ownership over specific properties and confirming the possession of more than 40 million acres by native corporations and paying them nearly one billion dollars for the lands the federal government proposed to retain in federal, state and private ownership. As I read through the details of the Act, I tried to comprehend Lieutenant Simms' interest. No joy.

Near the bottom of the stack was a publication from the General Services Administration or GSA, the federal agency that serves as landlord for most federal property. By then, I was almost finished with my fried rice.

The last of Lieutenant Simms' assorted paperwork was a page taken from a GSA notice of a public auction of federal real estate. The available properties included an obsolete mooring of the Army Corps of Engineers along the Ohio River; a former gunnery range at Fort Benjamin Harrison outside Indianapolis; an abandoned and inaccessible lighthouse in the Florida Keys; an office building on the periphery of the Hanford Nuclear Reservation. To my surprise, the list included two properties in Alaska, one of them on Kodiak. At first, I assumed it was a property adjacent to the old tracking station or the new space port. Then, in the detailed nomenclature, I found "R. 20 W. Sec. 7." I searched about for the lieutenant's topographical maps of Kodiak to confirm that the property in question lay on the North side of Barometer Mountain, squarely within the Coast Guard's ownership.

After so much reading, I stood to stretch and move after sitting so long in the desk chair that my butt felt numb. First, I went to the mini-fridge for a beer but decided on a slug of Jameson's instead. Then I paced about the room, sorting through the many questions this last discovery raised. Foremost among them, who could I trust in the Coast Guard command, either on the Base or at the Air Station? Why was Janet Simms too concerned to approach anyone with her knowledge or questions, not even the special agents on the Base? Was it possible this information was in any way connected to her death? That final question seemed so absurd that I pushed it out of my mind.

Instead, I focused on who I could approach for help with this new information. I had already been sent to sleep with the bears; I didn't want a repeat visit. I wasn't eager to give the bears a second chance. I finished the glass of whiskey and selected a cold Moosehead. I had no more reason to trust anyone in a command position than Janet Simms had, and she had rejected help from Frank Anker's office. Although Lieutenant Commander Andrews gave specific instructions not to contact him at work, I thought he might at least give me the name of someone on Kodiak he felt we could trust. Although he might be unhappy to hear from me, I am accustomed to having that effect on people.

27

I went to Frank Anker's office early, hoping to use a phone to call Andrews' office in Alameda. Frank headed out to teach a class on *chain of custody* for evidence at the fisheries law enforcement training center across the street. He told me to be certain to lock the door if I left before he returned. He didn't want to leave case files unattended.

I tried Andrews' line every 10 minutes for an hour. When no one picked up, I disconnected rather than leave a message that someone else might also overhear. Between calls to Alameda, I called other real estate agencies on the island to inquire whether Janet Simms ever contacted their office about the value of an acre of land on Kodiak. Negative results, or NEGRES as Operation Centers summarize unsuccessful searches. Most cooperated, but two offices declined my inquiry, believing secrecy about a land deal merited attorney/client or priest/penitent levels of protection. Finally, a little after 8 a.m. my time, Andrews picked up on the third ring. He sounded harried.

"Marty?" he demanded with considerable angst in his tone. "I just got out of the morning briefing, and I've got a meeting with the admiral at 9:30. In fact, I thought this was him calling to move it up."

"I'm sorry, sir. I need your help. I would say I've run up against a wall, but this is more like falling down a mineshaft."

"OK, I can give you five. Then I've got to prep for my meeting. We're going to be hosting a NATO delegation to talk about migrant interdiction. They're starting down in Miami, and the admiral invited them here to learn how to do it properly."

"We don't have time to go over everything that's happened here, but I need the name of someone on the island you trust, someone in the Base command if possible. Second choice would be over at the Communications Station."

"Hold on, let me see who's there. I've got a phone list here. A recent update." I heard rustling noises echo in the receiver as he moved things about on his desk. After a moment, he came back on the line. "Here we go, Jimmy, uh, James Avery, Lieutenant Commander. He's the lawyer in the Base legal office. Same year as me at the Academy. He played corner back. Wife is a lawyer, too. But she's civilian. They have two or three dogs, one of those big breeds, like Irish setters or wolfhounds."

"OK to mention your name to get a meeting?"

"If you must. Be discrete. You're familiar with the concept, right?"

"Did you have a nickname at the Academy that I can drop?"

Andrews laughed. "Not one that I'd tell you."

"Thanks for all your help, sir."

"You bet. Let's have dinner when you get back to the Lower 48." The line went quiet, and I thought he had hung up. "Oh, Marty. Good luck. Be careful."

I sat at Kathy Douglas' desk another moment, looking at the photos of her and her husband at their wedding. Both wore the new dress white uniforms. He had a ceremonial sword on his belt. In another framed photo, they wore scuba gear, perhaps from their honeymoon. I wondered where they went because they wore wetsuits. They looked like nice people. I recalled what Andrews had asked me when we were snowbound in the cabin back at Point Betsie. No, few special agents are much like me at all. Good for them.

Next, I called the legal office in the main Base building. a Petty

Officer Chitwood picked up on the second ring. Mister Avery had a full schedule for the morning, she explained, but there was a time when he could see me after lunch. His yeoman offered to pencil me in for 1400. I accepted.

With a few hours to spare, I drove to the Base exchange and went upstairs to the sporting goods section. Having already encountered Travis Pike's minions twice, I purchased an extra box each of .22 and .45 rounds. Somewhere I read that a Biblical scholar claimed paranoia is the beginning of wisdom. Wisdom aside, paranoia fosters preparation.

While waiting for my appointment, I wasted a little time in the music section. The racks featured a lot of performers I didn't recognize. While looking through a discount rack, I noticed an old cassette tape of Sade's first release. Remembering that the radio alarm in the lodge included a cassette player, I made a cheap impulse purchase.

When I went out to the parking lot, I found a sheet of paper wrapped around the Jeep's windshield wiper on the driver's side. No other vehicles nearby had a similar flier attached to the windscreen. Pulling it off the end of the blade, I folded it and placed it into my jacket pocket, not wanting anyone passing by to see me getting a message in this manner. Paranoia can have its downside, too.

As I headed for the Base building by the main gate, I unfolded the yellow sheet. The message was a single word, a name in fact: Ricci. The name meant nothing to me. I decided to start with Frank Anker. If he didn't recognize the name, I'd call Lieutenant j.g. Holland back, and then move on to Hannah Shangin if necessary.

The Wrangler lacked air conditioning to avoid over-taxing the four-cylinder engine when running in four-wheel drive. Alaska, during April, is a constant conflict between too warm and too cold. I stopped to unzip the Jeep's plastic window and fold it down, then started rolling to cool the rig's interior. Driving out the peninsula, I passed a black-hulled buoy tender and the white *Storis*, the oldest cutter in the Coast Guard fleet. I rounded the headland and started back toward the Base on the ocean side. In ten minutes, I rolled up in front of the Base HQ and headed up to the fourth floor on the elevator.

Petty Officer Chitwood stood at her desk, holding a phone to her ear, when I entered the Base legal office. She waved me toward a seating area with a low table covered in magazines from *Alaska Business Monthly* to *Proceedings of the Marine Safety Council*. At the center of the table sat several back issues of *Harvard Law Today*. Not junk mail, I assumed. From the half of the conversation I heard, the petty officer fended off a caller soliciting a donation for a local cause, perhaps a civic group. For her diminutive size, her voice took a rather forceful tone, almost threatening at times. With her blonde pixie haircut and owlish eyeglasses, she looked more elfin than ogre.

The wall behind her desk sported a large photo of Chitwood with a trophy bighorn sheep. Impressive. Add the cost of the state tag to the guide service, the hunt itself cost at least $5,000. In her lap, she cradled a high-powered rifle mounted with a large scope, a combo costing several thousand more. Of course, back home, my favorite fishing rod was a $1,000 Orvis with a $500 reel. I don't like to think how much I had invested in waders, creels, and flies over the years.

After ten minutes, an office door opened, and Lieutenant Commander Avery emerged. With his cropped hair and square jaw, he looked like the junior officer in a John Wayne war movie who would die in the first skirmish. He smiled and extended his hand. I thanked him for meeting me on short notice and asked if we could talk in his office. He motioned me in and closed the door behind me. When we sat at his conference table, I set my badge and military ID in front of him.

"Why do I recognize your name?" he asked.

"About the time you were at Harvard, I investigated a yeoman in the law enforcement office at the District Office. He did a runner when I found out he was selling information about investigations."

"No, doesn't sound familiar."

"I helped a friend of yours, Lieutenant Andrews, on a case in Lake Superior while he worked Intelligence at Headquarters."

"I could be wrong," he suggested.

"Years ago, I broke a commander's jaw for resisting arrest," I said. In retrospect, that case wasn't a career highlight.

"Bingo. That's it. Should I have any reason to worry?" Avery asked. "Are you investigating me?"

"No, sir." I opened the manila file folder and removed the property listing from the General Service Administration. I passed it to him, pointing to the key section.

After several minutes, he laid the paper on the table between us. "Should I recognize this?"

"That the Coast Guard is selling a tract of its land here?"

He stood. "Give me a few moments please. Can Ginny get you anything while I'm gone?" He headed for the door but stopped. "Please don't look at any papers on my desk. I'm preparing for a court martial." Then he went out the door and mentioned to his yeoman that he was going to the C.O.'s office.

When Avery returned, he paused at the door. "Do you mind if I ask Petty Officer Chitwood to come in and take notes?"

Although her involvement widened the sphere of people knowing about this land deal, I knew the petty officer handled confidential information in a legal office. No doubt she had been privy to at least one servicemember's Last Will and Testament or other personal documents. I nodded, and he motioned for her to join us. Chitwood settled on the sofa behind Avery and balanced a stenographer's notebook on her knee. She wore the first skirt I had noticed on Kodiak. Given the unpredictable nature of Alaska weather in the Spring, most women continue to wear slacks and knee-high rubber boots into June.

"I talked to the C.O. himself," Avery said. "Captain Benedetto has no idea how this notice made it into a GSA publication without his knowledge."

"May I show you the location of the property in question?" I asked. I flattened Janet Simms' map across the table. "See these sections on the map indicated in a highlighter pen?" With a forefinger, I traced around the boundary of Sections 5, 6, 7, and 8. "This map was in the possession of the late Lieutenant Simms before she died."

Avery sat back and glared at me. "You're here investigating the death of Lieutenant Simms? Agents must notify a command if investigations will occur within their authority. Why weren't we informed?"

"I apologize, sir," I said, holding up my hands. "I'm here at the request of the family. I did notify the special agents here the day I arrived."

He turned toward Chitwood and waved for her to stop recording our conversation. "Lieutenant Commander Andrews sent you?" he asked, the muscles of his square jaw clenching. "I knew he wasn't happy with the state troopers' findings."

"Yes, sir, he asked me to come up on my own time; it's not anything official." I shifted a bit as Chitwood began to scribble again. "But I found two curious things. First, when the trooper found Janet Simms, she had nothing you'd expect someone to carry outdoors on Kodiak. No bear bells, no bear spray, no map, no compass, no outdoor gear. What was she doing there? And then I came across this map. Once it roused my curiosity, then Lieutenant Holland shared with me this folder of material about land sales on Kodiak Island, including this notice from the General Services Administration. He received it from Miss Simms."

"Did Mister Holland happen to know how this notice reached GSA?"

"No, sir. In his defense, I'm not certain he was aware of its presence in the large stack of materials he gave me. If he was a part of something improper going on, I don't think he would have given me all this incriminating evidence." I paused, thinking if Mister Avery needed to be aware of anything else. "Sir, there's one other curious fact. Before she died, Miss Simms called Mister Andrews looking for the name of someone she could trust on Kodiak."

"And Mark didn't tell her to call me?"

"Well, sir, I don't know what they discussed or why she didn't call anyone here. She claimed she couldn't trust her command at the Air Station, the special agents on the island or anyone in the Base command."

"Over this?" Avery waved his hand over the GSA notice and the topographical map.

"Without the chance to interview the lieutenant, I can only guess."

Avery sat poring over the GSA land description and the lieutenant's map.

"Sir, if this were legitimate," I asked, "what would be the actual process to declare a property excess and for GSA to advertise it?"

"To be honest, I'm not familiar with the disposal process. Never had to do it. I know a few District Offices have gone through the process to dispose of automated lighthouses."

"Do you know how that works?" I asked.

"I'm not certain. Like I said, I've never participated in the process."

Petty Officer Chitwood sat forward on the sofa. "Excuse me, sir. I can help answer that. I worked in the legal office in Seattle when the district office disposed of a few parcels."

Avery turned toward her. "And do you know who initiates the disposal process? Is it the local Group office?"

"The district real property folks submit a request to GSA, and GSA will shop it around to other federal and state agencies. If there are no takers, then GSA asks non-profits, like historical societies. If nobody local expresses interest, then GSA auctions it off."

Her brief description of the process sounded accurate based on what I read in the GSA material.

"And where in the process does the local command get involved?" Avery asked her.

"Sir, if I recall, right from the start. Now lighthouses might be a little different than other real property because they have historical importance. At least once that I'm aware of, the admiral got involved in the negotiations over a lighthouse with the local historical group."

"But the local command was aware of the intended disposal?" he asked.

"As far as I know, yes, sir," she said.

"Well, Captain Benedetto was unaware of this published notice. That makes me believe this began in the District Office in Juneau."

Avery leaned back and stroked his firm jaw. He abruptly jumped forward. "Does Frank Anker know you're here conducting this investigation? What about the law enforcement staff down in Juneau?" His abrupt shift in focus from the GSA notice to my presence on Kodiak alarmed me.

"Yes, sir. I spoke with Kathy Douglass when I first got on the island. And Frank knew the next day. He informed Juneau. I've also talked with the Alaska State Troopers." Although we had covered this ground just moments earlier, I could see that he wanted some assurance given the turn this case was taking.

"Good, you've covered your bases. Thanks. I'm not sure where this will go next, but we need to do it all by the book. Any ideas why someone would do this?"

"Sir, the options are limited. Could it be an elaborate prank? Sure, but it would take someone with a knowledge of this GSA process as good as Petty Officer Chitwood."

"We don't have to worry about her," Avery said.

"Thank you, sir," Chitwood said.

"Behind Door Number Two, we have administrative mistake. Suppose an office in Juneau was training new employees how to submit a request to GSA, but it actually went to GSA by mistake." I said.

"Seems far-fetched. Wouldn't a limited number of staff need to know how to send a disposal proposal to GSA?" Avery observed.

"Excuse me, sir, the transmittal needs the district commander's signature as well," she said.

"Then we're left with what's behind Door Number Three, an intentional plot to sell Coast Guard land into the private sector. I'm guessing that right now, with this space port project, that land on Kodiak is at a premium."

"And someone would land a windfall profit?" Avery asked.

"The U.S. Treasury, sir," Chitwood said. "The funds don't even come back to the Coast Guard. But GSA should get fair market value when they sell it because any proceeds go toward the national debt."

"Thank you," Avery told her. "Can you see if you can find any records of Base Kodiak selling land in the past? Or even the 17th District in Juneau."

"Yes, sir. Do you want me to do that now?" she asked.

"Well, as soon as we finish here." Avery looked at me. "Which may be soon, unless you have more surprises for me to discuss."

"Isn't this enough?" I asked.

Chitwood closed her steno pad and stood. "I'll get right on this, sir."

After she left, I studied the lieutenant's map again. "Sir, here's an odd feature of this parcel for sale. It sits on the slope of the mountain, surrounded on two sides by federal land. I suspect the other sides belong to the Native corporation. If somebody buys the land, let's say to put up a housing development for space port employees, how do they get there?"

"There's no access?" He studied the map for a moment, then read the GSA notice again. Finally, he looked up at me. "I suppose I have some research on real estate law in my future." He pointed his thumb over his shoulder at the reams of paper stacked on his desk. "As if I don't have enough work. Thanks."

"One more service I provide," I said as we stood and shook hands.

28

For dinner that evening, I enjoyed a nice porterhouse smothered with mushrooms and onions alongside a baked potato and broccoli at the Anchor Club on Base. On a weeknight, there were few other patrons. I enjoyed an Alaskan Amber, bottled by the Alaskan Brewing Co. in Anchorage. Because it had limited distribution, I decided to have a second glass in lieu of a dessert.

A drizzle blowing in off the ocean greeted me when I walked out to the Wrangler. Once again, I found a sheet of paper wrapped around the wiper on the driver's side. I slipped it off and then climbed inside before I unrolled the page. The rain smeared the message despite my caution, but the word "Ricci" remained clear enough. I wondered if this memo came from the young man who had wiped down the Jeep's hood. After several days, the rain still beaded nicely on the Jeep's bonnet. On another topic, I decided it might be worthwhile to track down someone named Ricci tomorrow.

Given Kodiak's fickle weather, conditions changed as I drove from the Base into town. At the Buskin River, I went through a short burst of hail. When I reached the big turn over the harbor, the clouds parted to reveal a rainbow, but I needed the wipers for a quick cloud-burst as I passed the cannery.

Uncertain what I needed to do next, I turned into the business district and parked in the lot at the center of the business area. When I walked into the same bar, I saw Sage onstage performing a karaoke version of an old Stevie Nicks tune. I took a seat at the bar and ordered a Henry Weinhard with a whiskey chaser. I usually do things backward. Sage made a beeline toward me when she finished, ignoring her well-wishers at the tables. She hugged me.

"Hi. I wasn't sure I'd see you again. Somebody was in here brag-ging about him and a friend flying you into the refuge and leaving you behind for the bears."

"If you can help me identify him, that '*Somebody in here bragging*' will be doing prison time."

"Look, you didn't hear this from me, right? But Bruno keeps a surveillance camera running all the time. You can get *Somebody's* picture off that. He was wearing a Seattle Sonics sweatshirt."

"Thanks. Can I buy you a drink?"

"About time you got around to it." She flagged the bartender. "What he's having."

"When do you go home to Seattle?"

"Tomorrow. Can't wait. I'm kind of done with Kodiak. I'm cele-brating tonight. Like my outfit?" When she did a pirouette, her skirt swirled around her thighs. A guy at a nearby table whistled at her. Sage stopped, straightened her dress and climbed back onto the barstool.

"Yes, I like your outfit. Sounds like others do, too."

"Pigs. They've been bothering me all night. Bruno told them to leave me alone or leave his place."

I looked around the bar, trying to identify Bruno. "Stick close," I offered. "I come armed."

"So, you got your guns back after you got out of the refuge? *Some-body* said they left you without even a match."

I chuckled. "Wow, you heard chapter and verse of my little

escapade on ice. But it appears the boys weren't familiar with starting a fire using flint and steel."

"Hey, you got a favorite song?" she asked. "I've got another slot coming up soon. Rick has about every song since disco."

We both took slugs from our beer bottles.

"How about 'Black Velvet' by Alannah Myles?" I suggested.

"Yes, I love that song. I do it with my band, but we put in a long interlude with each instrument doing a solo. So sultry. You should see the mobbed dance floor when we do it at midnight."

"Sounds nice. How many pieces in your band?"

"Oh, it depends on who shows up. A lead guitar, drums, keyboards, sometimes bass, when she's straight. I play flute or sax. I've got a friend who plays an awesome trumpet when her boyfriend lets her come out."

"Been playing together long?"

"Geez, you're asking more questions than some labels we've auditioned for. You want to sponsor us to cut a demo tape?"

I studied the young woman for a moment, wondering if I was on the mark end of a grift. "What's that cost?"

"Serious? A five-song demo with copies to distribute could be 5K or fifty. Depends on what you want to put into rights and cover art."

"Let me think about it."

At that moment, the emcee called her up to the stage. It took a moment for him to shuffle through his collection for a ten-year-old hit. He had to restart the song because it jumped into the chorus without warning. Then Sage sang a flawless rendition. When she finished, the audience applauded vigorously, and three guys at a nearby table hooted and catcalled.

When she finished and came off stage, once again sweaty from the bright spotlights. She snatched a bar rag to wipe herself. "Sorry. Those lights are right on top of you. Place wasn't built to host a stage." She draped the towel over the back of her seat and took a sip of beer. "Sorry, I gotta go out and cool off a little."

I turned my attention back to my drinks and the television above the bar. The best I could tell, the game was Seattle Mariners vs.

Minnesota Twins. I couldn't hear the commentary, so I relied on the graphics at the bottom of the screen. It wasn't looking good for Seattle at the bottom of the fifth inning.

When the bottom of the sixth inning began, I looked around for Sage with NEGRES. Then I noticed her three rowdiest fans were no longer at their table, leaving a half-full pitcher of beer. I decided to investigate.

Despite walking around the bar's exterior, I didn't see Sage. I thought she had gone back to where she was staying to pack for her flight out, so I headed for the Wrangler. Then I heard several voices arguing from an alley beside the office supply store. From a distance, I recognized the colors of the dress Sage wore that evening. I climbed into the Wrangler and started the engine. Leaving the lights off in the bright parking lot, I wheeled the Jeep's nose into the alley entrance. Then I tugged on the headlights and flipped up the high beams.

As I expected, Sage and three young men turned their attention to the bright headlights, though they had to shield their eyes to see the vehicle. The men looked like the proverbial deer in the headlights. I didn't see any weapons, but they might conceal carry. Stepping out of the Wrangler, I removed the Colt from its holster.

"Good evening, gentlemen," I called from about two car lengths away. "Tell me if anyone recognizes this noise." I raised the Colt in the air and tugged back the slide to load a .45 round into the chamber. "Any guesses? No? That is the sound of a bullet being chambered in a 1911 Colt .45, a pistol with a firing rate of 85 rounds per minute."

Now that I had their complete attention, I let their tensions build. "Hey, let's do a little word problem. The three of you are about twenty feet away from me. How many rounds can an expert marksman fire in the time it takes you to cross that distance? In short, are your feet faster than my finger? While you boys think about that, Sage, come get in the Jeep."

She came down the alley with surprising speed and climbed into the passenger side of the Wrangler.

"Well, gentlemen, I hope this has been a learning experience for you. Let's never meet again, OK?"

With that grand exit, I stepped into the Jeep and put it into reverse. The three future perps made no effort to come after us. I took a long way around Kodiak village to come out by the AST post. No one appeared to be following us.

"Do you think I could bunk with you tonight? My host has a male friend she hopes will stay over."

"OK. Do you need to go get a bag?"

"No, I'm a pretty simple girl."

As the sky finally darkened, I drove down Mill Bay Road and turned up Thorsheim Street to reach the lodge. We went through the back entrance to avoid any suspicious questions. While she used the restroom, I walked down to the front desk to request an extra toothbrush. When I returned, she sat in front of the television watching a police procedural while sipping a beer. I stepped past her to reach the desk where I laid out my weapons: the Beretta from my ankle, the LE baton on my wrist, the survival knife from its sheath and finally, the 1911. After taking off the shoulder holster, I tugged off my belt and wrist brace. Then I realized she was watching me with great interest.

"You wear all that every day?" she asked.

I nodded. "Except when I'm working in my office. But you know, I feel more comfortable with it than not." I unbuttoned my shirt but left on my undershirt.

"I'd like to hang my dress, if you don't mind, because I'm planning to wear it on the plane. I like to look nice when I fly. I hate sitting next to people in track shorts and shower tongs." In seconds, she slipped her dress over her head and went to hang it by the front door.

"Do you mind if I rinse off in the shower?" she asked. "I feel kind of sweaty after performing under those lights."

After removing my trousers, I draped them over the back of the chair. Next I sat down to tug off the ankle holster. Then I laid down on the bed closest to the window. When she returned, she turned off the lights and took the other bed.

After dozing for about 45 minutes, I pulled down the blanket and sheet on the bed to lay underneath. Sage remained curled on the comforter of the other bed in a fetal position, wearing only her underwear.

Soon I was asleep, expecting to wake with the natural dawn. About an hour later, I roused when Sage slipped under the sheet on the bed where I slept.

"Sorry. Tonight scared me. They would have hurt me."

"No, they would have come to their senses," I said, not even believing myself.

"Still, thank you."

I shifted to give her room on the queen bed, realizing as I did that she was now naked. She draped a leg and an arm over me, bringing her face against my neck. "I'm not repulsive, am I?" she asked. She then moved to where she sat astride my hips. "Oh, that's a better sign. You're not a warrior monk, like in a kung fu movie."

"So, I'm not an old man like your father?"

"First, never mention a girl's father when she's naked on top of you. And second, you don't feel old now." She smiled down at me, her eyes wide and her blonde hair framing her face.

"I'm going to be sorry you're leaving town tomorrow," I said.

She leaned down, and she whispered into my ear, "Things work out, I'll change my flights."

29

Sage sat cross-legged on the other bed, wearing my shirt when I woke. "You know, thirty-five isn't that old."

"I never said it was. You decided I looked old," I said, sitting up and reaching for my trousers. I intended to shower, but I had no desire to sit unclothed while quizzed by a young woman who had shared my bed. "Too old, you said."

"We're only seven years apart. Why did you let me think you're ancient like my Dad?"

"Sometimes it's easier to let people believe what they want."

"But your face looks a lot older."

"Thanks, I guess. A little scuffle with a gorilla and a mirror. He tried to put me through it."

"And he set fire to your thigh?"

"No, that was a skunk with a handgun. Are we going to list all my imperfections? We should get breakfast first."

"I don't understand. I told you my brother was Golden Gloves. He never looked as banged up as you."

"Whole different set of rules." I paused, thinking for a moment. "Actually, he fought under set rules. People I deal with don't. I guess neither do you. Did you go through anything else besides my wallet?"

"I needed some cash to go get us coffee," she explained. She stood and brought me a mug.

"You went dressed like that?"

"No, I used your belt, and it looked like a regular shirt dress. They're the rage in Seattle."

"Future reference, I prefer a cold Coke in the morning. And when I'm done with my shower, I'd like to have my shirt back."

"Really?" she asked, unbuttoning the two top buttons. "You don't think I look pretty good in it?"

At that moment, the desk phone rang. "Yes, you do. Now excuse me."

Montgomery sounded very excited when I answered. "I hope your morning is free. Want to go flying with me?"

"Where are you? Aren't you still in Anchorage?" I asked.

"Came over on the final flight back last night. Found a message on my desk from a guy who was flying a guide and client out to the public cabin at Uganik Lake yesterday. Took the scenic route and reported seeing a blue de Havilland on Terror Lake. I've arranged with your friends out at the Air Station to give us a lift."

"You want me and not Frank Anker?"

"You can ID the guy who helped Joey Cross drop you at Terror Lake. Wouldn't you like to grab Pike's other accomplice?"

"How long do I have?"

"Wheels up at ten hundred."

"See you there." Hanging up the receiver, I smiled at Sage. "Go ahead and wear the shirt. I'm going to need a jersey for today's activities. Now I'm going to go shower. Think you could get me a Coke out of the machine down the hall?"

"You don't want me to come scrub your back?"

Shaking my head, I said, "I don't think my body can bear much more scrutiny. Besides, I thought you were flying home to Seattle today."

"Oh, that's how you are? One and done?"

"If you stay, hang the 'Do Not Disturb' sign, unless you want fresh towels."

With an electric razor, I tamed my scruffy chin. My cheeks remained tender from sporting duct tape for several hours. After letting the shower run to get warm, I squeezed into the narrow tub and soaped from toe to neck, then reversed to soap back down. With a dab of shampoo from the baby bottles provided by the hotel, I washed my hair and rinsed off completely. After I toweled, I dressed in underwear and trousers. Then I stepped into the cooler main room, releasing a cloud of steam.

"You want me to go get you something for breakfast?" Sage asked as I dressed.

"No, thank you." First, I pulled on a light cotton sweater and then rigged my shoulder harness over it. Between socks and shoes, I tugged my ankle holster up to my calf. Once dressed, I began filling the various empty holsters, including the double mag pouch for the Colt that hung on the harness opposite the pistol and above the sheath for the survival knife.

"Marty, do you need all that stuff this morning? It seems crazy."

When I finished putting the Beretta in place, I leaned forward, elbows on knees. "You said your brother joined the Marines. Have you seen a photo of him in camo with full battle gear?"

Nodding, she said, "Yes, that scares me, too, knowing my baby brother could go into combat."

"I might, too. Any cop could. Not combat, but there are times the bad guys want to kill you. A few years ago, I stumbled into a smuggling ring on Lake Superior. They killed two Coasties. Ten criminals died, as well."

"Did you kill anyone?" she asked.

I nodded.

"Weren't you afraid of those guys last night?"

"Sure, I worried they would do something stupid, like hurt you. And I wasn't certain they took me seriously. Three to one odds were in their favor."

"But what you told them about how fast you could fire? Wasn't that true?"

I stood and pulled on my new leather jacket. "Sure it was. 85

rounds per minute. But the gun only holds eight rounds at a time. Logistics were in their favor. Experience on mine. Now I have to go help a State Trooper make an arrest. Do you need cash?"

"No, I've got my bank card. I'll go find an ATM machine to make a withdrawal. Alaska *has been berry, berry good to me.*"

30

ontgomery met me in the parking lot outside the big blue hangar of the Air Station. He opened the tail of his SUV and offered me a variety of tactical gear that I declined, except for the Kevlar vest. He carried a Colt AR-15 slung across his chest, so I thought we packed sufficient firepower between us.

"You have Joey Cross sitting in a jail cell," I said. "Who flew the Beaver out to Terror Lake?"

"Don't know yet," Montgomery said. "FAA records show Cross has authorized two back-up pilots to fly his clients when he's not available. We'll see who is there to arrest."

The flight crew on the Coast Guard help seemed relieved that they only needed to give Montgomery and me a quick safety review after the mission briefing. The trooper had flown dozens of times on all three of Air Station Kodiak's aircraft: C-130, HH-60 and MH-65. I had flown on the now-retired H-3s before training for a short time in the incoming 60s and 65s. As I recall, about that time I began to have migraines during flight ops.

We were on the helo and settled against the back wall before the pilots started warming up the two General Electric engines. The crew had an extra headset connected to the aircraft's IC, so I deferred to Montgomery. He had a more current familiarity with Kodiak's geography than I did.

Soon we were airborne and heading out to sea to avoid any confusion with other air traffic at the airport. The FAA tower on a hill above the Base kept a regular watch on incoming and outgoing flights. Still, there are a surprising number of VFR pilots traveling in and out of Kodiak, which always made aviation a little dicey. I would never fly with a pilot who relied on visual landmarks to maintain course, given the vagaries of Alaska's weather. Too many aircraft met mountainous obstacles in Alaska's silky clouds.

Montgomery leaned close to speak into my ear. "I'm hoping if we go around the North end of the island, we can sneak into Terror Bay. I believe we can be across Terror Lake before they are able to destroy any evidence and ramp up the de Havilland. When the helo drops us, can you make sure the Beaver doesn't get started? The helo's going to hang over the far end of Terror Lake until we're ready for extraction. Good to go?"

Nodding, I checked each weapon I carried to ensure I was ready for whatever met us in the landing zone. Poaching wildlife was a new field for me; fisheries poaching is handled by regular fisheries LE patrols. The fascination of measuring someone else's catch of fish always eluded me, but I'm glad someone was willing to do it. Add the brevity of fishing and crabbing seasons to the mix, especially in January, and the conditions are ripe to strain available LE and SAR capabilities.

At two minutes away from the poachers' camp, the co-pilot began to give us a countdown to prepare. The rescue swimmer reminded us to wait to hop out of the aircraft until the helo was in contact with the ground to avoid the static shock. He reached over to remove the IC headset from Montgomery, who made a quick radio check on a small portable radio clipped to his AR-15 harness. The countdown continued as we came up the narrow valley from Terror Bay to the lake. The fog cleared as we came out into the open, and the Jayhawk picked up speed. Through the windscreen, I watched as we approached the blue Beaver at the South edge of the water.

Just short of the de Havilland's upright tail, the helo lifted over the same embankment I had wriggled up a few days earlier. After hovering for a moment to ensure a solid landing site, the HH-60 put down. The rescue swimmer gave us a slow count to ten on his fingers, then waved us out the starboard door. Montgomery went first, his AR-15 at the ready. Following his example, I pulled out my Colt and aimed it skyward. He knelt to study the camp through a small monocular. I crept toward the edge of the embankment to monitor any activity around the Beaver. Behind me, the Jayhawk lifted into the air and backed out over Terror Lake.

"Marty, I'm going to advance toward the tent," Montgomery said. "Anyone by the aircraft?"

"Not in view."

"OK, the helo has the Beaver in check. Follow me."

With his weapon level, the trooper executed a zig-zag approach to the nearest flap of the tent. Once there, he waved me forward. He lifted the flap to reveal the freezer and generator, which were now running. The tent smelled of carbon monoxide.

"Well, we know they're home," he said. "Where are they hiding? Shall we go through?"

"No, that's the way they'll be expecting. How about we divide and conquer. You go left; I go right?"

"I prefer safety in numbers," he said. "Let's stick together."

"Lead on."

I followed him down the left side of the tent at a snail's pace as we listened for any disturbances. At the end of the tent, he again knelt and studied the landscape with his monocular. "I'm stumped," he said. "Think they're out hunting?" Still on one knee, he straightened up to get a better elevation.

The first shot hit Montgomery in the left shoulder, beyond the protection of his bulletproof vest. The round then burned as it grazed my neck. The second round imbedded in his upper thigh. Montgomery collapsed onto his left side.

Grabbing the trooper's Kevlar vest, I dragged him back around the tent and inside. I closed the petcock on the fuel line of the generator to prevent us from dying of asphyxiation. The quiet might also allow us to hear the poachers' approach to the tent. Montgomery lay protected by both the refrigerator and the generator unless the hunters surrounded us. I put a tourniquet on his leg with my belt so he didn't bleed out. Then I took the radio out of his vest.

"CG Helo: AST One. Trooper down. Possible multiple shooters behind carcass dump south of tent. Can you disable shooters with heavy propwash, then return to original landing zone for recovery?"

After a moment, the helo pilot responded. "AST One. Will provide propwash until we take fire. Then evac and home. Confirm."

"Understood. Out." I acknowledged.

When I began unbuckling the harness holding his AR-15, Montgomery looked at me like seeing a friend grow a second head.

"Not my first trip to the OK Corral," I said, trying to reassure him. "Let me have your weapons along with any extra mags." I searched through the pockets on the front of his vest. "Oh, good. Plastic ties. Always useful." Besides the Colt AR-15, he handed over a Glock 22 that I tucked into the back of my trousers. "You familiar with a three-legged race? You keep your bad leg in the air while we make our way to the helo. Soon as you're aboard, the pilots are going to bug out. No argument. If we waste time, you lose your leg. Understood?"

He nodded. "Understood." He handed over several loaded clips for his weapons.

A bullet ripped through the canvas high above us.

"You're bleeding," he observed.

"Just a flesh wound." There's a line I've been waiting for years to use.

We heard the HH-60 pass overhead, and then I heard the unique sound of a Jayhawk as it accelerates to increase torque in the props. I knew the poachers were not having a fun time as the prop wash threw up anything not nailed in place. Anyone not wearing safety goggles was frantically rubbing their eye sockets.

"Get ready," I told Montgomery. "As soon as they come overhead, we're moving out. Any questions."

"What about you?"

"Bastards left me to die. Something kind of personal with me."

"Be careful. They don't fuck around," he warned.

"I noticed. When you get there, tell the hospital I'm AB positive. In case."

I heard the helo coming back above the tent and pulled Montgomery upright. With his arm over my shoulders and wounded leg between us, we hobbled toward the Jayhawk's landing site. I pushed as the rescue swimmer pulled, and we finally got the big trooper into the HH-60. I pulled the closest crewman toward me and pushed his helmet back. "Gunshot arm and leg. Tourniquet on leg ten minutes ago. If you have morphine aboard, give him something, but watch for shock. Don't forget to come back for me."

Crouching again, I turned and scrambled back to the tent as the helo rose and disappeared over the nearest ridge en route to Kodiak. Before I did anything else, I released the safety on the AR-15, then stepped out and shot a nice crisscross pattern in the Beaver's vertical stabilizer and rudder. Next, I used the Colt to put a few slugs in the floatplane's pontoons. Then I reloaded the .45 with a new clip.

Peering out the South end of the tent, I surveyed for signs of life. I assumed the shooters were still clustered behind the pile of bear corpses, wiping dust and sand from their eye sockets. Looking left and right, I didn't see any good avenue to approach a group that had already opened fire on us.

Then I remembered something Sir Arthur Conan Doyle attributed to Sherlock Holmes, "When you have eliminated all which is impossible, then whatever remains, however improbable, must be the truth." So, I decided that if an attack on the left or the right was impossible, the only solution, however improbable, would be to create a trap. An ambush by one.

After disconnecting the freezer from the generator, I pushed it out of the tent as far as I could in the muddy vegetation. Then I doubled back and removed the fuel line on the generator's fuel tank. Soon gasoline poured onto the dirt floor of the tent. I retreated to avoid getting fuel on my shoes. One round from the Colt into the fuel tank caused an impressive explosion.

Stepping to the corner of the tent, I shouted for the poachers to hear: "The Beaver isn't flying anywhere, so the only way out of here is under arrest. Unless you plan to walk back to Kodiak. Trust me, that's not easy. So you put down your weapons and come up here."

They replied with a volley of shots that shredded the remaining canvas of the tent.

As soon as their barrage finished, I scrambled over the lip of the embankment to settle behind a large clump of grass. I reloaded all my weapons, whether they were empty or not. Then I smeared mud across my forehead, cheeks, and chin. I hugged the dirt, hoping to avoid detection. My plan relied upon their group confusion.

After 15 minutes, I heard boots tramping in the mud above my head. Then I heard faint voices.

"Is the freezer still cold? The galls must stay frozen!"

"So far they are."

"I don't like this. Where's the other motherfucker?"

"Running like a pussy cop."

At that moment, I peered over the edge and confirmed they still carried their long guns. I rested the barrel of the AR-15 on the edge of the slope. Then I swept a round of bullets about a foot above their heads. When I poked my head back up, I saw four men sprawled on the ground and two crouched behind the freezer. A portable freezer does not provide a lot of protection for two grown men.

"Stay down unless you want another round, a little lower this time," I shouted. "You guys behind the freezer get rid of the rifles for the others and pitch them up the hill. The rest of you stay right where you are."

The two moved a little slow, so I fired two rounds from the .45 into the ground at their feet for inspiration. The bigger caliber provided clearer emphasis. In the end, they complied.

"Either of you want leniency from the DA?" I asked. Both men standing began to stumble toward me. "No! Only one gets the deal.

You in the brown flannel come here. Come get these zip ties and truss up your friends," I shouted. I instructed him to apply the zip ties to his friends' wrist and ankle.

I pulled out Montgomery's hand-held radio. "Air Station Kodiak; AST One. Situation contained. Six detainees for pick-up. ETA on relief?"

"AST One; AirSta Kodiak. Two HH-60s enroute your location. ETA ten minutes. Special Agent Anker aboard first. Any special instructions for the pilots?"

"AirSta; AST One. Approach safe. Clear."

With a little effort from the added weight of the extra weapons, I stood and walked around the prisoners with caution. They were an unsavory group, men who invested little in razors or barber services. I wondered where they spent the profits of this bear-butchering operation. With the scene secure, I went over to the man I recognized as Joey's accomplice. He still wore a Seattle Sonics sweatshirt that Sage recalled from the bar. To get his attention, I gave him a sharp kick to his hip bone. "Hi, remember me? Your friend is sitting in a cell in Kodiak. A cage is a good place for singing. I guess he's going to put you away for a lot of years." Then I walked away as he shouted denials. I went to the slope up from their camp to where their rifles lay. There I unloaded the six weapons and tossed them farther up the hill.

Frank Anker was waiting at the open door of the first HH-60 when it landed not far from the bound prisoners. Once the helo rested on the ground for a few seconds, he hopped down and came over to me in a hurry, his service revolver drawn. "Is this all of them?" he asked.

"At least all that would fit on a de Havilland Beaver when they came out."

"Good. How did you get them in custody?"

"I asked nice. After a few warning shots," I said. "You know what Big Al said about a kind word and a gun. And I set fire to their tent, so they might have a cold stay out here."

"You set fire to evidence?" Frank surveyed the scene of the crimes. "And why is that floatplane sinking?"

"I put a few rounds into it. Not going anywhere for a while."

"Montgomery was right." He glared at me. "You think you're Wyatt Earp."

"Didn't Wyatt come to Alaska after Tombstone?"

"I am going to lose my pension. Destroying evidence. Don't you know that warning shots are a violation of CGI policy? And bear poaching is way outside our wheelhouse."

"Come on," I said, pulling him by the elbow. "Why don't you go on the first flight to coordinate with local PD and Fish and Wildlife to arrange custody, unless you built a brig on Base. I'll come with the second."

He shook his head in disbelief. "Montgomery is in the ER now. They shot him first? Or was that you as well? The AST will decide whether to charge you."

"I don't think anyone's going to be pressing charges about warning shots and some property damage."

"You think that's your decision?" he asked. "I think it's a fact."

"You think the AST are going to recommend charges over a shot-up floatplane? These poachers fired first and hit Montgomery twice. I pulled him out of the line of fire and put him on a helo to safety. Then it was six to one, and they fired on me. You were thinking I should wait for them to hunt me down with .30-06, 200 grain Bear Claws? And yes, I know what they loaded because I emptied their weapons. Besides, all the evidence the wildlife trooper needs is in that freezer. Or piled 20 yards south."

"I still think I should put you in cuffs," Frank said.

"Know what Wyatt Earp told the Tombstone sheriff?" I asked. "On his way to the corral, he said, 'I won't be arrested today.'"

31

By the time the helo carrying me and the second batch of three poachers arrived at the Air Station, Frank and the first group of three were already on their way to the jail. Kathy Douglass met me on the tarmac, ready to escort the remaining criminals downtown with the assistance of a few instructors from the fisheries law enforcement training center.

Kathy pulled me aside. "Boy, you set Frank off."

"Yeah, I get it. He saw a weapon. Hurt his feelings, did it?"

"Me, I would have shot you myself," she said as we walked through the hangar to the parking lot.

"Thanks. What's happening on this end?" I asked.

"Montgomery is in surgery to remove the bullet from his leg. Almost nicked the femoral artery, so the tourniquet was a smart move. Wound on his arm was a through and through."

I pointed to my neck. "I noticed."

She looked but ignored my injury incurred in the line of duty. "I've got Fish and Wildlife on the way, and a wildlife trooper is coming over from Homer. Look, Frank told me to notify Juneau. Of course, they'll hear it from the Air Station anyway so I'm in no hurry."

"Thanks for the storm warnings." I smiled. "Can I give you Montgomery's hardware to return?"

We walked over to the gray K-car assigned to the special agents. She unlocked the trunk. I unfolded a red tartan blanket inside, then removed the harness holding the AR-15, which I unloaded and ejected the round from the chamber. I laid the rifle across the blanket. I then removed Montgomery's Glock .22 from my waistband and repeated the process of unloading and clearing the chamber. Finally, I clicked off the hand-held radio and placed it with the Kevlar vest on top of the weapons. I had an extra clip for each weapon.

"Nothing else?" she asked. "No sharp sticks?"

"Just my acerbic wit."

"Oh, that's your super power?" She walked to the driver's door. "Take my advice. Steer clear of Frank for a day or two. He'll calm down when he knows it's not going to screw anything up for him." At the driver's door, she paused and looked back at me. "By the way, a mud mask should come off after 20 minutes."

My reflection in the rear window of the K-car shocked me. When she drove off in the Chrysler, I walked to the Wrangler. Again, I found a sheet of paper from a yellow pad wrapped around the driver's wiper on the windscreen. Again, same message: Ricci. But at the moment, I had a more pressing matter of personal hygiene.

32

To avoid startling guests or staff in the lobby or lounge, I walked in the back door of the Baranof. Unfortunately, there was no way to sneak into my room. When I did, Sage screamed. But she stopped immediately and stared at me with wide eyes.

"Sorry. I wasn't sure you would still be here," I said, removing my jacket, then unholstering and unloading my Colt. I laid the pistol on the dresser and unhooked the shoulder harness. Next, I shucked the LE baton and then the survival knife. Finally, I stripped off the sweater I had worn all morning.

Sage shrieked again. I stepped in front of the desk mirror where I could see the dried mud smeared on my forehead and cheeks in the reflection. The slight wound on my neck had soaked my undershirt from collar to waist with bright red blood.

"Are you ok? Were you shot?" she asked.

"I was only grazed. The trooper with me took two rounds and is in the hospital now. I'm the lucky one."

Dropping the tabloid magazine she was reading, she climbed off the bed and came over to me. "Let's get you cleaned up." She tugged the bloody t-shirt out of my trousers and pulled it over my head. In the corner of the room sat a laundry hamper soon to be full of bloody and muddy clothes. She pushed me into the narrow bathroom and instructed me to sit on the toilet lid. After draping a towel across my lap, she went at my face with a soaking washcloth and soap.

"I've got some moisturizer in my purse. That will help when you're out of the mud."

"I'm not a make-up kinda guy," I said.

"It's not lipstick. It'll keep your face from peeling off. You don't use sun block either, do you?"

"Getting rather personal, aren't you?"

"You didn't mind getting rather personal last night, did you?" she replied.

"Absolutely not. Did you?"

"I led that dance."

"Happily enough, I hope."

"Very. How did you get mud in your ears?"

Turning my head, I looked at my reflection in the mirror. She had scrubbed off the dirt and mud from my face, but my hair and neck were filthy. "Let me take a shower. If I don't meet your standards when I'm done, you can finish the rest with a scrub brush."

She handed me a shower towel, "Don't tempt me." Then she left, closing the door behind her.

33

After a steamy shower, I wrapped a towel around my waist and draped another over my shoulders. Then I went into the main room, barefooted and damp hair. I wasn't expecting new guests. When I saw that Frank Anker and Kathy Douglass sat at the end of the two beds, they shocked me.

"Hi. Anybody knock on this island?" I asked. "Or wait for an invite?"

"Your lady friend let us in," Kathy said.

"Are you here on a warrant?" I asked.

"Not unless you really want one. Wouldn't be hard to get for you," Frank said. "I talked with Sergeant Corcoran of the AST post. He said thanks for pulling Montgomery to safety and saving his life with that tourniquet. Corcoran doesn't plan to file any charges about shooting up the de Havilland. And he's not too worried about evidence, other than the gallbladders in the freezer. Later today he's going out to collect them with a few coolers and ice packs. He's got Joey Cross as a cooperating witness now, but he may get one of these other clowns to flip for the right deal."

"That's all good news. Thank you," I said. "You could have called me. They make these things called telephones. Perhaps you've seen one."

"There's more," Kathy said. "Juneau told us to help you with your other investigation on the island."

I stared at the two of them for a moment. "I don't mean to be rude. But do you mind stepping outside while I dress? I don't feel comfortable having this conversation in a mini-toga."

They stood and headed for the door.

"Thank you. If you see my friend, ask her to wait for me in the lounge. We're discussing funding for her band's demo tape."

Kathy gave my towel a disapproving look and then looked at the unmade beds. "Business meeting, huh?"

Once they were gone, I dressed, minus any weapons I left on the dresser. When I felt comfortable, I opened the door and closed it behind them.

"Thanks. I'm a modest guy," I said. "So, what does Juneau want?"

"In short?" Kathy asked. "You off Kodiak and preferably out of the state. As soon as possible, even if you're packed in ice."

"Let's speak hypothetically," Frank said. "Suppose an officer working for the admiral in charge of Pacific Area had concerns about the tragic and gruesome death of a relative. Unhappy with the official investigation, the officer might ask someone to review the case."

"Too bad. I was hoping we were speaking hypothetically about packing me in ice," I said. "If we can get that off the table, I suppose an officer might express concern about the death of his sister-in-law," I agreed.

"So, Juneau asks why a special agent from Outside is sniffing around Kodiak and gets into unrelated trouble. This business with Travis Pike and these bear poachers is way, way outside our wheelhouse. We assume it's all related to your kerfuffle up in Lake Superior."

I nodded. "That's my assumption, too. And that's what Pike admitted to Montgomery. I hope it's admissible because Pike kept talking after hearing his Miranda rights. But we need to separate these two things. Pike wants to kill me on behalf of his friends in God's Own Patriots – that's all Crisp Point. He happened to hire somebody with a de Havilland who is also involved in bear poaching."

"Couldn't just keep things simple?" Frank asked.

"Here's what we know about the Simms' investigation," Kathy said. "You talked with Lieutenant Holland, at least twice. And you talked with Lieutenant Commander Avery."

Frank leaned forward on the bed. "Is there something you learned about Lieutenant Simms' death that needs further investigation?"

I took a sip of flat Coke from the can Sage had bought hours earlier. What remained tasted like the coke syrup my grandmother administered for upset stomachs. "Before we get into anything, you need to know that Lieutenant Simms didn't want to involve you two, or anyone in her command. Whatever it was, she thought the matter was too sensitive for anyone local to help."

As if by defensive instinct, Kathy put her hand on the badge clipped to her belt. "Now that you've been investigating her death, do you agree with her?"

"This is the first I've heard of any concerns about our integrity," Frank said with a snarl.

"Look, I don't know why she said that. Maybe she had no reason at all. She may not have trusted anyone on Kodiak. Period."

Frank raised his hands as if to stop traffic. "Does it matter what she thought before the accident? A bear killed her. Period. End of story."

"No argument," I agreed. There was no evidence of another cause of death, but the bear's role was rather obvious. She could not have survived that attack.

"Yet here you are," Kathy said.

"No argument," I said. "Look, some of this you know. Some you may not. And I need you to keep it all confidential until I can figure out what it means."

"We have orders to help you," Frank said. "Nothing personal, but Juneau would like any further investigation wrapped up."

"ASAP, the boss said," she added.

"Wow, usually takes more than a week for people to want me to leave," I said. "Let me bring you up to date on what I've learned and where I plan to go next."

Over the next hour, I described my visits with Holland, Avery, Montgomery, and Marilyn Solverson. I didn't mention Hannah Shangin or Anton, the beer-guzzling Malamute. I showed them the bulky folder Janet gave to Holland. Then I spread the copy of Janet's topographical map with specific sections highlighted. Finally, I shared with them the real property auction notice from GSA.

"Now you think Janet Simms uncovered a plan to sell Coast Guard real estate without authorization?" Kathy asked.

"I don't know yet. We need to learn a few things from the legal eagles before we draw any conclusions."

"So how can we help?" Frank asked in his usual gruff manner.

"Help me solve another angle to all this. I keep finding a sheet of paper like this on the Jeep I'm driving." I handed them the most recent note from earlier in the day. "Who is Ricci?"

"David Ricci is also a lieutenant at the Air Station, a H-65 pilot," she said. "Been here three years, same as me. We came over on the ferry at the time. I remember because he brought over an 18-foot Crestliner fishing boat that made my husband drool."

"Maybe we can talk to him Monday if he's not flying."

"Sure, but now that Juneau has gotten involved we'll have to notify the command we'll be talking to him," Frank said, taking a pen and small notepad from his breast pocket. "No more flying below the radar."

"Apart from a pricey fishing boat, do you know anything about Ricci?" I asked.

"I see him on Sundays in chapel," Kathy said. "Good voice in the hymns. I know he volunteers down at the high school's anti-gang programs in the afternoons."

"After Legal resolves their question about land disposal, and we get an interview with Ricci next week, any other issues to resolve?" Frank asked me, holding his pen poised over his notebook.

I settled on the desk chair and sipped from the old can of Coke again. "Yeah, the big question. Why was Janet Simms out there in the first place? What was she doing without any outdoor gear? No mention in her day planner of plans with a friend or co-worker to go do any of the usual activities. Any ideas?"

"We'd had the usual month of autumn fog. Nice sunny day, so Captain Benedetto granted sunshine liberty for Base employees at lunchtime, at least for anyone not on duty. Then Captain Lord at the Air Station granted liberty as well," she explained. "I don't know about the other commands. Not something that happened often, so people take advantage of it when it does. Could be she didn't have time to make arrangements to meet someone that afternoon. But she didn't want to miss a sunny day."

I stared at the two of them. "That's it? By coincidence, she put those numbers in her day planner. Then the day turns nice, and everyone gets liberty out of the blue. And she encounters a bear? A perfect storm of bad luck?"

Frank spoke first. "Guess we'll know more when we talk to Legal and Ricci.

"Here, I brought you a present," she said, fishing a bottle of Hoppe's Elite Gun Oil out of her over-sized purse. "I thought after playing in the mud that your pistol might need attention."

"Thank you. I only have a small bottle of oil with me."

"Anything else we can do for you on a Friday afternoon?" he asked.

"Yeah, small thing. Who's managing the beach house for the chiefs now?" I asked.

Kathy raised her hand. "Happens to be my turn. I got out of being secretary or treasurer by volunteering for the beach house."

"Any chance it's available tonight?"

"Sure." She opened her purse and drew out a pair of keys on a single leather fob. "Would you like to go visit?"

"Yes, if I may, I haven't been there in years. Still free for chiefs, right?"

"There's a party tomorrow night, so drop the key off with Base Security in the main building tomorrow morning."

With that, they ended their interrogation and left me in relative peace. A moment later, Frank knocked. "Can I assume you're not going to open any new lines of inquiry while you're here? No questions about the island's historic price gouging or such."

I raised three fingers on my right hand. "Scout's honor."

Frank gave me a quizzical look. "There was a troop that had you as a member?"

"Maybe not for long," I said. "Have a nice weekend."

34

C lean but tired, I took some change from the small stash of coins I'd been accumulating during the week. I headed down the hallway, searching for the soda machine and Sage. As I passed through the lobby, Lily flagged me down. This time she did not announce my identity aloud. On a small message form was a brief note: "Saturday. 1 p.m. Site of bear attack." I thanked Lily and headed into the lounge. Sage looked up when I came in.

Waving a magazine at me, she asked, "Do you know how many times I've read this through? I can tell you how to lose 50 pounds in 10 days and still make ideal spring desserts. Oh, and I've memorized the Kodiak Daily Mirror."

"All good to know. I'll quiz you during dinner."

"Is that your idea of an invitation?"

"Didn't I tell you I was raised by jackals?"

"No, you failed to mention that. But it explains a lot." She stood and hoisted a duffel bag over her shoulder. "I went and got my stuff up at my friend's place. Do I have time to freshen up before we go? I'd like to change, too."

"OK, but the longer you take, the less inviting your dinner

options. Now I'm offering steak, chicken, or seafood. In a few hours, it's going to be burgers and fries in a bag."

"Come on, then. Stop wasting my time."

We walked up the hallway so she could spend 15 minutes closed in the bathroom. When she emerged, she wore a silky blouse and slacks rather than the same dress she had worn for 24 hours.

We drove back to the Coast Guard Base and up the hill to the Anchor Club. I found a space for the Wrangler at the upper end of the parking lot, which was crowded tonight. We waited only five minutes for a table and another five to order. I recommended the Henry Weinhard's, and she nodded in approval.

"I'm surprised you know it," she said. "It's a Seattle brewery."

"Good beer knows no geographic boundaries. It's the ones named for their home city, like Milwaukee's Ale or Iron City Suds, that you need to avoid."

"A regular ale philosopher."

"Everyone needs something to believe in," I said. "I believe I'll have a beer." I ordered a New York strip, and she had the crab.

"You want to know the sad thing about crab?" she asked. "The crabbers are right here, but they have to pack the crab on ice and send it to San Francisco. Then it comes back here. Some stupid business contract so you can't buy fresh crab off the boat in Kodiak."

"I heard that before, but I didn't want to believe it. I knew a lot of Coasties when I was stationed here who owned boats to fish for halibut or keep traps for crab."

"Sad but true." She looked about the restaurant. "This is nice. All this time, I thought being in the military is a sacrifice."

"This is a little different. Spend a few days on a fisheries patrol, and the galley goop starts to be a little like gruel."

"Still, it's nice here for me. With you. Thanks. Listen, I want you to know that I don't get in bed with a guy because he saves my ass. I've had a grand total of two boyfriends. Period. One went into the seminary. The other decided to get in touch with his leather side."

"Ouch." I reached into my jacket pocket and withdrew a $20 from Andrews' bank envelope. I placed it on the table between us. "I can beat that. I paid for a counselor to tell my ex-wife that she wanted to leave me. A form of anti-marriage counseling, I guess."

"Sweet. Therapist have a side business as a divorce lawyer?"

"Perhaps. And the only other woman who tried to seduce me planned to murder me."

Sage pushed the bill across the table toward me. "You win. Keep your money."

"Thanks. You up for dessert? I'm going to have another beer while you do."

"Why can't I have another beer?" she asked. "You think all girls are chocolate fiends?"

"Sorry. I apologize. You have whatever you want."

When the waiter arrived, she ordered a champagne cocktail instead of a Weinhard's. We sat for several minutes, sipping our drinks. Finally, she spoke up.

"Listen, I called home today. Don't worry, I didn't charge it to your room. I have a phone card for my travels. My brother's up for deployment to Bosnia. He's coming home on a week's leave Sunday before he goes. I made flight arrangements for tomorrow."

"Bosnia? I can't imagine what's expected of the troops heading there."

"My mom wants help putting together a little party for him." Sage held up a small notebook in which she had been making notes. "I've got three pages of names so far. I'll think of more on the plane. I need time to call people on the list when I get home. And time to get the band together."

"Wasn't there a Belushi movie about getting the band together?"

After leaving a nice tip for the waiter, we headed into the cool evening. In the parking lot, I found another note wrapped around the Jeep's windshield wiper. I began to feel trapped in a Hitchcock movie. With the note secure in the glovebox, we headed off the Base and turned toward town. Beyond the airport and Buskin River Inn, I turned right onto a gravel road that continued past the Fish and Wildlife Refuge Center. The road went up a short incline to a pair of steel pipes closing the road, locked in the middle with a padlock on a chain. With the key from Kathy, I hopped out and unlocked the gate and swung the arms open. We drove on up to a wide gravel parking area outside a large wooden building.

"Come with me," I said, leading the way. I unlocked the door and turned on one set of lights, revealing a large empty room. The beach house is maintained by the Chief Petty Officer's Association and used for a variety of parties and receptions. The house included a bar and kitchen. I placed the Sade tape in the stereo equipment behind the bar, and soon the first song, *Is it a Crime*, began to play through the speakers.

I walked back across the wide floor to where Sage stood looking out the large windows overlooking a bluff facing out on the bay. Lights of boats and buoys flickered on the waves. I took her left hand in mine and turned her toward me. When she stepped closer, I placed my right palm against the small of her back, and we swayed together to Sade. When the first song finished, I went back to the bar and laid my Colt and survival knife there.

When I returned, she gave me a shy smile. "So have I disarmed the Beast?"

"Not denying I'm the Beast," I said, slipping my hand back around her waist. "But I still have a pistol on my ankle."

"Can't let a girl have her fairy tale, can you?"

"I'm hardly a fairy tale, in anyone's imagination."

She snuggled her face against my chest. "Come on, let a damsel have her white knight until the dragon devours him."

We danced together through *The Sweetest Taboo* until the system played *You're Not the Man*. She raised her head and fixed me with a stare. "You aren't, are you?"

I listened to the lyrics a moment about a man who could do no wrong. "Not even close," I answered.

"You know that an empty promise should include a promise, right?" she asked.

"Let's go outside, there's something else I want you to see."

I led her to a split-rail fence along the crest of the sandy embankment facing the ocean. Away from the lights of the beach house, the dazzling show of starlight illuminated the night. The Milky Way appeared as a ghostly swirl.

"Wow, it's beautiful. It reminds me of one night sailing on that crabber from Seattle out to Dutch Harbor. I had the helm on a midwatch. So beautiful with the Northern Lights all across the starboard sky."

"You were probably the only woman on a crabbing boat. You weren't worried?" I asked.

"Nah. The skipper knew my dad, so he laid down the law before we got underway. Besides, I wore this." She held up her forearm, revealing a leather thong with a six-inch tail of silver ball bearings dangling from her wrist. "Gift from my mother. She armed all the women in the commune. Put a throttle on the whole free love thing. Gives someone a heck of a whack. Wish I had worn it last night."

"You'll warn me first, right? I wasn't expecting a damsel in distress to come armed."

"Never underestimate a girl in a band." Sage shivered in a breeze off the water and crossed her arms. "Can we go back to the lodge before I get a chill?"

"Yes, let me go lock up the house. Can you handle a manual? Want to start the Jeep to get the heater running?"

Snatching the keys from my hand, she headed for the driver's seat. "I love to drive a stick. Can I drive to the Baranof?"

When the Jeep's engine roared to life and revved to about 8000 rpm, I felt a shiver of regret, which my Grandmother called someone walking on my grave. In this case, it seemed more like hopscotch. Shaking off the willies, I went inside the beach house to turn off the lights and gather my armament. I turned off the stereo system and ejected the tape. Soon, we had locked the gate and were on the way back to Kodiak village.

Along the way, she sang to a Bonnie Raitt song on the radio. "Of all the singers in the world, I wish I had her voice. It just sounds like raw emotion," Sage said when the song ended.

On the North end of town, we went to the market on the Northside and bought a six-pack of Molson and pretzels.

Back in the lodge, I loaded the beer into the micro-fridge while she went to the vending machine for soda to mix with whiskey. She also brought back a bucket of ice that she tucked into the mini-freezer. Again, I offloaded all my weapons. Then she remembered a copy of her band's demo tape stowed in her duffel bag. She fished it out and plugged it into the combination alarm clock/radio/tape player.

"When those agents came to the door, I told them we were talking about you sponsoring my demo. I suppose we should actually talk about it."

"Good. We had our stories straight. Not that I need an alibi; I'm here on vacation."

Her finger poised over the play button, she gave me a look of concern. "You ever hear of Disneyland? Or cruise ships?"

The demo included three covers and two originals composed by Sage and the band's keyboard player. Sage wrote the first tune about the power of attraction, featuring a piano riff that rose and fell like a rainstorm. Next came a sweet, slow version of *Love me Tender*, followed by a remake of *These Eyes* from The Guess Who that grew in intensity toward a wail. Besides the obvious reasons, those two songs sounded completely different when performed by a girl band. Next came the second original, a ballad of a painful break-up, actually desertion, Sage explained, that used the bass to lay the beat rather than the drums. The tape ended with a song she said came from an English duo, a sultry blues ballad with the jarring lyric: *You slipped through my fingers like a razor through leather. And I can't get these blues on the run.*

When the tape player clicked off, she gave me an expectant look. "What did you think?" she asked, a tone of excitement obvious in her voice.

"Well, I liked the song choices and how you switched up instruments in different ways. I don't know the musical terms for that. Can we listen again?"

"We wanted to make the songs sound different, not just karaoke versions of hits. People can get that on a jukebox." While she rewound the tape, I stood and walked to the micro-fridge. I dropped a couple of ice cubes in each of the ceramic mugs by the coffee maker. At the desk, I filled the mugs with just enough whiskey to float the ice. As the tape played, we sat opposite each other on the twin queen beds, using the nightstand to hold our drinks.

When the demo finished a second time, I asked, "So, after you've been working up here for the winter, then paying for your bass player's rehab, how much do you still need for production work and duplication?"

"I've always heard you should never mix business with pleasure." She stood and began unbuttoning her blouse. Stepping toward me, she asked, "Shouldn't pleasure come first?"

35

We woke early enough to have reindeer sausage and eggs out at the King's Diner on Lily Lake. We listened to her demo on the Jeep's cassette deck on the ride out. Sage seemed surprised that I knew of a local institution. She expressed greater shock when the same waitress from my prior visit recognized me and called me by name.

"Is it good that everyone in town knows a secret agent?" she asked.

"I wouldn't say everyone. Yes, a front desk clerk and a waitress. Besides, I'm not a secret agent. Those jobs have great theme music. And I don't have a license to kill." The only experience I have in common with James Bond is being in someone's crosshairs.

"Would you use one?"

"If I had to," I said.

Our conversation paused when our breakfast plates arrived.

"What time is your flight?" I asked. "I don't want to make you late." Personally, I find discussing violence at breakfast unappetizing.

She gave me a surprised look. "Come on, Marty. You know what flying out of Kodiak is like. Scheduled time and departure time are related like unicorns to horses."

Laughing, I covered my mouth with a napkin and held up the

other hand for her to stop the riff. "So true. I've spent days at the Anchorage airport waiting for the weather to clear on this end."

"They suggested I arrive at least ninety minutes early. The new flight plans state: Departure time determined by when we can see blue sky."

"That's about right."

"What do you have planned after I leave town? A night out on Kodiak? An evening at the Breakers?"

"First, I owe a visit to Trooper Montgomery at the hospital. He may have taken a bullet that could have been mine."

"Charming thought," she said.

"But I do have a mysterious date this afternoon. I was asked to meet someone out where one of the pilots died. I'm going to go see who wants to chat."

She put her napkin over her half-finished breakfast. "You're taking someone with you, right? One of those agents who came to the room yesterday?"

"I don't think I need adult supervision," I protested.

Sage rested her hand on mine. "Look, I know I have no right to ask this, but please take someone with you. People dropped you in the refuge and shot your friend. I don't think you should take chances."

I tapped the .45 holstered at my chest through my jacket. "Like Indiana Jones said, 'You know what a cautious fellow I am.'"

"Didn't he end up in a pit of vipers?"

Nearby diners in the crowded restaurant on a Saturday morning appeared to take an increasing interest in our conversation. Already *persona non grata* in Juneau's 17th Coast Guard District offices, I concluded being less conspicuous might be the better part of valor.

After a brief stop at the Baranof to collect her duffel bag, we drove on to the Kodiak airport, still listening to her demo tape. Once inside, she bought a ticket on the first PenAir flight over to Anchorage. The nice woman behind the counter explained that the outbound flight would experience a delay while the inbound flight waited for a window to punch through the fog hovering over the airport. This meant the airline might combine or cancel flights to get back on its operating schedule. As soon as the announcement for the flight came over the intercom, Sage cleared security screening and sat in a separate waiting area.

Climbing into the Wrangler, I checked my diver's watch. Visiting hours were beginning at Kodiak Island Borough Hospital. I felt disappointed that Sage had cut her stay on Kodiak short. As if I needed to salt my wounds, her voice came through the Jeep's speakers when I turned the Wrangler's ignition. In her rush to leave, she had left her demo in the Wrangler's tape deck. I had to admit that spending time with an attractive young woman was a pleasure I had mostly forgotten.

Listening to her eclectic mix, I drove back into the village. The hospital is a single-floor brick building with perhaps a dozen patient rooms. The nice woman at the nurse's station directed me to the left down the hallway. Montgomery shared a room with a recent survivor of an emergency surgery for a gangrenous appendix. He sported some type of intubation through his nose and seemed to be the happy recipient of morphine. In comparison, the trooper looked ready to go home at a minute's notice. When I entered, Montgomery pushed himself higher in his inclined bed.

"Finally come to set me free?" he asked. Overnight, his stubble had grown into a dark beard.

"Do you recall getting shot twice yesterday?" I asked. "Nothing personal, but wouldn't a day to let that thigh heal a little make sense?" I did not tell him that this advice in no way reflected my personal history. Working that case on Lake Superior, I instructed a corpsman to tape up a dislocated shoulder and bandage a gunshot so I could get on with the investigation. I had no other choice. I had made a promise to the wife of one of the missing crewmen and a commitment to the Commandant of the Coast Guard.

"I always heard you should get right back up on the horse that threw you."

"Did a horse shoot you in the leg?" I asked.

"That would be one trick pony," he mused.

"Glad you're in good spirits. Cute nurses to keep you company?"

"Sure, but they're all married to pilots out at the Air Station. Except for the one married to the C.O. of the *Storis*."

"Ouch. Better behave yourself."

"Thanks. What are your plans for the day?"

"I received an invite to meet at exactly 1300 in the location where Lieutenant Simms died."

"Oh? Who's your back-up?" he asked.

"You think I'll need it?"

"Wouldn't hurt." He raised his hand to point at his leg. "Looks like I may be indisposed at that time."

I sat on the chair at the side of his bed near the window. "You think there's a chance the bear is still hanging out, waiting to ambush me?"

The trooper shifted in his bed, so he faced me and motioned for me to move closer. He pointed over his shoulder at his roommate. "This is a small community, so you can't tell who knows you're here or why."

I leaned toward him. "You think your roommate is faking?"

Montgomery seemed to ignore me. "Pike found you by chance. Somebody else might be looking for you with malicious intent."

"If there's a coven of assassins after Marty Galloway, they're on the far side of Cook Inlet," I said.

"OK, it's your funeral."

"Enjoy the wake." I fished a $20 bill out of my wallet. "Here, I owe you a couple of drinks, dead or alive."

"I don't think this is a joke." He took my money just the same. "Do you have a suspicion who it is?"

"A pilot at the Air Station. All week long someone's been leaving a name on my vehicle. He may be reaching out with information."

"I expect I'll get released Monday or Tuesday whenever my surgeon gets back from a kayak expedition around Sitinak. I will gladly help you then."

From rescuing an injured hunter years earlier, I knew that Sitinak Island sat at the far Southern end of the Kodiak Archipelago.

"Sitinak? South of Akhiok? How did he even get out there?"

"Oh, he told me all about it. Him and an old Army buddy chartered a floatplane to drop them off and fetch them when they get done. Strapped their kayaks to the plane's float struts."

"OK, I guess it's a better way to experience Alaska than riding the bus into Denali. Listen, I don't have any way to cancel this afternoon and reschedule for when you've got your strength back."

"Hold on, I'm as strong as ever. It just hurts like hell when I try to stand upright."

"For now, I have to go out to the Base and drop off some keys. I'll visit you later with the usual magazines and candies."

"Remember that I'm partial to caramels. Good luck, Marty. Be careful out there."

As I left, I thought once again that if my luck ran out, any care would be futile.

36

Base Security occupies the basement of the main admin building inside the front gate. I parked the Wrangler on the street and walked past the flagpole and through the double doors. First, I returned the key to the beach house for the next renter. Then I showed my badge and ID to the watchstander, a tall young man with a high and tight haircut. I asked if the Base maintained a supply of tactical gear from which I might borrow a bulletproof vest for a few hours. As a third-class petty officer, he didn't want to take on that responsibility. After a quick call to the chief boatswain's mate in charge of security, the watchstander unlocked the door to the storage room for me. He showed me the sign-out logbook, then left me to search for myself. I left after 15 minutes with a vest slung over my shoulder.

In the relative privacy of the empty parking lot above the Anchor Club, I stripped off my jacket, zipped myself into the vest and slipped my leather jacket on back over it. As the morning fog thinned, the early afternoon became warm. I removed the canvas top of the Jeep's half door, then drove around Nyman Peninsula to kill a little time until I was ready to go up to Bear Creek.

At 12:50, I drove to the wide spot up the dirt road from the

Communications Station. So far as I could see, no other vehicles traveled the same track as I went. With my .45 tucked inside my vest and jacket, I moved the Beretta to a hip pocket of my trousers. In the early afternoon, a wisp of a moon peaked through a sheer curtain of fog. I climbed out of the Jeep and walked down over the embankment toward the creek, which had begun to subside from its flood stage a few days earlier when I first arrived.

The breeze coming down the valley tousled the remnants of yellow tape on the wooden pegs placed by the AST around the actual site. The grass and weeds within the perimeter struggled to regain their footing after the crowd of first responders trampled the area at the end of the last growing season.

The first blow hit me full in the sternum, like a punch to the solar plexus hard enough to knock the breath out of my lungs. The report of the weapon echoed around me. Another strike hit my back at the bottom of my right shoulder blade. The second shot resounded up through the valley above Bear Creek between Pillar and Pyramid Mountains. Breathless, I dropped to my knees, looking frantically for shelter from snipers perched on the mountains above both sides of the creek. NEGRES. A third shot kicked up sand in front of me, a miss by a round from behind likely targeting my skull.

As I leaned to the right to retrieve my Colt from under my left arm, I felt a second round from the front strike in my breast pocket. Despite the Kevlar, the strike numbed my hand. When I looked down, I saw the round half protruding from the leather jacket. Both shooters clearly spent time on the range.

Pinned down between two snipers, I weighed my options in a hurry. Nothing on the Wrangler's body provided enough protection from high-powered rifle fire. The surrounding grass offered no cover. I had one choice — hope the depth of Bear Creek was sufficient to distort a rifle shot fired over a long distance. With the best deep breath I could manage despite the pain in my ribs, I stood and fired a round from the Colt toward each shooter in rapid succession. There was no hope of hitting anyone at that range with a pistol, but return fire might distract them while I staggered toward the stream.

The water chilled me to the core as I waded to waist depth before plunging as deep into the center channel as I could. When swimming in the Bering Sea to rescue a crabber knocked overboard, I at least wore an insulated dry suit. Here I had only my leather jacket. I began to shake. I scrabbled my way along in the gravel at the bottom. Submerging and rising only to gasp a quick breath, I floated downstream in the rapid spring runoff. Holding my breath was all the more painful given the blows to my ribcage. I wasn't certain how much of a shield I gained from the water, but it seemed smarter than remaining directly in their sights.

Bear Creek flows into the Buskin River, which passes Kodiak Airport on its way to St. Paul Harbor. Although that route offered plenty of refuge, I risked hypothermia and unconsciousness if I stayed in the cold waters that distance. About 100 yards downstream from where I stumbled into a shooting gallery, I crawled onto the gravelly bank and hid in the sparse shrubs. Breathing remained painful; I gasped for air and, with effort, removed my jacket and the vest to let my shirt dry. I collected three flattened slugs that fell onto the ground when the vest came off. Then I planned my next moves.

37

From where I crawled out of the creek, a radio tower took a ghostly shape in the oncoming fog. Too bad an earlier haze provided no cover while I was the living target on a shooting range. The Communications Station building itself lurked a short distance beyond the tower, obscured in the mist. From there, I would be able to contact Base Security; then, they could transport me to the Base clinic or down to the hospital. Still a distance to cross without getting myself shot.

With effort, I pushed my battered body erect, then stumbled forward. I moved low and slow, one arm wrapped across my chest to keep anything internal from shifting about. In the other hand, I dragged my jacket and Kevlar vest, grateful for its presence earlier. Somehow two shooters had neglected to shoot me in the head. Not that I complained. I rather like my brain matter on the inside of my skull. I suppose the pair could have been trying to scare me off looking into Janet Simms's death. But if I had not worn a Kevlar vest when they opened fire, I would be more dead than frightened.

Moving and listening for any vehicles on the dirt road, I stumbled along the gravel road toward assistance. As I passed the antenna tower, a white Ford Bronco with a roof rack of blue lights emerged from the gloom. I waved an arm to catch the patrol's attention. The same young man who earlier manned the security desk in the main building rolled down his window when he came alongside me.

"Everything OK, Chief?" he asked.

"No, I could use some help. Well, a fair amount of help actually. Do you know if anyone is on duty at the clinic?"

"Yes, Chief. This morning I transported a young woman from the *Firebush* who burned her hand in the galley. The Officer of the Day didn't want to risk a problem on his watch."

"Great. Could you give me a ride over there?"

"Sure, but do you mind unloading your weapon first?" For a security officer, he sounded almost apologetic to be making such a reasonable request.

Not wanting to complicate either his day or mine, I turned away from his rig to aim my pistol at the ground and expel the clip. Then I jacked the slide to eject the round from the chamber. With a grunt, I bent and picked up the bullet from the ground. I shuffled around the front of the Ford and pulled myself up into his rig. On his radio, he gave the clinic advance warning that we were on our way over. Along the way, I asked him to keep an eye on the abandoned Jeep and watch for anyone leaving the area with long rifles. I expected NEGRES; the fog provided perfect cover for anyone sneaking away.

A corpsman met me at the door to let me into the closed clinic. They maintained a skeleton staff on the weekends to handle emergencies. She put me in an exam room and returned several minutes to take my temperature and other vital statistics. Petty Officer Jenkins looked alarmed when her electronic thermometer gave three successive readings hovering just above 96 degrees. I asked for a warm blanket while I waited for the doctor on duty.

Before the doc on duty arrived, I examined the fresh ventilation in my new jacket. Bullet holes can really reduce the value of good leather. When the physician came in, I recognized Doctor Douglass immediately from the photo on his wife's desk in the special agent's office. He shook my hand. "My wife says you've had a rather eventful week on Kodiak. From the notes, it looks like the duty corpsman found your core body temp low."

"I took a little dip in Bear Creek, above Buskin River," I explained. "I figure I'll warm up eventually, sir. But could you check my ribs? Just to make certain I haven't broken anything."

"What happened that you think you cracked a rib?" he asked as he took notes on the evaluation sheet.

"I was out near where Lieutenant Simms died when two snipers started using me for target practice. With high-powered rifles by the look of these rounds." I held out my hand, showing him the slugs from the vest I had worn. "Lucky for me, Base Security had loaned me Kevlar. It fared worse than I did."

He examined the slugs closely, shaking his head. Then he chuckled. "I can't wait to tell Kathy about this. Nothing personal, but she and Frank have a bet on whether you make it off the island in one piece."

Beginning to unbutton my shirt, I said, "Can't say that I blame them. The way the week has gone, I'd lay odds against."

Doctor Douglass helped me remove my outer shirt by tugging at the sleeves and then pulled the t-shirt over my head. When I was half-naked, he walked around me, tapping his forefinger on his lips pensively. "Yes, you were lucky to be wearing a vest, but I wouldn't celebrate yet. I'd like you to go down to the hospital for x-rays and maybe a CAT scan."

"I've had ribs five and six cracked on the right side of my sternum before. But the shooter was carrying a pistol and standing a few feet from me."

He pulled on a pair of nylon examination gloves. "This may hurt," he warned as he began to palpate the dark bruises across my chest and back. At one point, his exam caused me to inhale sharply; then, I choked in pain. His touch across my back evinced similar reactions. I breathed easy when he stripped off the gloves and pitched them into a bin.

"If you want something to help you sleep, I can prescribe Percocet," he offered.

I shook my head. "No thanks. I'm not a fan. Not a good idea for me to get woozy now. As you know, the odds of me leaving Kodiak are already running against. I wonder which way Kathy is betting."

He chose not to address his wife's wager. "OK. Sit tight. I'm going to call down to the hospital about x-rays. Depending upon what the x-rays show, we may need to get that CAT scan done. And I'll write out a script for a few Ultram to help you sleep. It's milder, but if you don't like narcotics, split a pill in half. Or take a shot of whiskey, but not both unless you are miserable. Understand? Think of pain on a one out of ten. When you get to a seven, take a med. Then take a couple of hot showers and use a large warm compress. You can ignore pain, but it won't ignore you."

"Thanks. If you ever thought of being a motivational speaker, please don't."

38

Ceiling tiles have a fascinating illusion of uniqueness. With nothing else to focus on while waiting on a gurney for someone to transport me out to a trailer in the hospital's parking lot that housed their new CAT scan unit. First, I compared the corners of two adjacent panels, looking for any similarity in the pattern to the holes there. Then I added a third panel. As I prepared to add a fourth to the comparison process, a voice interrupted my concentration.

"Galloway! What are you doing here?"

I turned my head to the right and saw Montgomery's face. He sat in a wheelchair, still wearing the usual flowery hospital garb.

"It's after visiting hours. I had to sneak in to see you. Like my cover story?"

"You forgot my candies."

"Busy afternoon," I said in my defense.

"So I heard. A nurse told me what happened. Her husband is the security guard who rescued you."

"Like that comedian said, 'It's a small island, but I'd hate to paint it.'"

The trooper chuckled. "So, you didn't take my advice this morning, did you?"

"Not exactly," I said. "But I wore Kevlar. That's like back-up, right?"

"You found a vest that can pick the shooters out in a line-up?"

"Not any more than I can. They knew what they were doing: elevated positions, distance, crossfire."

"Prior sniper training, you think?" He shifted so he could raise himself enough to look down on me. "What happened to the 'This isn't my first gunfight' guy?"

"I never said what happened in that corral. At least I don't have an actual GSW this time around."

"Did anybody offer you witness protection last time around?" he asked.

"I guess everyone got busy and forgot."

"And now you're just here for the Jell-O?" he asked, shaking his head.

"And I'm going to rescue you, remember?"

"No, you were going to bring me caramels."

"Excuse me, gentlemen, may I interrupt this gabfest?" A nurse came into view next to Montgomery. She wore hair swept up in a white surgical bonnet, blue surgical mask hung around her neck. "Mister Galloway, we've got an emergency coming in From a Coast Guard medevac. There was an accident on a fishing vessel by King Cove. Doctor Lang would like to send you home. I'll have discharge instructions for you. If you have trouble breathing, the doctor wants you to come back in immediately." She left to ready my paperwork.

"You have a place to go?" Montgomery asked.

"I'm good. I haven't checked out yet."

"Way this keeps unfolding, you may check-out for good first."

"I appreciate your support. I may hang around just to irritate you."

"I don't think Frank Anker will go along with that. But I've got a spare bedroom I'll rent you in case. Cheaper, but no maid service."

"I'm kidding. I have a real job to get back to." I started to roll onto my side in order to sit up, with the ultimate goals of standing and dressing. Montgomery maneuvered his wheelchair and then locked its wheels so he could offer his good hand to help pull me upright. When I exhaled, I felt a sharp stab of pain. "I've broken ribs before. You'd think I'd be used to it by now."

"You have Achilles' ribs?" he asked.

"Shouldn't you go check on your roommate?" Being the butt of his jokes began to sour on me. I struggled to get dressed in my shirt.

He shook his head. "No, I was thrown out. This Lieutenant Commander Avery is here from the Base Legal office. My roomie is doing a Last Will and Testament. The surgeon told the guy yesterday that there might still be gangrene in his system. Not the most encouraging thing to hear a week after surgery."

"Ouch."

"Yeah, the guy's wife really lit into the doc afterward."

"I'll bet that doesn't happen too often," I observed, pulling on my shirt. "Did you say he's an old Army doctor?"

"Yes, he's got the bedside manner of a drill instructor," he said. "But on the bright side, I'll bet my roomie's widow'll look good in black."

I stopped buttoning to stare at him. "Don't tell your roomie that."

Montgomery brayed with laughter as he wheeled himself away.

39

When Helen, the nurse, asked if I had any questions before I signed the discharge instructions, I nodded. "Is all this gauze around me doing anything?"

"Doctor Douglass ordered it before he sent you over, didn't he?" Helen asked. The way she held her clipboard displayed an enormous diamond on her wedding ring finger, as Montgomery would have predicted. "I suppose he intended to prevent any broken ribs from shifting. You don't want a jagged rib to pierce your lungs or pericardial sac."

"But if I don't have any broken skin, then the gauze isn't keeping anything from falling out or creeping in, right?"

"As long as you have it when we discharge from the hospital."

"Understood. Thank you kindly." I signed her form, pressing hard to get through four carbon copies.

Helen maneuvered over a wheelchair to push me out. When I started to object, she gave me the standard spiel about hospital liability. Would make more sense to me if instead they just didn't put down wax on all the floors throughout the building. Out front, Helen helped me into the passenger seat of a mini-van taxi. The driver was Filipino, likely descended from those brought as stewards on whaling ships as far back as three centuries ago. He knew exactly how to get up to Buskin Lake, then took me the extra distance to where the Wrangler sat parked on the gravel. He even got out to help me get up into the Jeep. I thanked him and tipped an amount equal to the fare. As I turned the Wrangler around, I could no longer see the tops of the radio towers for the dense fog settling over the island.

When I got back to the lodge room, my first task was to take a sip of whiskey straight from the bottle. By then, I felt warmer than after diving into the Buskin. I unbuttoned my shirt, still damp from the creek, then decided the dry gauze was too scratchy to keep on, especially as it served no purpose. I discovered that Base Security had taken the extra step of depositing my weapons in the dresser's top drawer for safe-keeping. I suppose Lily had granted them access because of the incident with Pike. Generous on the part of Base Security, I thought, considering they would need to trash the vest I had borrowed. High-powered rifle rounds are likely to break down any vest's integrity.

I pitched the damp shirt into the laundry hamper. Beer in one hand and survival knife in the other, I went into the bathroom. Cutting the gauze where the corpsman taped down the bitter end, I began to unwrap, like undressing a mummy. Gradually a mosaic of blue, purple, red and black emerged on my chest. When I closed the bathroom door, a full-length mirror hanging on its backside revealed a bruise on the right side of my spine below my shoulder blade, about the size of a baseball. At least no damage would be visible to anyone, unlike the scars on my face left behind after my misadventure in Northern Michigan.

Leaning against the bathroom counter, I realized that I needed to remove my boots so they could dry out, along with my trousers that were still wet from the creek. With little appetite for the pain involved in the bending and twisting, I took another sip of beer as if that would alleviate the matter and contemplated the advantage of an Ultram.

A knock sounded at the room door. With Montgomery hospitalized, I deduced either Frank Anker or Kathy Douglass had come to gloat. I draped a shower towel over my shoulders and went to answer.

"Do you always answer the door half naked?" Sage asked.

"What are you doing here?" I asked in surprise. "I thought you'd be halfway to Seattle by now."

"You didn't notice any fog around the island today?" With a fore-finger, she lifted the edge of my towel out of the way. "You didn't ask for back-up today, did you?"

"Maybe yes; maybe no. I've been hearing that question a lot today."

"Then I wasn't the only one to think you needed help."

"No, but that's not why you're here, is it?"

"The lady at the ticket counter said they released the pilots until at least 9 tonight. Even then, they won't predict when the inbound flight would punch through."

"And you thought you'd hang out here?"

"Not in the hallway, no. Think you might invite me in soon?" She brushed past me on her way into the room. "So how bad is it?" she asked. She dropped her duffel bag on the bed closest to the door. When I lowered the towel, she gasped. "What did they use on you, a baseball bat?"

"No, rifles. A couple hundred yards. Fortunately, I wore a vest."

"Small blessing. OK, is there anything I can do for you?" She sat on the bed, staring at my collage of bruising.

"Actually, I could use some help." I sat next to her. "I went into a stream to get out of their lines of fire. Can you help take my boots off so I can dry them, along with these damp trousers?"

Sage laughed. "That's a come-on I never imagined hearing." She pulled the wooden desk chair over in front of me. "Put your foot up here." She unknotted each boot in turn and then tugged my khakis off.

"I should take a hot shower. The doctor said it might help." I decided to skip any mention that I had been swimming in waters that potentially host giardia, which can cause skin problems along with the abdominal affliction. I lifted my feet, and she pulled my socks off. With a dry pair of underwear in hand, I headed for the shower.

When I had the water hot and strong enough, I stepped into the tub. Soaping up my body and trying to wash my hair, I discovered any strenuous reach proved more painful than I expected. I may have been too loud in expressing my discomfort. After a few moments, the curtain shifted aside, and Sage stepped into the tub.

"Why do you look so shocked?" she said. "I helped clean you yesterday. And you've seen me naked before."

Handing her the little rectangle of soap and the washrag, I said, "I wasn't expecting anything good to come of this, that's all."

"Don't you get any ideas." She sounded serious. "You're in no condition. Do you hear me?"

Surrendering, I stood as still as possible while she brushed my torso with the soapy washrag. Then I turned so she could reach my back. Bracing my hands against the shower wall, I leaned forward so she could wash my hair. She stepped out to allow me to rinse head to toe. I took extra time to let the hot water run over my back and chest. When I finished, she stood dressed and ready with a pair of towels to wipe me down. When I came into the main room, she also helped me dress. Finally, I requested a beer.

"Canadian or Golden?" she asked.

"I guess I'll take a Molson."

"Good choice," she said, handing me an open bottle.

She then mulled over our dinner choices on the island while I field stripped both weapons and wiped the parts with the Hoppe lubricating oil Kathy had gifted me. Pistols are like the pets in the movie *Gremlins*. Never get them wet.

"Now when are you going home for your brother's visit?"

"If you will take me out to the airport by 7 in the morning, I'll stay tonight."

I smiled. "Now that's an offer I can't refuse."

40

When the alarm sounded at 0500, I rolled onto my side to find Sage staring at my face. Her eyes opened a little wider in surprise.

"What's wrong?" she asked. "Why are you looking at me that way?"

"Astonishment."

"Uh-oh. Why?"

"Look at me. This face. These battle scars. I'm not the kind of man women flock to. Sure, not young women who look like you."

"I think there's a compliment in there. Thanks." She leaned forward to kiss me, careful not to bump my bruised chest. "I'm not the kind of woman men take seriously. And you're fun. Even a little dangerous."

"Don't let the International Man of Mystery thing fool you. I'm a cop, of sorts."

"I'd like to take a shower before my flight. Then can we go back to that diner for breakfast? I'll never find reindeer in Seattle."

We managed it all, including her shower and a nice breakfast, yet still made it to the airport just a few minutes after 0700.

"Can we say good-bye out here?" she asked. "I hate to get

emotional in public, and I might today. You won't go get yourself killed, will you?"

"On purpose?"

"I'm serious. I know what happened in just the past few days."

"No, I have no intention of dying up here."

"Do you promise?"

"Yes."

She leaned over and kissed my cheek. Then she hopped out and went into the terminal.

Mission accomplished, I drove over to the Base Security office. The same petty officer who loaned me a vest was back on duty. "Good morning, Chief," he said. "How may I help you?"

"Any chance the Base keeps a metal detector around?"

"Not that I know of. But I could make a few calls to see if anyone on the crew has a personal unit."

I spent the morning at the security desk until one of the other petty officers on the security team stopped by with his personal detector while on his way to the chapel. After providing me with five minutes of instruction on his model, he rushed off to take his young family to morning service. I loaded the device into the front seat of the Jeep and set off into the dense fog. When I reached the same parking site above Bear Creek, the mist began to clear. With the detector functioning, I went down to the same area where I had scrabbled about on the ground the day before. I established a search pattern in a rectangular parallel to the stream bed. For 45 minutes, I walked in rows about two feet apart, making progressive passes down the slope. Finally, I hit an anomaly in the ground. I knelt and used my knife to dig around the object so I could lift it out of the soil without damaging it. The first target turned out to be a filet knife. I continued walking the grid for another 20 minutes when I hit another positive alert. Excavating with my knife to avoid damaging any evidence, I located a bullet that looked pristine. The impact in the sand seemed to cause little damage. I compared it to those that fell out of my clothing the day before. Likely match, but not conclusive. No way to know how long the slug waited in the sand to be found.

After returning the metal detector to the Base Security desk, I went downtown to consult with the most knowledgeable people about rifles and their ammunition on the island. The two clerks at Big Ray's Alaskan Outfitters seemed excited when I entered. They appeared relieved to have something to do on a Sunday morning before church services ended when business would likely increase.

"How can we help you this morning?" the closest man asked.

"I'm hoping you can tell me the caliber of these rounds," I said, setting the pristine round and the three slugs on the counter between us. "No rush."

"What do you think, Larry?" the clerk asked over his shoulder. He looked back at me. "Larry's our resident gunnery sergeant; I'm more the fly-tying wizard."

The older gentleman came to the counter and peered at the slugs. "Sure, I have a good idea about these. Hang on a second." Larry opened a large cabinet containing shelves filled with boxes of ammunition. He returned to the counter a moment later with a black box. Opening the container, he removed a plastic tray containing new cartridges and laid a bullet next to the projectiles I carried. "Here's my best guess. A .300 Magnum intended for a Weatherby .300. This one of yours is almost pristine, so I could pull the bullet out of a new casing to compare them if you think it's necessary to be that certain."

I pushed the other slugs from my vest toward him. "Could these four be from one box, fired by the same type weapon? You said likely a Weatherby?"

Larry picked one up and peered at it like a jeweler appraising a diamond. "I'd say it's pretty likely." He went back to the ammo locker and returned with a box of Winchester rounds. He stood two bullets upright next to each other. "Look at the different lengths of the casings. Smart shooters are careful because brass is pretty elastic, so a casing can spread or stretch when it gets fired. Mixing ammo is a good way to foul a weapon."

"A lot of Weatherby's on the island?" I asked. "With so many hunters here?"

"Not so many as other rifles. More Marlin 1895s and Winchester

70s. Have you seen the little Sitka deer on this island? You could knock them down with a BB gun. Hit one with a round like this, wouldn't be enough left to make a sausage. You'd need a Weatherby for our bears, or caribou and elk up on the mainland."

The other clerk spoke up, "So what's this all about? Because the troopers could send these off to Anchorage for their ballistics people to test. They could tell you who was leading the Stanley Cup playoffs when these cartridges were manufactured."

"That's OK. I don't need to know their genealogy. But let me buy that box of Weatherby shells." With that investment, I was well on my way to depleting the cash Andrews gave me back in Michigan.

I wondered who on Kodiak invested in Weatherby rifles. They are nice hunting rifles, but pricey. I simply didn't like being anyone's prey.

———

41

On any Sunday morning back home, I would likely be on the firing range, practicing with each pistol in either hand. On those days when the range closes to host competitions, I find Sunday mornings depressing, like the Johnny Cash song, *Sunday mornin' comin' down.*

Yes, there was plenty to look forward to on the coming weekdays, including interviews with Lieutenant Ricci, Lieutenant Commander Avery and Petty Officer Chitwood, as well as preparing a final report to Mister Andrews. No doubt, I also needed to check-in with my boss back in Cleveland to make certain I still had an open billet waiting for me when I returned.

That left Sunday afternoon with nothing left to do. I felt tempted to go back into Big Ray's to purchase a suitable rod, reel, flies, and a non-resident fishing license to spend a relaxing afternoon fishing. Instead, I concluded I didn't have the upper body flexibility for decent casting on a Kodiak stream, even without the gauze wrapping. Fishing should never be physically painful. I headed back out toward the airport and passed the Base on the left and Old Womens Mountain on the right. In another few miles, I stopped to top off the Jeep at the gas station in Bells Flats. In the little grocery store, I purchased a sandwich for lunch. Next door in the liquor store, I bought an inexpensive cooler that I filled with two bottles of beer, the sandwich, and a small bag of ice. I loaded the cooler into the back seat and headed out Kodiak Island Highway in the opposite direction from the segment that goes North to Anton Larson Bay. Like that road, this gravelly dirt segment did not merit the term "highway." Vehicles kick up clouds of dust that can be seen miles off.

This road hugs the coastline as though traced with a No. 2 pencil. The first segment where it strays crosses the shoulder of Heitman Mountain over Zaimka Ridge. On my prior tour of duty, I hiked up the mountain about 900 feet to a broad lake as flat as a pane of glass. The state had recently begun stocking the lake with rainbow trout, and I spent a pleasant afternoon with a line in the water.

A few miles farther along, I drove down onto a long beach that faced Kalsin Island. After removing the Jeep's canvas half door, I popped in Sage's demo tape. With the turkey and Swiss on rye and a beer, I sat on a beach comprised of gray cinder-like dust that likely settled after the 1912 Novarupta eruption. The waves rolled in with a tempo that matched the bass line on the band's first original track on the tape.

A short, high-pitched shriek sounded above me. I stood so I could turn to look over the Jeep. Perched on a branch at the top of a dead tree sat a bald eagle. He remained for several minutes, repeating his one-note cry several times. I assumed he was calling to a nearby mate. Knowing the species is monogamous, I wondered if he was alerting a female to a potential nest site high above Kalsin Bay. After a few moments, he flew off and swooped down toward the water to seize a fish as large as his own body. Most of an eagle's size is in its seven-foot wingspan. The predator returned to the same tree and began to tear at the fish. Soon a female appeared to join the male eagle on the limb and share their meal. After wrapping the remaining sandwich and emptying the last of the beer bottle onto the ground, I climbed back into the Wrangler and continued down the "Highway," leaving the eagles to enjoy their feast in peace.

After crossing the Olds River and Kalsin Creek, I turned left and went up Pasagshak Point Road. The road went overland away from the ocean and through a narrow valley before coming back down to the coastline of Pasagshak Bay. Beyond Lake Rose Tead, a hiking trail wanders out to the Pasagshak Peninsula headland. If you sit there quietly, you can hear the songs of the whales. On this visit, I continued toward Fossil Beach because I had heard that the rancher there had swapped his cattle for bison from Wyoming because predation by bears ravaged his steers. Bison know how to respond as a herd to fend off hungry bears. Bison also have no trouble in harsh winters.

I wanted to see the bison. And I saw them. Up close and personal. I came across the herd as the space port construction site came into view. The big, shaggy animals stood on the right-hand side of the road. I stopped the Jeep and killed the engine to study the bison, at least 50 in the group. One looked as large as the Wrangler.

When I reached to turn the ignition on in preparation of leaving, a calf wandered in front of the Jeep. I thought it was crossing the road, but it stopped. Then an adult followed and stood next to it. After ten minutes, the entire herd surrounded the vehicle completely. I turned the key back off to avoid draining the battery. I worried that if a large bison bull became irritated by the presence of a red Jeep, the animal might knock the vehicle onto its side. I could see that the Jeep's body did not afford enough protection to stop a newborn calf. Accepting that I wasn't going anywhere until the bison herd approved, I reached into the cooler in the backseat and removed the second beer.

An hour passed as the herd sauntered across the road at its own pace. When only stragglers remained, I started the engine and drove in a wide circle around them. No revving. No sharp acceleration. No loud music. There was no way to predict how they would act or react. When I reached the trailhead for the Pasagshak Peninsula Trail, I stopped to dig through the tapes in the console. I found a classic Bob Seger tape and popped it in for the ride back into town.

42

W hen I reached the lodge, I called Frank Anker's home. While his wife seemed very pleasant when she answered, her husband sounded angry to be disturbed on a Sunday evening. His mood improved when I invited him for a beer in my room. Or we could meet someplace like the Buskin River Inn or the lounge in the Baranof. He opted for the latter.

When he arrived 20 minutes later, I sat at a table as far from the bar as possible. I thought we should strategize for Monday in a more secluded atmosphere. He wore a Chicago Bulls jersey, which I thought said a lot about the man. The Bulls roster included Jordan. Frank liked sure things.

"What's so important we couldn't do this tomorrow?" he demanded to know. "I was about to open a very nice bottle of wine. I purchased a Chateau Margaux 1995 last time I was in Anchorage. A single bottle runs more than a hundred dollars."

"Ouch. Then you don't want to spoil your taste buds with a house wine here. How about a beer?" I asked, motioning for the waitress. "I once had a wine steward suggest a light beer to cleanse the palate before wine tasting."

Frank ordered a bottle of Alaskan Pale Ale. "Hard to picture you in a place so swanky it had a sommelier." He lifted his jersey to remove a pack of unfiltered Camels from a shirt pocket. A Zippo light came from a pants pocket.

"You haven't seen my refined side."

"Is this it?" he asked, looking about the lounge as he ignited a cigarette.

"What do you expect? We're on Kodiak. At least the waitress isn't wearing hip waders."

He took a sip of ale and then looked at the bottle in surprise. "Not bad. Now what couldn't wait until tomorrow?"

"You've heard about my little misadventure up on Bear Creek yesterday?"

"Sure. Everyone on the island has. Even the bears are laughing about it."

"Rude bears." From a pocket, I removed two rounds that I set on the table between us: a fresh .300 Weatherby Magnum cartridge taken new from the box and the rather pristine projectile I recovered from the sandy soil where the snipers missed their target, a humble Coast Guard special agent.

Frank sat forward and gave them a careful inspection. "Looks like a close match," he agreed. "What caliber weapon?"

"If they're an actual match, then a .300 fired by a Weatherby."

"Somebody meant business," he observed.

"Somebodies," I reminded him.

"Can you prove a Weatherby fired it?"

"I'm not a gunsmith, but the .300 Weatherby Magnum has a longer shell casing. Could cause a problem if you mix rounds, even with similar calibers."

Frank inspected the rounds another moment. "Now you're a forensic ballistics expert?"

"No, but I can listen to the people who are. Want to know about hunting ammunition, talk to the people who sell it."

"How many times this week someone try to kill you?" He leaned away from the table to relight the cigarette that appeared to have extinguished on its own.

"More than I'd like to ponder. So down at Big Ray's they say there aren't too many Weatherby rifles on the island. They're hunting rifles with a lot of stopping power. Good for taking down trophy animals."

"Or a special agent?" he asked, with a discomforting chuckle.

"OK, but nobody wants my head on their wall." I thought of the collection of trophies mounted in the great room of the Solverson's home.

"You'd be surprised." He laughed again. "Do you think we're looking for a pair of big game hunters or a set of assassins?"

"I don't know that yet."

Frank motioned to the waitress to bring two more beers. "Assuming this wasn't just a random, but a well-coordinated attack with high-powered rifles, do you think this connects to Lieutenant Simms or to this land deal? Or both?"

"Well, I've got a hunch."

"Oh, this sounds like trouble," Frank said as the fresh beers arrived; his in a brown bottle, mine in green glass. "Am I going to regret this conversation?" He leaned back, and his deep inhalation caused the end of his cigarette to flare bright red. He turned his head and exhaled away from the table.

"Hear me out first. Thursday afternoon I talked to the Base legal officer with his petty officer present. Now she happens to know all about the process for disposing of property through GSA. Coincidentally, on the wall behind her desk is a photo of Petty Officer Chitwood posing with a trophy big horn sheep. Looked like she had a pricey hunting rifle."

"Coincidence doesn't get you to a search warrant," Frank said. "Any reason to think it was her shooting at you? I'm not saying that I'd blame her."

Probably my stare appeared angrier on the opposite side of the table than I intended.

Frank stubbed his smoke in the ashtray and raised his hands. "Look, I'm not being a jerk here. I want to be certain what we're working with. From where I sit, here's what you got: a yeoman familiar with property disposal; a yeoman who can handle a rifle; a yeoman who knows why you are in Kodiak. Look, I'm going to 'fess up. Before I became CGI, I was a yeoman; I understood land transfers; I'm an Expert shot; and I have more reason to want to shoot you than most people on the island."

"Can you repeat that directly into my wristwatch?" I joked, resting my forearm across the tabletop.

Frank leaned forward. "For the record, Marty Galloway is a huge pain in the ass."

"So much for your retirement gift."

"Again, why am I here?" he asked. "I don't think a hunch is going to go far with either the captain or Juneau. One of the main reasons Coasties come to Alaska is the hunting; everyone else comes for fishing. Most homes in Coast Guard housing are going to have a hunting rifle. We're not going door to door looking for one."

"OK, how about teasing Petty Officer Chitwood." I moved the box of new Weatherby 300 shells from a chair to the tabletop. "Make an excuse to ask about taking the big horn. Then politely put these on the table, without any comment. Watch her reaction. Let her think we know more than we do."

"Are you a card shark? Looks like you're trying to bluff five aces with two jokers in your hand."

"Maybe. The bluff is all in the play."

"While Kathy and I go make wild accusations, what are you going to be up to?"

"Assuming there's no connection between Lieutenant Simms and this land business, then the land issue is, as you would say, outside of my wheelhouse. I need to focus on her death. I plan to talk with Lieutenant Ricci, wrap it all up and go back to Cleveland. If I have time, I'll look into my own attempted murder."

"And you'll set it all straight with her family? Including anyone in Pacific Area?"

"Of course. That's my intention. And I'll leave you to handle the land thing."

Frank stood and walked to the bar. When he returned, he carried a pair of cocktail glasses with a shot of alcohol in each. He set one in front of me. With hesitation, I raised my glass and sniffed. The tequila mixed both sweet and spicy scents. "Let's drink to that." He raised his glass. "Tell me, Galloway. I've known a lot of special agents over the years. You're not like anyone else I've met. I can't put my finger on it. You're different."

"Oh, I'll agree with that. I make that clear to anyone who asks. I'm not here to mar the reputation of any other agents."

"So how did you get in? The screening is a little more rigorous than drawing Binky from a matchbook."

With little choice, I raised my arm and extended my wrist toward him. Frank reached over to twist my black metal bracelet to where he could read it. "Lieutenant Martin Galloway?" He stared at me closely. "You're related to *him*?"

"Directly. I assume Admiral Thorne helped my application along as a result. I couldn't fly on a helo any longer. I suspect he stepped in to help keep me on active duty."

Frank released my wrist and nodded. "Well, OK, then. That explains a lot. Listen, no more surprises, right? Kathy and I will handle the land issue. You'll talk with Mister Ricci and stamp 'Case Closed.' Any problems?"

"Fine with me." I nodded in agreement. "Especially if it takes the target off my back."

We clinked glasses again and slugged down the last of the tequila.

43

Sitting outside Captain Lord's office at the Air Station, I realized that I would not present him with the best of reasons to interview one of his young officers. I imagined the conversation going along these lines: *"Captain, Mister Ricci's name has appeared on my windshield several times. May I question him and possibly impugn his name? No sir, you don't need to throw me out of your office personally, but thank you."*

I started to wish I had asked Frank Anker or Kathy Douglass to do this while I spoke with Mister Avery. I would have liked to watch Petty Officer Chitwood's face when I showed her the box of .300 Weatherby Magnums. No doubt she had an interesting alibi that the agents could debunk with little effort.

Finally, the young yeoman who manned the front desk of the office shared by the C.O. and X.O. of Air Station motioned me over. The first-class petty officer was a spit-polish example of everything I had failed to achieve before I migrated from dress uniforms to casual work clothes. He towered over me by four inches and his biceps stretched his shirt sleeves tight. The petty officer knocked for permission to enter, then opened the door to the captain's office and announced my name. I thanked him as I entered. I first approached the captain's somewhat expansive oak desk. He looked like most pilots I knew from my time in aviation; he was tall and lean, with an angular face under close-cropped hair. Perhaps it had something to do with squeezing into the seats of a cockpit.

"Good morning, Captain," I said, standing at something approximating attention. "Thank you for taking the time to see me this morning."

Captain Lord nodded. "And this is Lieutenant Ricci." Ricci sat in a high-backed leather chair facing the captain's desk. He leaned forward to twist to his right to see me. He gave a slight wave.

"Good morning, sir," I said.

Captain Lord soon made clear that he intended to control our conversation. "Galloway, I understand you served here with some distinction as a rescue swimmer. With that in mind, I asked Mister Ricci to cooperate with your inquiries now. I hope you won't abuse his cooperation."

"Not my intention, Captain. I only have a few questions I'd like to ask."

"Why don't you have a seat then?" the captain asked.

I settled in the leather chair next to where Ricci sat. I took out my notebook. "Is it OK if I record your answers?"

"Of course," Ricci said.

From the quaver in his voice, I could hear he was as nervous as I was conducting this interview in front of Captain Lord. The lieutenant's fingers tapped anxiously on the arms of the chair. I thought I could put him at ease by explaining my purpose in asking questions.

"Sir, I'd like to clarify that my questions are not part of an official investigation. Although I am a Coast Guard Special Agent, I am here on annual leave at the request of the family of Lieutenant Janet Simms. I wish to be clear that there is no suggestion of any wrongdoing on your part. I hope that the questions I have may help me paint a full picture for her family of what transpired that afternoon. Are you comfortable answering my questions?"

The lieutenant looked from me to his commanding officer. "What do you think, Captain? Should I?"

"I am not a lawyer, but I believe you can trust Galloway when he says this is not that type of inquiry. I've made a few calls. Most people praised Galloway's integrity. I reviewed the case where he earned the Coast Guard Medal. He's shown true mettle."

"Thank you, sir," I said.

"OK, let's proceed then," Ricci said.

"Thank you. I understand you knew Lieutenant Simms as a fellow pilot. Did you ever speak with her on occasions or topics other than work at the Air Station?"

"Anytime, ever? Yes, I'm sure I did."

At that moment, vigorous knocking sounded on the captain's door.

"Yes, who is it?" Captain Lord called.

His yeoman burst through the door. "Excuse me, sir. I have an urgent call for Special Agent Galloway. The caller says it's an emergency."

"Would you excuse me?" I asked, standing from my seated position. "Sounds like we may need to postpone our conversation." Nodding my head toward Captain Lord, I executed a left turn and went into the outer office. "Which phone?" I asked, puzzling over who would be calling me so frantically.

"This way," the well-creased petty officer said. "I have a private office where you can take the call."

I followed him down the hall to where he opened a door for me. From my prior time at the Air Station, I thought that door led down to an exterior exit. When I stepped through, I found only a stairwell of metal steps heading down.

44

Being stupid and recognizing your own stupidity beforehand are two very different functions. On the top landing of the steel-grate stairs, I recognized this as some type of trap. The petty officer's hand on my left shoulder confirmed my stupidity.

"The real agents arrested Ginny in her office this morning. They thought you could handle me?" the petty officer asked. He did not bother to introduce himself as the spouse of Ginny Chitwood.

Stupid as I may be, I recognized that pitching down those steps would do nothing for my overall health. Getting a grip on his hand, I stepped backward into him and dropped to one knee. Pulling his weight down over me, I sent him tumbling instead.

His output of profanity was prodigious for a man engaged in an ungainly display of gymnastics and gravity. Still, Chitwood *maritus* managed to halt his downward momentum. With a loud grunt, he pulled himself erect and started back up the stairs. He waved his hands toward his chest, inviting me to come down to fight him. Given his height and weight advantage, I stayed in place, with secure footing on the upper landing and a firm grasp on each handrail. When Chitwood reached the third step below me, I brought a knee to my waist and planted a snap kick on his face. His head recoiled like a crash-test dummy experiencing whiplash. He teetered for a moment, eyes rolling up in his head before closing. I reached to grab his shirt, an initial reaction before I stayed my hand. Rather than go with him, I let him fall alone. He landed on his back before momentum carried his legs over him. His body came to rest, face down, about halfway to the ground floor. He did not move.

I went back into the captain's office and knocked at his inner door. With his permission, I stepped inside.

"Captain, would you contact Base Security? We're going to need medics, security, and one of the special agents."

Standing, he asked, "What's happened?"

"We've had an accident," I explained. "Petty Officer Chitwood slipped up on the stairs."

45

F rank handed me a cup of coffee that I accepted to avoid appearing ungrateful. Then he settled behind his desk. No sign of Special Agent Douglass.

"Exciting morning around here. One Chitwood in jail; the other in the hospital with a broken nose, broken wrist, one dislocated shoulder and three fractured ribs." He stared at me intently. "Any idea how Bill Chitwood incurred those injuries?"

"He's clumsy?"

"You're going to have to do better than that. We sure didn't find a banana peel."

"You saw him. You think I could take him down?"

"The doctor said his nose got flattened, like he walked into a wall or something. Given the missing teeth, looks like his chin hit the step not his nose."

"The stairs can be *treacherous*," I said, quoting one of my favorite old movies. I did not plan to share with Frank any information pertaining to the 2nd degree black belt in tae kwon do I had earned since the problems I encountered solving the conspiracy of gun smuggling at Crisp Point. Better to let everyone think a clumsy oaf tumbled down the steps on his own.

"You missed a bit of fun this morning. Kathy and I went in, all business like, and asked to see Mister Avery. We went into his office, and Avery called Chitwood in like we needed a note-taker. She gets all set up, and Kathy puts the box of shells on the table. Petty Officer Chitwood turned white, burst into tears and confessed to everything but Irangate."

"I guess you gave her one phone call, so then her husband came after me."

Frank sat back and smiled like a Cheshire cat.

"Oh, is this where I guess what happens next?" I asked. "I'll take Miss Ptomaine in the mess hall with a beef stew."

At that moment, Kathy came in, carrying a white foam container and a tall paper cup with a straw protruding from its lid. "Hi, boys. Sorry to break up the meeting of the He-Man's Woman Hater's Club."

"Special Agent Galloway was just telling me about meeting Ginny Chitwood's husband. A very different greeting from ours."

"What, no tears?" She shed her jacket and settled at her desk.

"I wouldn't say that exactly. Even a little whimpering."

"Oh? I'm sorry I missed it. But I enjoyed locking little Ginny up behind bars." She bit into her burger with gusto.

Frank placed his hands behind his head and gazed at the ceiling. "Husband and wife snipers. That's a first for me."

"I'm hoping it's a last for me," I said.

"Which of them missed the head shot, do you suppose?" Kathy asked.

I held up my bullet-pocked jacket for their inspection. "I would rather not speculate on that."

"Did the husband admit to ambushing Marty?" she asked Frank. "The wife admits to the land scam, but she is still claiming she had nothing to do with Saturday. And, for what it's worth, there was no gunshot residue on her hands when I swabbed her. I didn't detect the smell of vinegar, so she didn't clean with vinegar and hydrogen peroxide. Maybe Bill had a different partner in crime?"

"I'm afraid it may be a little while before he can tell us much with his jaw wired shut." Frank stood. "I'm heading to the hospital to swab him for gunshot residue, and then I'm going to lunch."

Blue smoke shrouded Frank just as the doorway framed his exit. I watched Kathy shake her head in frustration. "Right on the line. He's always right on the line so I can't really say anything."

"I guess I'm heading out to grab a bite, as well. Anchor Club still have a good menu for lunch?" I asked.

"Yes. The mess hall usually has a good spread, too, and you'll save a few bucks."

After lunch, I found my way back to the Baranof. I didn't owe anyone an accounting for my time, so I tuned the radio to a Mariners game somewhere on the West Coast. Against my better judgment, I laid down and didn't wake until early evening, which made sleeping that night all the more challenging.

46

Friends have told me they sometimes wake happy with a memory of some childhood event, like pony rides at a birthday party or a first day of school. I envy them. Dreams haunt me. They are most often about bodies –– the corpses we recovered of those hopeless who jumped from the Golden Gate Bridge or the unlucky lost in the Pacific or the Bering when their vessel sank without warning in hostile waves. Whether in a 41-footer stationed in San Francisco Bay or on an H-3 flying out of Kodiak, I often had the task of retrieving the remains before they disappeared into the depths.

That night, the nightmares began at the Fort Point small boat station where I worked as one of the "Bodysnatchers" under the Golden Gate. Our primary responsibilities included recovering the remains of individuals who jumped from the high span. Impact of landing on water from that height is similar to landing on cement. Never the romantic or gentle passing people may think. The two most common causes of death are drowning from involuntarily inhaling the Bay water or trauma to the internal organs caused by the body's impact on the water's surface.

Alaska lacked such high bridges; most rescues were generally more mundane. The H-3 flew a lot of medical evacuations, MEDE-VACS, for crewmen from trawlers or crabbers after hands or limbs got caught up in winches or other deck gear. At times, we rescued hunters or hikers wounded by accident with firearms or axes. Frequently we responded to medical crises in remote Native villages or on cruise ships. Once I delivered a young woman's first baby halfway between Karluk and Kodiak.

Another night in Alaska reminded me of a hunter we once rescued near King Salmon after a bear attack left his leg nearly amputated above the knee. The helo lowered me and maintained a hover nearby that allowed the crew to keep a look-out to warn me if the bear returned. I administered the first aid necessary, including a tourniquet above the wound, to prepare him for hoisting into the H-3. He bordered on shock, so I hesitated to administer any significant narcotic. An ambulance waiting at the Air Station took him to the island hospital where someone far more competent than me performed the amputation.

Recalling his injuries, I woke and sat on the side of the bed. The autopsy photos of Lieutenant Simms cycled through my head two or three times. That hunter was fortunate that firing his rifle once or twice scared away his attacker. Janet Simms was not so lucky.

As the alarm clock ticked closer to 3 a.m., I attempted to rest against the pillows and close my eyes. Instead, I remembered other encounters with the dying and the dead as survivors and corpses merged into a blur of rescue or recovery.

When another hour passed that way, I rolled on my side to watch the minutes click past on the digital clock. Toward the end of his life, my grandfather, a veteran of a world war in Europe and a police action in Asia, confided in me, "At my age, sleep is vastly over-rated."

Like four generations before me, I joined the Coast Guard to save lives. Service took my father's life. And I have spent too much time among the dead. It is not what I signed up for.

47

The clock continued to roll toward dawn until I finally surrendered and turned off the alarm. After shaving, I stepped into a shower as hot as I could endure. The cool morning air seemed rather bracing when I stepped outside, and I felt fully awake when I started the Jeep. The national news from Washington played on KMXT as I drove out to the Base.

The importance of our meeting at Base Kodiak had increased significantly over the past twenty-four hours. When I arrived with Frank and Kathy, Lieutenant Commander Avery led us to Captain Benedetto's office, where he sat at a large conference table with Commander Nakashima, his executive officer. They could not have been more different in appearance –– him an obvious choice for center on the Academy football team; her more comfortable on the tennis courts. He wore gray hair in a brush cut; her blonde hair fell in pixie fashion below her ears.

Splayed across the tabletop were several different types of maps of the Coast Guard Base and aerial photography of the area surrounding Buskin Lake and the Communications Station. The captain spoke first. I wished his question was not directed at me. "So, why would someone think they could sell part of my command without my notice?" His tone made the question sound almost accusatory.

"If I may, sir," Mister Avery interjected. "This appears to be a crime of opportunity. The section at issue is remote and unused. We have no roads that go up there. And the process to auction it isn't something that we would monitor. I had never seen a copy of this GSA notice until Galloway brought it to my attention."

"Someone tell me how this GSA auction thing works," the captain said.

Avery shared what he had learned from Petty Officer Chitwood and his own legal research. From the notes that Captain Benedetto wrote on a yellow legal pad, I could see his concern about how this could get past everyone both here and at the District Office in Juneau. When Avery finished, Commander Nakashima assumed the questioning.

"If GSA auctions real estate, they receive some renumeration, correct?" she asked.

"Yes, Commander," Avery said. "At least fair market value. Otherwise, they rebid it."

"This parcel is almost four full sections of land, each more than 600 acres. Do we have an approximate value?" Nakashima was going right to the heart of the matter.

"Likely upwards of a several million," Avery answered.

"Would it matter that the parcel is on the side of a mountain? Or surrounded by other federal or native land, making it inaccessible?" Her questions made me wonder if she was also a lawyer.

"I've been researching that issue, but I haven't found a clear answer. Among Lieutenant Simms' materials were copies of the Alaska Native Claims Settlement Act of 1971," Avery said. "The Act suggests that a private owner would be granted access across federal land, at least in the case of forests and parks. But the Navy established the Base here in 1960, well before the Act passed. The Coast Guard took possession of the Base and other lands on Kodiak in 1972. I don't know if this Settlement applies here or not."

The captain's pen stopped moving across the pad. "I'm sure all this legal stuff is fascinating to lawyers. Here's what I want to know. You said the auction opening bid could be millions of dollars. Where would a pair of petty officers find that kind of money?"

"If I may, Captain," Kathy said, "the other thing that has puzzled me about the Chitwoods is what they were planning to do with the land. If they started selling it off themselves, wouldn't someone connect the sale back to them? I don't know the statute right off hand, but no doubt selling government land without authorization is a crime."

"Title 18, Section 641, I think," Frank said. "I looked it up. And then I called the office in Juneau that handles real estate. They contacted GSA and requested a copy of the authorization they received."

"OK. Who signed the authorization?" Captain Benedetto demanded.

"The signature belongs to Rear Admiral, Lower Half, Richard FitzHenry," Frank said.

"What? Without consulting me?" the captain's expression mixed surprise and anger. "Are you certain?"

"To be honest, no, Captain," Frank said. "Surprised me to hear the District Commander would authorize it and neither the Base legal officer or C.O. wasn't aware of it. I asked for a copy and also asked about other recent land disposals."

"Are there others?" the X.O. asked.

"Yes, ma'am. Two years ago, the admiral authorized the sale of a parcel of land adjacent to the old Air Station Annette, which moved and became Air Station Sitka."

"I'm going to call the admiral as soon as we finish," the captain said.

"I don't believe he'll know anything about either disposal. I took an FBI class on forgeries a few years back, so I compared the two signatures," Frank explained. "They matched. Perfectly."

"I didn't think that was possible," I said.

"It's not," Frank replied. "Ask a person to sign their name five times and there will be slight variations in all five."

"So how did it happen on these documents?" the captain asked.

"One of two ways, Captain," Frank said. "Either a skilled forger or an Autopen."

Avery spoke up. "Would someone need access to the admiral's Autopen or could they reproduce his signature using an existing letter?"

"Either would work?" Frank said.

Kathy leaned forward and raised her hand. "Captain, we'll need your authorization to search the Chitwood's' quarters to see if they have an Autopen."

"What happened to that parcel at the old station Annette?" Benedetto asked. "Did GSA put it up for auction?"

"Yes, Captain," Frank said. "I found that GSA advertised it, but I could find no record that it ever sold. Maybe it was a test run for this sale."

The captain laughed. "Or nobody wants to live in Sitka."

48

When we left Captain Benedetto's office, I pulled Kathy and Frank aside in front of the elevator. "Can we meet at your office? I have another suspect we should interview."

"About the land or about Lieutenant Simms?" Frank asked.

"Yes."

At that moment, Avery called my name from the door of his outer office and motioned me over. As I approached, he led the way into his office and closed the door behind me.

"Have a seat, please," he said, settling behind his office desk. "Galloway, can I speak with you in confidence?"

I nodded.

"Thanks. Look, I understand you're on leave. That's fine. And perhaps it was my mistake to include you in that meeting just now."

At that moment, a light rap sounded on his office door. Commander Nakashima let herself in and sat in the chair next to me, facing Avery. I felt impressed by how they had organized this conversation without any mention during our prior meeting. Did cadets at the Academy learn telepathy?

"We've just started, ma'am. Galloway, as I said, we'd like to request your confidentiality on this matter. We cannot risk any suggestion that Admiral FitzHenry became involved in a conspiracy to defraud the government. You can understand the danger of accusing a flag officer of any such crime."

"Let me underscore what Mister Avery said," the X.O. said. "Until we know exactly what happened with those signatures, we can't risk any public speculation."

"Yes, ma'am," I said, nodding in compliance. "Even though I am on leave, I still consider anything I learn as part of my inquiries to require the greatest discretion."

"Have you shared any of your suspicions with Mark?" he asked. "Mister Andrews, I mean."

"No, sir. At his request."

"Marty, you need to understand the sensitivity of these issues given Mister Andrews' position on the staff of the Pacific Area Commander," she explained. I assumed this concern meant Fitz-Henry was up for a second star. Any controversy at this juncture might turn his hopes into a shooting star.

I felt more than a little insulted that Commander Nakashima thought it necessary to explain admiral games to me. Having spent a week fishing on a powerboat a few years prior with the then-Commandant of the Coast Guard, I thought I had a more in-depth knowledge of flag-rank politics than most in the Service. I had met Admiral Thorne after my father's patrol boat was sunk by friendly fire in Viet Nam, and Thorne kept tabs on my family and my career ever since. Even after he retired.

"Yes, ma'am, I appreciate the delicacy of the situation. At this point, I am still struggling to understand whether or not the land issue links to Lieutenant Simms' death. If you'll excuse me, I have a meeting with Frank Anker and Kathy Douglass to go over that issue."

"I have one more request," she said. "The captain and I would like you to brief us before you discuss the issue with anyone outside the command. Understand?"

"Understood. I would like to request permission to involve the State Troopers if the investigation takes us into their jurisdiction."

Avery and Nakashima exchanged looks before both nodded. "OK," she said. "On a need-to-know basis only."

When she stood, I understood that I had been dismissed.

49

When I arrived in the special agent's office on the opposite side of the Base, they sat at their desks sipping coffee from foam cups. They looked up at me in surprise.

"What got you called to the principal's office?" Frank asked.

"They thought I would report the admiral to McGruff, the Crime Dog," I explained. "You know what they say, 'Loose lips sink stars.'"

Kathy held out a coffee cup toward me. "Fresh from the cafeteria this morning. Not as warm now, I'm afraid."

Although it wasn't my preference, I accepted so as not to be any more of a jerk than I had been so far on this intrusion into their domain. "What do you both have planned for next steps?" I asked.

"I thought I should go visit Ginny Chitwood downtown before she gets transferred to federal detention in Anchorage," Frank said. "In case she has decided to talk. Her husband will be a guest at the hospital a few more days. He's not going anywhere with that bed handcuffed to his wrist and leg"

"You think she will cop a plea?" Kathy asked. "She's gotta know you're in no position to give her any kind of deal. Or either one of them, for that matter."

"OK, but I want to know why they thought they could get away with it," he explained.

"Meanwhile, I'll be drafting a warrant for Captain Benedetto's signature to search their Base housing," she said. "I'm going looking for a pair of Weatherby rifles and an Autopen machine. Anything else? Well, if you don't see me again, it means I found their stash of a million plus dollars in cash."

"Will they still have anything in their house?" I asked. "They would have gone back to look for my body, that's common sense. If they didn't find me, or my astonishingly good-looking corpse, didn't they know the game was up? They could have dumped everything and made their great escape in the 36 hours before they ended up in the cooler like Steve McQueen."

Kathy stood and came around to lean against the front of her desk. "OK, gentlemen, here's something that's been bothering me. Galloway gets invited out to Bear Creek on Saturday afternoon. The Chitwoods' ambush fails. Galloway goes off to the hospital, then he returns the next morning to gather slugs that match their weapons, which aren't very common here."

"Remember to write all this up for Juneau," Frank said.

She raised a finger, asking for a moment to finish her thoughts. "Galloway's got a good point. So why did they even hang around for another thirty-six hours? Rather than hiding evidence, why not leave? There's more than one way off the island. What, they were waiting to get arrested?"

We sat in silence for several minutes. Frank ignored his ringing desk phone.

"If I may theorize for a moment?" I asked. "As we discussed this morning, the Chitwoods wouldn't have the money to buy this many acres at auction. Right? And they would have trouble disposing the land if the auction went through. Agreed? We should assume what?"

"They have a partner," Kathy said.

"Who got nervous and told the Chitwoods to kill you," Frank said.

"And why would two decorated petty officers obey an order to commit murder and then hang around?" I asked.

"Because if they didn't do as told, they wouldn't get their share of profits from the land sales," Frank said.

"And they couldn't leave earlier because they didn't have the permission of the boss running the scheme," Kathy added.

"That, lady and gentleman, constitutes a conspiracy," I said. "Actually several: Theft of government property. Forgery of an official document. Attempted murder of federal agent."

"Only attempted theft of government property," Frank corrected. "We caught on in time. Well, *you* caught on in time." He nodded in my direction.

"While we do the hard work," Kathy asked me, "what are you going to be doing?"

"I will be asking AST if we could conduct an interview with a civilian in town."

"No hints about who?" Frank asked. "I thought Juneau wanted us to play in the same sandbox."

"Understood. But this is definitely the state trooper's sandbox."

50

At the AST post, Sergeant Liam Corcoran appeared quite harried for mid-morning on a Tuesday. Sleeves rolled to the elbows, he came down the hall with a mug in one hand and a topographical map in the other, a pencil tucked behind his ear and bifocals slipping down his nose. Looking at his wiry frame, I wondered if he had wrestled in high school or college. The tattoo down the inside of his right arm read, "Semper" in script. The other arm bore the word, "Fidelis."

"Good morning, Galloway," he said. "Please tell me you're not here to ask for my help. It's just me right now. Montgomery is on bed rest for two weeks. I told him yesterday that if I see him in the office again, that I'm writing him up for disciplinary action. Even if I don't charge you, I still blame you."

"Wait, I stopped him from bleeding. And I never saw that belt again, not that I'd want a blood-stained leather belt back. So no other post can loan you help until he's back?"

"Are you kidding? We're in stupid season; everyone's coming off five months of cabin fever. Suddenly all the idiots have to try DUI limits and see if last year's game laws are still in effect. Can't tell you how many people forget that where there was a foot of ice on a river last month is now an inch, and snowmobiles don't swim."

"Think of the job security," I said.

"I've got plenty without any help. Fifteen hours of daylight and every male in Alaska wants to be Sergeant Winklepance."

"So now may not the best time to come asking for a favor?"

He stared at me like I expected him to produce a moose from a hip pocket. "I'll put you on my calendar for after the Termination Dust falls in October."

At least I knew Termination Dust referred to the first snowfall of the year. I was still trying to puzzle out the meaning of "Sergeant Winklepance" – but I assumed he did not intend to be flattering. "Look, if you could make an arrest, I'll transport the prisoner to Anchorage."

"Oh, it's that easy, is it?" Corcoran asked. "No warrant. No arraignment? No bail? No ROR? Do you need me to spell that out?"

"No, I understand 'Released on Own Recognizance.' I don't think it's likely in this situation. Conspiracy to murder a federal officer will generally get a magistrate's attention."

The sergeant sipped from his mug. "Depends. Were you the federal agent in question?"

"Do you have someplace I can brief you on what we're dealing with?"

"Sure, come on back to my office," he said. "You can see I've got nothing else going on this morning."

In Corcoran's tidy office, we sat on opposite sides of a narrow metal desk with fake wood accents. He listened as I explained the past three days, interrupting only on those occasions when he already knew what had happened. He followed along, scribbling notes on a pad of paper. When I finished my explanation, he looked up and set his pen aside. "OK, so who do you think is the criminal mastermind and Uncle Pennybags behind this scheme?"

"Aunt Pennybags, in this case," I corrected, "And like the original Pennybags, they seem to be building a land monopoly on the island."

Corcoran sat back in his chair and looked at me in astonishment.

"You want to go after the most powerful power couple on the island? They're in line behind only the Native corporation? And you think an arrest will fly? No grand jury? Nothing?"

"Imminent risk of flight," I said.

"Sure. Her attorney was a speaker in the state legislature. Her prior lawyer was a former governor."

"Well, I've got 'Friends in Low Places.'"

He laughed. "OK, but don't sing. How about this? If the U.S. Attorney in Anchorage tells you they are looking into this matter, I'll go chat with the Solversons and suggest that the Chitwoods implicated them in a scheme."

My turn to express surprise. "You don't think that will create a flight risk?"

"You've got some kind of suspicious mind. So why don't you go to the USA before we make any move?"

Standing, I extended my hand. "OK, let's hold off on contact with the Solversons. I'll talk with Frank about approaching his boss in Juneau, then we'll likely go to the USA in Anchorage. But I may be back with an arrest warrant."

"Sure, call first. With Montgomery lollygagging, I'm busier than a musher with a hungry team and a half cup of kibble."

51

The special agents were already huddled back in their office when I arrived. In obvious excitement, Kathy waved me over to a conference table where she stood with Frank. She wore cotton gloves for handling evidence. Laid out on the tabletop sat a large device with a spindly arm protruding over it.

"As expected, one Autopen," she said. "Confiscated under a legal search warrant executed on the Chitwoods' housing unit. Complete with photos. And as a bonus, I found their bank statements in a desk. They would have trouble coming up with a million dollars cash, or even a tenth of that. Also in the desk: a GSA auction notice."

"Pretty good haul for a few hours," Frank said.

"Wait until you see this," she said. She removed a yellow notepad from a paper bag. Across the top sheet, someone had scratched a broad swath with a lead pencil. "I managed to raise the word 'Ricci.' I'm guessing they have been leaving clues on your Jeep to confuse you. And trust me, if you want to know any rumors, ask a yeoman."

Frank walked to her desk. I followed along. "So, is there anything you didn't find?" he asked.

She shook her head slowly, reluctant to dump her complete findings on us at once.

I reached up to wriggle a forefinger through the bullet hole in the chest of my leather jacket. "Nothing missing?"

"No. I didn't find any weapons. Nothing," she said. "You should see the place. Like a shrine to some guy named Thomas Kinkade. Pictures of lighthouses and cabins in snowy winter scenes on every wall. Kind of creepy, like going to an art museum for elves. But here's something I thought might bring back some memories for Marty." She pulled the gloves back on to handle evidence. From her bag, she produced a black VHS video tape and held it aloft. "*Attack on Crisp Point* sounds like a John Wayne Western, doesn't it?"

Frank shrugged and headed back toward his desk. "I've already seen it. It's more like a Marx Brother's movie." From a desk drawer, he removed a pack of cigarettes and a Zippo lighter. He coaxed out a fresh cigarette before he stopped himself. He held the pack upright and shook the cigarette back inside. "Sorry, I forgot."

Kathy chuckled and looked at me. "Frank sometimes forgets there's no smoking in federal buildings now by presidential executive order."

"Hey, I didn't vote for him," Frank groused.

Kathy laughed at him. "Come on, Frank. A little break will do your lungs some good." She looked at me but pointed at Frank. "Frank's going to be the first person to get black lung without going near a coal mine."

"Lots of things cause cancer. Can't ban the world," he protested. "Maybe you didn't find a rifle, but I found gunshot residue up to Chitwood's elbows and on his cheek."

"Let's look at this as two separate issues," she said. "First the land fraud. Ginny knew the process, and we have an Autopen and a GSA notice. Then there's trying to kill Galloway. Ginny may not have participated, but she recognized the Magnum rounds. And her hubby was covered in GSR. Galloway survived the ambush Saturday, so Bill then tried to assault him at the AirSta."

"I can't wait to hear a clever defense lawyer try to spin all this," Frank said. "We've got motive, opportunity, method, and assault on a federal agent."

"Yes, we've got proof of *mens rea* carved in stone," I said. I wandered back to sit in a chair in front of Frank's desk. "Here's the next challenge. Any smart prosecutor is going to want the rifle Bill used, preferably with his fingerprints. For now, all we can prove with gunshot residue is that he fired a weapon, but no idea what, when or where. And I'm sure the USA would like to know the identity of Bill's accomplice on Bear Creek."

"I don't like the sound of this, do you?" Kathy asked Frank. "I feel like he's dumping all the work on us."

"That's one way to look at it," I said. "Or you could think of this as giving you credit for wrapping up this potential fraud against the government."

Kathy held up a stack of bank statements. "We agreed that the Chitwoods would not have the money to buy 600 acres at auction, let along four whole sections. And somebody else would have to sell the property in the future."

"Not necessarily," I said. "What if somebody intended to build there. Maybe a massive housing project?"

"Housing for engineers out at the new spaceport?"

"Sorry, boys. How do you suppose they would keep that partnership secret on this island?" Kathy asked.

"You keep it all in the family," I said. I hoped my amateur profiling made sense.

Frank settled back in his chair. "This involves the person you believe is their accomplice?"

"To a ninety nine point nine percent of certainty," I said.

"You're not sure, then," Kathy said.

Frank gave her an approving smile, then turned to me. "Why don't you tell us your suspicions?"

"I discussed this with Sergeant Corcoran. He thought we should ask the USA or the FBI to come to talk with the individuals in question to establish some reasonable suspicion."

"And they would fly out here based upon...?" he left the question dangle.

"I've got a hunch," I said.

"Oh, you've got a hunch. And based on that hard guess, you think the FBI will come flying out to Kodiak?"

Kathy excused herself from our discussion to answer her ringing phone. While she had a quiet conversation, Frank and I continued talking about how to proceed.

"Look, Marty, I am not saying you're wrong; however, I don't think we can show probable cause for your other suspect like we can with the Chitwoods. Does said person have a name?"

"Marilyn Solverson. And her husband Hans."

Once again, Frank stared at me like looking at Sasquatch. "You don't swing on the meatballs, do you?"

"Only the pitches I get."

Kathy hung up her receiver and turned to face us. "Well, gentlemen, that was Mister Avery. The Chitwoods have lawyered up."

"That's a game-changer," Frank said.

"Avery thought they made an interesting choice of lawyer. Not a name you find under Criminal Law in the phonebook."

"Oh?" Franks and I said in unison.

"Walter Alexander Riggs. Former governor of Alaska."

Frank turned to look at me. "We're benched. This game just moved to the big leagues."

52

When I returned to the office of the Air Station's commanding officer on the following day, the yeoman who greeted me had allowed me to use the operation's boss' telephone a few days earlier. She now filled in for the otherwise detained Petty Officer William Chitwood. She stood when I explained the purpose of my visit and knocked on the C.O.'s door. To my surprise, Captain Lord came out of his office to greet me.

"Galloway, I'm very sorry about the incident yesterday with Chitwood. I'm relieved to see you were not hurt in the fracas."

"No, Captain, all things considered, only thing bruised is my pride."

"Come into my office," the captain said. "Petty Officer López, would you locate Mister Ricci and ask him to report to my office?" The captain turned to me. "Come in, Chief. Would you like something to drink while we wait? Coffee?"

"No, thank you, Captain. I'm fine."

He led me into his office and motioned toward one of the leather office chairs. "This may take a few moments. I asked to have Mister Ricci pulled from the flight rotation for the day, but the op center may need to page him. And I'd swear Alexander Graham Bell made our pagers himself."

I hesitated before I sat. "Captain, I don't mind waiting in your outer office. I don't want to distract you from important work."

Captain Lord gave me the same benevolent smile all senior officers have for enlisted members as if their commissioning bestowed upon them the hidden answer to Life, the Universe, and Everything. "No, actually, I'm curious what you have learned about the Chitwoods. I would never have expected Bill and Ginny to engage in anything under-handed, let alone criminal."

To maintain the integrity of the investigation, I gave the captain only the *Reader's Digest Condensed* version of the alleged land swindle, excluding any mention of Rear Admiral FitzHenry, Marilyn Solverson, or Anton. But the captain seemed satisfied.

"And may I ask you something on another topic?" he asked.

"Of course, sir."

"Have you uncovered any information pertaining to Lieutenant Simms' death of which I should be aware? I was her commanding officer, and I had the unfortunate responsibility of informing her mother. Family notifications are the worst part of this job."

"I understand, Captain. I have served as a funeral escort. I have not yet found any evidence to indicate anything other than what the state troopers report indicates."

At that moment, a knock came on his office door, and López stepped inside. "Captain, Mister Ricci is here."

"Thank you. Please ask him to come in."

Lieutenant Ricci entered, still wearing his blue flight coveralls. He walked so stiffly that I expected him to salute. Instead, he stood at attention until invited to sit. His nervousness had nothing to do with my questioning. Every minute a junior officer spends before their C.O. could constitute a potential black mark when it comes to their Officer Evaluation Report. The captain motioned toward the seat adjacent to mine. If it is possible to sit at attention, Ricci managed it.

"Mister Ricci, let me remind you of what we discussed yesterday. Galloway is a special agent in the Ninth District, but he is here at the request of Lieutenant Simms' family. As such, you are under no obligation to answer his questions."

"I understand, Captain," Ricci said.

"Sir, I'd like to add that I have not asked to speak with you because I suspect you may have done something inappropriate or in any way illegal," I said. "I am wondering only if you can provide me with any information about why Miss Simms would have gone up to Bear Creek."

"I will try," Ricci said.

"To begin, how did you know Miss Simms?"

Ricci relaxed in his seat from rigid attention and turned to face me. "There aren't many single officers on Base. Kodiak isn't that high on the list of duty locations for bachelors. It was pretty clear that she wasn't getting a lot of social invites, so my fiancée and I started inviting her over to our place when we had something planned. She always brought wine, sometimes a cheese and crackers thing."

"Ever go to her apartment?" I asked.

"No, I never did. Nor Wendy, so far as I know. That's my girlfriend."

With a smile, I nodded. "How often would you say you met her outside work? Weekly? Monthly?"

Ricci sat back and scratched his short sideburn with an index finger. "When I first got here, I'd say weekly. But then monthly after Wendy finished her residency and moved up from Chicago."

"Wendy didn't like Miss Simms? Or your relationship with her?"

"No, it wasn't that at all. Wendy and I have been apart for a while. She did her residency at a hospital in Chicago. I was on the *Polar Sea* when it went to the North Pole." He paused to give his captain a nervous look. "We wanted to spend some time alone together."

Admitting any sexual contact outside marriage, even consensual, may be problematic for a young officer with career ambitions. The Uniform Code of Military Justice was written in 1950 in such broad language that a C.O. could find a lot of reasons to end a career if they so choose, thanks to Article 133. "Conduct unbecoming an officer and gentleman" is, as the lawyers say, in the eyes of the officer's C.O. I decided Ricci might be more relaxed and forthcoming if we spoke privately.

"Captain, I've taken up a lot of your time already," I said. "If Mister Ricci is comfortable, I'd like him to accompany me over to Bear Creek."

"Lieutenant, do you concur?" Captain Lord asked. "You are under no obligation."

"Yes, sir. Anything I can do to help the Simms family."

Ricci and I stood and left. As we reached the door, I thought I heard an audible sigh of relief. Ricci stopped to speak with Petty Officer López. "I'm going off Base with Special Agent Galloway. Would you please notify the Ops Center to page me if they need me. I'll be up by the Comms Station."

As we headed down the same stairwell I had nearly tumbled down the day before, Ricci's verbal dam broke. "Thank you. I like the captain, but I get so nervous around him. He's more than the C.O.; he was on the original team to select the HH-65 back 20 years ago. He's a pioneer."

We walked over to the Wrangler. "I thought you might be more comfortable out here. I don't know Captain Lord, but any C.O. can be intimidating."

"Well, thanks. Look, I want to be clear, there was never anything between Janet, uh, Miss Simms, and myself. Ever."

"No kinky Tupperware parties or anything of that nature?"

He laughed for the first time since I'd met him. A good sign. "Are you kidding? Wendy is not into either kinky or Tupperware. She's a Chicago Miracle Mile girl. Father owns six banks around the city; mother is a state senator."

"I'm curious; how did Wendy and Janet get along?"

"Fine. Yeah, when Wendy got here she may have been a little jealous, but she realized she had nothing to worry about."

At that time, we turned from the main route into town onto the so-called highway that led up to Buskin Lake and the Communications Station. I did not bother to stop and change the Jeep's hubs into four-wheel drive. In a short distance, I turned up the gravel two-track that wound up along Bear Creek. I stopped the Wrangler above the site of Janet's death and climbed out.

After several minutes, Ricci stepped down from the rig and followed me down to the area where the crime scene tape still fluttered on the pegs. He seemed reluctant to be there. "Sorry. I haven't been back here since that day."

"As I said, sir, my main question is whether you know why she would have come out here. She had no fishing gear; no camera or binoculars."

He shrugged in silence.

"I understand it was Sunshine Liberty for most of the commands on Base," I said. "So, she couldn't have planned to come here in advance."

"No, I guess not. I was flying a training mission when the C.O. called it. I didn't know about the liberty until I got back to the Base."

"Any idea if Lieutenant Simms invited someone else to come hiking with her when she didn't reach you?"

Ricci fell silent. He stared up the slope of Pyramid Mountain. As an experienced angler, I knew how to let the fly float on the water in front of the quarry to see if he snagged it. After several minutes of silence, he finally turned toward me and spoke in a voice as quiet as a breeze.

"Maybe she did, but when I got her message, I came over."

"Sorry, sir, you came over that afternoon?" I did not recall reading that detail in the AST reports.

"Yes. Wendy was interviewing down at the hospital for a job, so I came to meet Janet."

"Sir, I'm not accusing you of anything, but did you see what happened to Miss Simms?"

He drew a ragged breath. "I saw the bear, if that's what you mean. It was on top of her. She was not moving. At all. Nothing. It was already tearing into her." He dropped to his knees on the rocky surface.

"Sir, what did you do then?"

"I tried to distract it. Yelling, shouting, waving my arms. That bear ignored me; it stayed right on top of her."

For a moment, I feared he would vomit from remembering the scene of the bear's attack. I knelt next to the lieutenant on the gravelly ground and put a hand on his shoulder. "Sounds to me like there was nothing you could do at that point. If she wasn't fighting back, she was dead by then."

"I tell myself that."

We knelt there on the slope overlooking Bear Creek for several minutes. I allowed him to rest a moment before I continued questioning. "And then you left?"

"I didn't know what else to do. I couldn't stop the bear, and I couldn't watch what it was doing."

"I'm sorry to keep asking questions, sir. Why didn't you report it?" His eyes stared at the dirt in front of him. Yet, I felt I had no choice but to continue my questions while he continued to cooperate. "You were not responsible for a bear attack."

"I guess I panicked. By the time I got my thoughts together, somebody had found her body. I started to come back but saw a lot of rescue vehicles," he explained. "I took a little time to think about what I should do."

"Why were you so concerned?"

"I didn't want to cause gossip." His head drooped. "She was dead, and I thought only of myself."

"As I said, sir, there was nothing you could have done at that point."

"I want to believe that, but I still think about that bear. It destroyed her."

"Tell me, sir, have you told anyone else what you told me here?"

"No. Well, I told Wendy. Now you. That's all."

I wanted to change the subject to relieve his anguish. "Sir, did you see anyone else when you came out here?"

He thought that over a moment or two. "Yes, two cars. I saw Holland's old Monte Carlo down by the lake. After I came past it, I was nearly run off the road by a truck coming out like a bat out of hell."

"Did you recognize it?"

"Does it really matter?" he asked, looking puzzled.

"Whoever drove it may have been the last person to see Lieutenant Simms alive."

"OK, it was boxy. I thought it was a Isuzu Trooper. Maybe a Jeep or a Land Rover." He turned to look at me. "You don't think I should have done more?"

"Sir?"

"To stop the bear?"

"Not unless you have a shirt with a big yellow S under your coveralls. You tried to frighten it, but he didn't budge. If you'd provoked it any farther, he would have attacked you as well. Without a rifle, there was nothing you could have done." For emphasis, I added, "Nothing, sir."

Ricci stood and brushed gravel and dirt off the knees and the seat of his uniform coveralls. "Thank you. I hope it will help me sleep through the night."

"Another year," I said as I scrabbled to stand. "Takes a while after you've seen something horrible like that."

When we returned to the Wrangler, I hoped that Janet Simms did not suffer long during the attack. But I knew Ricci would suffer the memory for a long time to come.

53

After returning Ricci to the Air Station, I drove over to the special agents' office on the far side of the hill. Their gray sedan sat outside, and they sat inside. Both carried on phone conversations when I entered. They both looked up and waved, but neither ended their calls to greet me. I sat in the desk chair opposite Frank's desk. He scowled at me.

Kathy's phone conversation ended first. "So how does one man create so much work for so many people?" she asked.

"Oh? Frank been busy?"

"Right. Frank would never poke a sleeping bear. You must like to wander around this island kicking as many bears as you can find."

Frank's call came to an abrupt end when he swore and slammed the receiver into the desk unit. "God, Juneau! They are angry that the Chitwoods have gone radio silent and found a high-price lawyer. And now the USA wants to take the case. Juneau is all for handing the Chitwoods over for federal charges rather than letting the admiral convene a court martial."

"Why is the USA asking for work?" she asked. "Could let us clean up our own mess."

"Because the USA's office want to flip our couple on the Solversons, who the Coast Guard can't touch," Frank said. "They want to prosecute them together in hopes that someone will flip on the other. And the FBI is coming over to interview the Solversons."

"When?" I asked.

Frank shrugged. "All I got out of Juneau was soon."

"I'm no lawyer," Kathy said, "but this seems like a good way to get someone to cooperate. And I wouldn't care who sings, as long as the Chitwoods receive dishonorable discharges."

"And prison time," I said, "I'm good, as long as nobody forgets charges of attempted murder of a federal agent against the Chitwoods. You've got the hospital report, but I'm happy to give you photographic evidence if you need it."

"Trust me, no one wants you to take your shirt off," Frank said.

Kathy laughed. "Tell me, Galloway, after a trip to the bear refuge and the hospital, did you resolve what you actually came here for? What about Travis Pike?"

"Good question," Frank said. "Are you ready to go home? There's a Space-A flight this morning over to Anchorage."

"Here's your hat. What's your hurry?" I quipped. "First, Pike told Trooper Montgomery that he was acting on behalf of God's Own Patriots, which connects to the missing Coasties in Lake Superior. With regard to Lieutenant Simms, I can reassure the family now."

"You spoke to Lieutenant Ricci?" she asked.

"Yes. Good conversation." I thought it best not to elaborate.

"If the admiral wants to turn everything over to the USA, are you going to stick around?" Frank asked, in a more earnest tone the second time around.

"I'm starting to think you don't enjoy the pleasure of my company."

"Damn, you're slow," Kathy said.

"No, it's not that," Frank protested. "I don't need this much excitement before retirement."

"What Frank means is that he doesn't want anything to screw up his thirty years."

"Understood." First, I thought through an inventory of tasks to complete before leaving Kodiak, such as returning the Wrangler. I considered visiting Hannah and Anton, but realized I couldn't tell them any more than they already knew.

"You're being quiet, Galloway," Frank said. "Should I worry about what you have planned next?"

I stood and stretched gingerly to avoid irritating any recently damaged body parts. "No, making a little mental memo of what I need to do to get ready to go. As a priest once told me, 'You never know what you can do until you try undoing what you've done.'"

"You're Catholic?" Kathy asked in surprise.

"Yep, every Saturday evening at Our Lady of Perpetual Regret. Why do you ask?"

"I don't mean anything by it. I am, too. I guess I didn't match your reputation with an altar boy." Her apology sounded earnest.

"I'm a retired altar boy," I said. "Look, could I borrow a phone for a moment for a quick call?"

"Use my phone. I'm heading out to lunch anyway," Frank said as he stood and headed for the door.

"Look at the time," she said. "I guess I'm late for lunch, too."

With that, I picked up the receiver on Frank's desk phone and dialed a number at the 486 prefix on Kodiak.

A husky voice answered. "Solverson Realty."

54

Not all fog is created equal. Think of it as a cloud hugging the ground. Aviators describe fog in terms of how it develops and how it impacts visibility. In some situations, moist air over a cooler surface creates radiation fog as the temperature falls. At other times, cool air flowing over warm water causes a steaming fog or Arctic sea smoke. Fog conditions make flying in or out of the airports in Adak and Unalaska along the Aleutian Chain especially dicey.

Although my preference meant little to the density of the air's moisture, I woke that morning hoping for clear conditions. No luck. On what I intended to be my last morning on Kodiak, a dense, shallow fog hung over the town and the port. Ground fog significantly reduces visibility up to just about the first story of most buildings. Once airborne above a shallow fog, pilots may find anywhere up to unlimited visibility.

Standing outside the Baranof Lodge's back door, I struggled to see the bright red Jeep in the lot, but I had no trouble recognizing the surrounding buildings. Using structures in town and Pillar Mountain as landmarks, I navigated out to the airport and headed back up the Kodiak Island Highway. Just beyond the Communication Station's radio tower, I turned up the familiar two-track to where I saw the yellow crime scene tape. Standing along the gravel road, I could not see the rushing stream down the slope from me.

From the haze came the sound of footsteps crunching the gravel. Slowly a figure emerged into visibility. Marilyn Solverson appeared into view within six feet before her features were recognizable. She wore a stylish double-breasted leather coat over khaki trousers and knee-high boots.

"I appreciate your punctuality," she said. "What do you have that you think would be of interest to me?"

"We'll get to that. First, I want to know about the day Lieutenant Simms died. A witness recognized your Land Rover leaving the scene. Were you scouting parcels you wanted Ginny Chitwood to send to auction next?"

"Does it matter now?" Her voice betrayed exasperation.

"Yes, it very much matters."

"That pilot figured it out somehow. What did she know about land transfers?"

"Quite a lot, actually." I said. "Back in Boston, before she became a pilot, she helped transfer several lighthouses to other organizations. You chose the wrong Coastie."

"Somehow she knew all about the Chitwoods. She thought I would help her trap them."

"So you decided to get rid of her?"

"No. I didn't hurt her. A bee landed on her neck. When she tried to brush it off, it bit her. I've never seen someone have a reaction like that."

"She went into anaphylactic shock?"

Marilyn nodded. "I suppose. She fell down, holding her throat. Her face puffed up. I didn't know how to help her. Then I heard the bear huffing and snorting. It came down the stream and right toward us. I ran for my truck because I thought there might be something to scare it off. When I looked back, the bear was on top of her. It ripped at her head."

"You left her?"

She gasped. "I did. I thought I could get help." Her voice was low and quiet. She appeared to shudder, as if shaking off the memory. "That's not why you called me out here."

"That's correct." Holding up a cassette tape, I said, "I think you might want the only copy of a phone conversation between Bill Chitwood and your husband, Hans, planning how to ambush me out here on Saturday. I think that's worth what you were going to give the Chitwoods. I'll give you until Monday to get the cash together."

Marilyn laughed. "You think the state will charge us?"

"No, probably not. But the U.S. Attorney in Anchorage may. At the moment, you're standing on Coast Guard property, which is federal jurisdiction."

Abruptly Marilyn withdrew a small pistol from a coat pocket. "Give me the tape. What kind of idiot brings the evidence to a blackmail?" The gun looked about the same size as my Beretta.

I tossed the tape a little high for her reach. We watched it disappear into the mist. When she turned to search for it, I stepped forward and shoved her from behind. Her pistol fired. Then a larger caliber weapon fired somewhere above me; it's slug slammed into the hood of the Jeep. I threw myself behind the Wrangler for whatever protection it offered. The shot sounded like it came from the slope on Pyramid Mountain. The situation seemed all too familiar. I drew my Colt, even knowing I could see no target through the fog.

A second weapon fired from across the creek on the slope of Pillar Mountain.

"Don't reload! You only get one warning," a woman's voice instructed through a megaphone. "Frank's a marksman, and his next shot will be a bulls-eye," a woman called out from somewhere on a mountain slope above me. "Lie face-down. Now spread-eagle. You're under arrest."

I stood and turned to give the same instruction to Marilyn Solverson. She was gone. I went searching through the fog. Somewhere in the mist, I heard an engine start. Suddenly the shadow of a large vehicle came racing out of the gloom toward me. I jumped out of the way, but the Land Rover veered toward me, missing my leg by a matter of inches. Recovering my balance, I sprinted to the Jeep. On the front seat sat a two-way radio.

"Base Security, Agent 3. BOLO for black Land Rover traveling Southeast toward main road. Contain above CommSta. Notify AST of Land Rover's possible presence on road into Kodiak. Request arrest."

"Agent 1, Agent 2. Nice shot there. Took the gumption out of Hans. I'm going to haul him down to Agent 3 now."

"Agent 2, Agent 1. Get him in handcuffs before transport." Nice of Frank to direct Kathy's arrest of Hans Solverson on the radio.

"Base Security, Agent 3. Is Marilyn Solverson in custody?"

"Agent 3, Base Security. NEGRES at this time. Ground fog hampering search."

When I tried to start the Wrangler's engine, it revved to life and sputtered out. I eased the spring closures on each side of the hood and opened the engine compartment. Steam sizzled through a large hole in the radiator.

"Base, Agent 3. I'm going to need a tow truck at my location."

"Agent 3, Agent 1. ETA your location in 15. Contact with Agent 2?"

"Agent 1, Agent 3. Negative."

Kathy sounded tired when she skipped proper radio protocol. "Permission to drag Hans on his butt. I'd make better speed getting to Marty's location."

Within 10 minutes, Kathy emerged through the white shroud lingering just above ground level, still dragging Hans by his arm. "Next time, I want to be the sniper."

"That'll be between you and Frank," I said. I stepped toward Hans. "We seem unable to locate Marilyn. Any suggestions?"

He laughed. Then he spat in my face.

"Don't take it personal," Kathy said. "He's been like that all morning." With a well-placed shin across the back of his knees, Kathy brought Hans to the ground on his belly. "Now behave yourself. I'm from Nebraska, and I'm a goat-tying champ."

I opened the tailgate on the Wrangler and removed the small toolbox there. Inside I located exactly what the occasion required. After walking back to the front of the Jeep, Kathy and Hans came into view again. I tossed the roll of duct tape to Kathy. "I'm all for helping him retain his right to remain silent. Eight inches, ear to ear, that should do it."

"A little something on the ankles?" she asked after covering his lower face.

"If you think he's a flight risk," I suggested. "His accomplice remains at large." I failed to time her performance, but she made quick work of wrapping tape around his ankles. No doubt she was well within the 45-second threshold for a rodeo competitor.

At that moment, the gray K-car emerged from the gloom. Kathy leaned toward me. "I'm going to tell Frank that the duct tape was your idea."

"Don't forget the spit when you tell him."

Frank bolted from the K-car. "Security and AST don't have her yet. Where the hell is she?"

"Did she go up the valley the other way?" Kathy asked.

"Nowhere to go. The road dead-ends at Anton Larsen Bay."

"She could meet a boat," I suggested.

"Would she leave her husband and take off?" Kathy rolled Hans on his back. "Know where your wife went?"

Hans turned his face away from us.

"That's it!" I shouted as I ran toward the K-car's passenger side. "Come on, Frank. She's meeting a floatplane."

The driver's door slammed closed, and Frank ground the ignition a few seconds too long. The K-car lurched into gear and fish-tailed as Frank floored the gas pedal. He swung us in a tight circle, and we headed back down the two-track toward where the CommSta tower rose above the shallow fog. Using the two-way radio mounted on the dashboard, I contacted the AirSta.

"Air Station Kodiak, Agent 3: Any assets currently airborne?"

"Agent 3, Kodiak: Negative."

"Kodiak, Agent 3: Request weather conditions at Anton Larson Bay."

"Agent, Kodiak: Sea smoke with limited visibility to 500 feet.

Stratus ceiling at 900 to 1,000 feet. Visibility at 2,000 feet estimated one mile or less."

"AirSta Kodiak, Agent 3: Roger that. Clear." I put the mic back into the clip on the dash.

"Sailing out of Anton Larsen Bay would be risky, and flying out is impossible." He eased off the accelerator when we entered a particularly dense bank of fog as we passed the Base winter recreation area.

I rested my head against the window, staring out at the whiteness. "That depends on whether somebody can convince a pilot to try it. And Marilyn Solverson can be quite persuasive. She's probably carrying a lot of cash."

He leaned forward, gripping the top of the steering wheel with both hands. He looked a little like the groundhog learning to drive a pick-up truck in the Bill Murray movie. "Don't drive angry," I said.

He turned his head quickly and gave me a brief questioning look. "You're so strange." His attention went back to the road up through a pass. "So, you think she'll talk someone into flying in these conditions?"

"Sure, it only gets hairy on take-off and landing. Most of the time, you stay in those few hundred feet between the ground fog and the clouds." I pointed at the rearview mirror mounted on the windshield. "Your field of vision is wide and low, like a letterbox. But once they get out of the bay, they're over open water all the way to the mainland."

"Could we get an aircraft after them?"

I laughed. "Not likely. Way outside acceptable Coast Guard parameters. Visibility can go from unlimited to zero in minutes."

The car swung left, and the rear tires bit into the gravel along the berm of the road.

"Sorry," Frank said. "Didn't see that turn coming."

"Careful. I think we're heading down toward the bay. After we pass the gaging station on the Red Cloud River, it's all wetlands along the right hand side."

"Got it." With one hand, he reached into a shirt pocket for a pack of unfiltered Camels. He punched in the lighter on the dashboard and shook out a single cigarette. "Yeah, I know what the president said. He ain't here. You going to report me to Kathy?"

"Just don't run off the road and wreck us. You get me killed, my Congressman's getting a very strongly worded letter."

In a couple of miles, my side of the road turned from grass to water. The warm water of Anton Larsen Bay helped burn off some of the fog, and our visibility improved. The ceiling lifted to 50 feet, and visibility improved to a quarter mile, permitting us to see the width of the bay.

"Binoculars on the floor of the backseat. Can you reach back and get them?" he asked.

I did as he requested while he pulled the car into a small opening where the road rounded a headland. Our view spanned from the northern edge of Larsen Island on our left across the bay to where a steep slope rose into the foggy shroud on the East side. A fishing skiff with one occupant drifted about 20 yards offshore. Frank tapped my shoulder and pointed down the road to our left. A few hundred yards away a Range Rover sat on the shoreline.

Frank and I both drew weapons as we approached the truck, and we each took a side. After confirming the rig was empty, I opened the passenger door. The interior smelled of lavender potpourri. Frank leaned in on the driver's side.

"Let's leave everything for the troopers to tag and fingerprint," he said.

"Including that Weatherby rifle in the backseat?"

"Especially that. If we don't find Chitwood's prints, we may have trouble making our case. But grab that scarf. Let's flag that fisherman."

The scarf Marilyn left behind looked more burnt pumpkin than international orange, but when Frank blasted the truck's horn and waved the scarf, the fisherman looked our way. He started the boat's outboard motor and began puttering toward us. As he approached the shoreline, we both stowed our weapons. We waited for the potential witness to arrive. "What's actually on that tape you gave her?"

"Turnabout is fair play," I said. "I gave her Travis Pike's latest and greatest. Scraped the label off so she wouldn't suspect."

"A Travis Pike recording? You're one mean bastard."

"Nothing I haven't heard before."

As the boat neared the shoreline, Frank waved his badge. "Thanks for coming in. We won't hold you up long. Did you see the woman who drove this truck over here?"

"Just for a minute, sure. Then she was gone into nowhere," the fisherman called. I wondered if he retired from the Coast Guard and elected to remain on Kodiak. A number of military retirees stayed for the hunting or fishing. The annual distribution of state revenue from the oil fields didn't exactly scare anyone away either.

"Did she leave on a boat?" Frank asked.

The older gentleman shook his head. "Not for long. She rowed out to get onto a floatplane. Left the skiff adrift out there somewhere. Flew out on a Cessna 185, I think. Maybe 1980 or 81."

"You know your aircraft," Frank said, sounding impressed.

"Well, I should," he said. "22 years with FAA, ten in the tower here. Then Reagan fired all of us. But the fishing here is good."

"See which way they flew?" I asked.

"See? No. Not in the soup we had this morning. Surface viz on the water about 20 yards. But they were likely going out over Kizhuyah Bay, then steer for Anchorage. If not, there's plenty of places to put down a floatplane on the mainland."

We thanked the former air traffic controller and returned to the K-car. Without a filter, Frank's cigarette burned steadily toward the nub. "Call it in. Tell Base Security to stand down. We lost her."

55

When he appeared at the baggage carousel, Andrews sported a polo shirt and a tennis sweater draped around his neck with the sleeves knotted at their cuffs. He wore khaki trousers and deck shoes. His appearance surprised me because I had never seen him out of uniform before his arrival at Chicago's Midway. On a Saturday morning, most of the inbound passengers were late-arriving business travelers, likely held up from a week-long work excursion. They still wore business suits sans ties, with their shirt collars unbuttoned at the neck. The few women among them wore work-out clothes, as if they traveled better prepared for their return than the men. Perhaps they simply were tired after a week spent in skirt and heels.

Another feature of Andrews' appearance struck me in the bright lights of the terminal. Somehow in Michigan I had failed to observe the graying of the hair at his temples.

"Marty, good to see you again," Andrews said as he extended his hand in greeting. "And nicer without all the snow."

"Thank you for flying over, sir. This'll be easier with you here."

"It's a weekend. You can drop the 'sir.'" he said. "Considering I nearly got you killed once or twice."

"Three times, sir."

His left eyebrow went up. "Oh? I didn't get a full accounting."

"We've got a three-hour drive ahead, so I'll catch you up. With X-rays if you'd like."

"I don't think that's necessary."

We exited the terminal and headed to short-term parking. Arriving from Alaska earlier that morning, I had already retrieved from long-term parking my Grand Wagoneer, undamaged, to my great relief. We paid at the gate and merged onto the highway in quick order. About 20 minutes into the drive, he demanded a stop at a rest area built above the highway where he could get a cup of gourmet coffee and a bear claw. I took the opportunity to top off the Jeep so that we wouldn't need any other stops en route to Indianapolis except for personal relief.

Once we were back on the highway, he said, "Did your musical tastes change while you were in Alaska?" Andrews asked. "Up in Michigan, it was classical and jazz, with a little Native American flute. This is an eclectic collection on one tape."

We listened to the audition tape by Sage's band again, so I explained its origin, minus the naughty bits, as Monty Python would say. "If you'd prefer, you can try to find something on the radio?"

"No thanks. All that talk about the president? Think of all the school books they could have bought with all the millions spent investigating him."

"If it's OK, sir, I try to be as apolitical as possible," I explained. "Stupid politics got us involved in a war that killed my father."

"I'm sorry, Marty," he said. "So let me tell you what I know about Kodiak already, then you can fill me on what I've missed." He described how I ended up in the Chitwoods' shooting gallery and two days fell into another Chitwood trap. "So now the rest?"

"Let's say that there are three different stories from Kodiak," I said. First, I described my encounter with Travis Pike and a few members of God's Own Patriots. During their search of the Solverson home, the FBI found a check stub made out to Travis Pike, which her assistant explained was to cover my disappearance.

Then, I told him about my return to the refuge with Trooper Montgomery to catch the bear poachers. Finally, we got into the details of the land deal involving the Chitwoods and their likely accomplices.

He turned in his seat to stare at me. "You stirred all that up in ten days?"

"I didn't go looking for anything else; it all kind of found me."

"Or shot at you," he said.

"Would you like to talk about Janet now? Or wait until we reach Indy?"

"Let's finish the land deal. So how did you identify the Chitwoods' accomplices?"

"We needed to answer a couple of questions about the Chitwoods. First, a search of their housing unit didn't find any hunting rifles, which seemed odd because we knew they went on at least one hunt for big horn sheep. And they needed somebody to bid on the land at auction. Janet had spoken to a real estate person on the island. Turns out that person had a collection of big game trophies in her home. It kind of fell together after that."

When he sipped from his coffee, I saw his name scrawled on the cup in black marker. "Why not leave the Solversons for the FBI and the USA in Anchorage?" he asked.

"Two reasons really, sir. We didn't think we had enough to even question them. Second, I knew she was near the place Janet died when it happened, and I wanted to know what Marilyn saw."

"Tell me later." Andrews turned to sit forward in his seat, watching through the passenger windows as the industrial parts of northern Indiana passed by. Eventually, he turned back toward me. "Sorry, I don't like to think that I could have helped Janet."

"I'm not certain that's true, at least not how Marilyn tells it. We may find out more from her husband as the FBI leans on him."

"What did you get by luring them out?"

"Attempted bribery, attempted murder of a federal agent, assault, resisting arrest, fleeing custody, flight to avoid prosecution. Better, it was all on federal property, so the USA has jurisdiction. If Hans didn't know everything that Marilyn was up to, he's probably not a happy man right now."

After Gary, we turned South and entered the endless corn and wheat fields. Once we had heard Sage's tape twice, I handed Andrews a flat brown case from the back seat containing 36 cassette tapes. "You can find something in here."

"Not my first round draft picks, but... Hold on, you have a Chick Corea tape?" he asked in surprise.

"Sorry, am I not supposed to?"

"No, I'm just surprised that's all." Andrews hesitated. "What did you learn about Janet's death?"

I turned down the volume of the radio so I could quietly recite Marilyn's description of events at Bear Creek on the afternoon Janet Simms was mauled to death by a Kodiak bear. Then I explained the trap Frank, Kathy and I sprang to capture the Solversons but which Marilyn had evaded, leaving Hans to face the consequences alone.

Andrews sat silently for 30 minutes before he spoke again. "Wait, that makes no sense. Janet couldn't be allergic to bees. You can't enlist or go to OCS with allergies. You certainly can't become a pilot."

"Maybe she didn't know. Or maybe she developed allergies as she aged. The autopsy described some petechial hemorrhaging. With all the other injuries, the coroner didn't make much of it. But it could show lack of oxygen."

"Did this woman try to help Janet?"

"From what she said, there wasn't time before the bear chased her off. And she left."

"You believe her?" he asked.

"I don't see any reason for her to lie. She already planned to flee the country."

"I don't understand how she escaped. Why didn't Base Security and the Troopers have the whole area closed down?"

"She evaded us in the fog. We chased her across the island in zero viz, but she had a float plane waiting. We thought she'd fly into Anchorage, but she went directly to Dillingham. From there, she took a private jet to Kamchatka or Vladivostok."

"And we don't have extradition treaty with Russia."

"Mister Avery says there's a treaty in the works. I bet Russia is just a stopover."

"Really? You couldn't predict she had a plane waiting, but now you know her travel plans?" He playfully poked my shoulder so I would know he was joking.

"Yes, sir. Both Marilyn and Hans are big game hunters. There was a space on their wall for a Siberian ibex."

"Sorry, what's a Siberian ibex?"

"Kind of an antelope. I had to go to the Base library to look it up."

"That's fine, but she can't add it to her collection in the Kodiak house. Not without a stopover in a federal prison first."

"Maybe she'll start her collection over in a new mansion. Now she's got all their money and all the time in the world."

56

During the next two hours, we enjoyed the Chick Corea tape twice. Andrews simply couldn't settle upon another artist in my collection, despite my suggestions. When we reached the I-465 beltway around Indianapolis, I tuned in to an AM station to listen for traffic reports. On a Saturday afternoon, the only slowdown on the highway came before the exit to the shopping centers. At the East 56th Street exit, I made the right to head in the opposite direction from Fort Benjamin Harrison, the Army post. At Keystone Avenue, I turned left. In a mile and a half, I pulled up in front of Valeria's Taqueria.

"Sorry, sir, I need to run a quick errand. Are you hungry?" I asked.

After 15 minutes spent with the owner and her grandson, I left with a letter guaranteeing Tall Boy and his friends food for a month to be charged against one of my credit cards up to a pre-set limit. The owner's initial reluctance disappeared when the young man explained how much food a group of 15 or so teenage boys could consume in a month. With gratuity, the restaurant's income could prove substantial.

As we arrived at Gloria Simms' address, Andrews looked around to ensure there would be no trouble. "Be careful. There's a bunch of punks who hang out around here in some of the abandoned homes."

"Yes, I met them on my last visit. We have a truce, of sorts." I handed him the letter from Valeria's. "You've heard of winning hearts and minds through stomachs?"

"You think this will change their minds about mugging you and stealing your Jeep?" he asked.

"Oh, you, of little faith," I said. "It worked well enough last time I was here. Five pizzas and two hundred bucks got me a Grand Wagoneer security detail. And this," I said, pointing to the Taqueria note, "is for protecting your mother-in-law's place while I've been gone."

"So, I'm supposed to show up every month and bribe them?"

I opened the door of the Jeep and started to climb out. "No, sir, we all do what works for us. I'm good with bribery if it means one less hassle in my life."

"Funny, your reputation is more pugilistic. I have said a lot to defend you over the years. Look, Galloway, your name isn't all shamrocks and leprechauns in any admirals' mess."

"I sure hope not, sir," I said, turning back to face the Jeep's passenger seat. "Because they wouldn't like what I say about them."

"OK, don't tell me then."

To my surprise, I didn't see Tall Boy or any of his friends loitering about the neighborhood. I assumed they would arrive in short order.

Andrews rang the doorbell once before entering the Simms' kitchen door. Not comfortable intruding into her home, I lingered at the threshold until I saw Gloria come into the kitchen. From her blue scrubs, it appeared she was either coming from, or going to, work. After hugging Andrews, she extended her hand toward me.

"Hello, Marty," she said. "Come inside. No need to hang around out there."

"Thank you. I didn't want to bust in on you," I said.

"You mean like someone else?" she asked, pointing toward Andrews. "Like this bull in the China shop? I'm used to it. Come on in. Can I get either of you something to drink? Or lunch?"

When we both declined, she led us into the living room, where I'd rifled through the moving cartons containing Janet's possessions. At that moment, I recalled an entire box in the back seat of the Grand Wagoneer. I promised to bring it inside before we left that afternoon. Changing his mind, Andrews requested a glass of ice water.

"How are you going to approach this?" he asked after she had left.

"Well, as gently as I can. But she may make some assumptions."

"I don't want her upset with any unnecessary details."

At that moment, Gloria entered the room. "What shouldn't I know?" she asked.

Andrews stared at me, even though he had raised the matter.

"Nothing, ma'am," I said. "By unnecessary details he meant some other things that came up during my time on Kodiak, like some bear poaching."

"Oh, that's terrible. I've read about killing bears for their gall bladders." She handed a tall glass to Andrews.

"Yes, that was it exactly. Gallbladders and claws for medicinal use in Asia. But that had nothing to do with Janet's death."

"Marty, why don't you start by telling Gloria what else you discovered while you were on Kodiak?" he asked.

I settled back on the sofa, hoping to appear more relaxed than urgent. "If I may, I'd like to ask a question. Gloria, as a child, was Janet allergic to anything? Maybe peanuts, shrimp, dogs, or bee stings?"

"No, never. She ate PBJ sandwiches, and we went to Red Lobster on special occasions. I don't recall when she was bitten by a bee or wasp. Why do you ask about that?"

I took a deep breath. "The autopsy identified petechial hemorrhaging. That suggests she may have had trouble breathing."

"No, she didn't have allergies." She paused for a moment as she considered my questions. "I don't understand. They told me that a bear attacked her." As a nurse, Gloria would understand the implications of an allergy and anaphylaxis.

By Andrews' look, I could see he thought a more thorough explanation was in order, so I continued. "She may have developed an allergy later in life and not known about it. If she was bitten by a bee, she may have had an anaphylactic reaction. The petechial hemorrhaging might indicate she stopped breathing before the bear even came along."

"If that's true, she wouldn't have suffered so much pain," Gloria said. "All this time, I've thought about her being conscious while that animal ripped her apart. Imagine the terror she would have felt." She sat in silence for several minutes, occasionally dabbing a tear from a cheek. Neither Andrews nor I intruded on her thoughts. Finally, she said, "It's never good to lose a child. A parent is supposed to go first. But if it happens, you hope she suffered as little as possible."

"Gloria, is there anything we can do for you?" Andrews asked.

She stood abruptly as though trying to get away from the subject of our conversation. "No, I have to get ready for work. I'm due at the hospital in an hour. Marty, would you bring back that box you took?"

"Of course, let me go get it," I said, standing and heading for the outside door.

"Just a moment," she said, coming into the kitchen behind me. When I turned, she embraced me. "Thank you. I'm relieved to think Janet didn't suffer. At least that's my hope." I felt her tears on my cheek when she hugged me.

"Mine, too," I whispered. "I hope she did not suffer at the end."

Outside, I found Tall Boy leaning against the faux paneling on the side of my Wagoneer. "Find everything OK inside?" he asked.

"Yes. Thank you. And here's my end of the bargain." From the inside pocket of my jacket, I removed the letter from the taqueria. "Here's the deal. Write all the names in your group on the back. Give this letter to Valeria or her grandson. Then your friends just need to give their name when they go in. The costs will charge to my credit card. But it's not intended for large parties. Understood?"

He nodded as he read the letter, then extended his hand. "I didn't think you'd show again."

"A deal is a deal. Important that a man keeps his word," I said.

"That's true, man." He turned and started to walk away, but stopped and held up the letter "Thank you." Then he continued up the street alone. No cohorts in sight. I lowered the window on the tailgate and removed the packing box. After closing up the Jeep, I took the box inside the house.

Andrews stood in the kitchen, pouring coffee into an oversized ceramic mug. After I placed the box on the kitchen table, he motioned me back outside. "Gloria would like a few moments to herself," he said. We sat on the top step of her porch. "So, Marty, have you considered working in Alameda? We have an opening for a special agent coming up. I could put in a good word with the Vice Admiral."

"No, sir, I couldn't let you throw away your career that way."

His face showed a blank expression. "Sorry?"

"There's not a word you could say about me that Vice Admiral French would consider good. He was in charge of the International Affairs Office in D.C. when I dragged Petty Officer Morgenstern back from Mexico. Captain French wanted me court-martialed, if he couldn't skip the formality and go straight to execution and dishonorable discharge. I was lucky that Admiral Thorne still liked me."

"So what are you going to do next?"

We walked toward the Jeep. "Sir, I was early enlistment, a week out of high school. So I have about two years left. I'm thinking about trying to get a billet in Cleveland with fewer chances of getting abducted. Or shot again, for that matter. Either one might upset my mother. You know they have these new jobs for career counselors. Or I could be the admiral's driver; I know a little about evasive driving tactics."

"No way to persuade you to hang around until I make captain? I could use a good senior enlisted advisor."

"I think you're talking another five years or so," I said. "That's a long, long time when you've acquired as many enemies as I have."

Andrews chuckled. "Which enemies are you referring to? God's Own Patriots? Or admirals?"

"Both, sir. I'm not stupid. Admiral Thorne liked me. Now that he's retired, there'll be a lot of folks who wouldn't mind seeing me disappear. Maybe if I keep my head down, I'll see it through to retirement."

Andrews chuckled. "I know. Thorne sent me to work for French to give me cover from the blowback after he retired." He stood and stepped off the porch. "Who the hell am I kidding? I won't make O-5, let alone captain. Turns out Captain Benedetto called my admiral to say thanks for helping uncover this land plot. He couldn't help but drop my name."

"Sorry, sir. I tried to keep your name out of it. But who else would ask me to go there?"

Andrews looked off in the distance for a long few moments. Then he seemed to rouse himself. "Hell, what would I have done if I made O-6? Skipper a cutter all over the Pacific? Endless fisheries patrols? I hate fish." He turned back toward me. "Driving back to Cleveland today? What is that, six hours?"

"Today I'm only driving to the airport here."

"Really?" Andrews leaned against the Jeep's fender. "Where are you headed now?"

"West, sir. I have to return something to a friend in Seattle. And I'm going to invest some funds in the entertainment business."

"Well, thank you. From me and Gloria both." As we shook hands, he gripped mine with both of his own. "And from my wife, Angela."

When he released my arm, I stepped back and snapped to attention. "In case I don't have the chance if you do make captain, sir." Although we were both dressed in civies, I raised my right hand in a salute.

Andrews returned my gesture. "At ease, Chief. Good luck. Be careful."

BT

ACKNOWLEDGMENTS

The author wishes to thank several people who provided assistance in preparing this book, including:

- Kate Arbogast
- Marguerite Arbogast
- Peter Ehni, Ph.D.
- Barbara Voulgaris, PACS, U.S.C.G.R. (Ret.)

ABOUT THE AUTHOR

Kenneth Arbogast, M.Ed., M.A., was a chief petty officer in the U.S. Coast Guard. His assignments included the USCGC *Mackinaw*, Coast Guard Headquarters, First Coast Guard District, Boston, Fort Benjamin Harrison and Kodiak, Alaska. His decorations include a Joint Service Commendation Medal, Coast Guard Commendation Medal with two stars, Joint Service Achievement Medal, and Coast Guard Achievement Medal with one star among others. He later worked for the U.S. Forest Service as a forest public affairs officer and tribal liaison.

www.ingramcontent.com/pod-product-compliance
Lightning Source LLC
Chambersburg PA
CBHW070740180626
46818CB00007B/2924